WHERE FIREFLIES GLOW

KAVERY MADAPA

Copyright © 2024 KAVERY MADAPA

All rights reserved

The characters and events portrayed in this book are fictitious. Any similarity to real persons, living or dead, is coincidental and not intended by the author.

No part of this book may be reproduced, or stored in a retrieval system, or transmitted in any form or by any means, electronic, mechanical, photocopying, recording, or otherwise, without express written permission of the publisher.

ISBN-13: 9798884280809
ISBN-10: 1477123456

Cover design by: Alyssa Scott
Library of Congress Control Number: 2018675309
Printed in the United States of America

To the dreamer in all of us

CONTENTS

Title Page
Copyright
Dedication
Introduction
ONE 1
TWO 11
THREE 22
FOUR 36
FIVE 50
SIX 65
SEVEN 79
EIGHT 93
NINE 99
TEN 111
ELEVEN 116
TWELVE 126
THIRTEEN 137
FOURTEEN 151
FIFTEEN 165
SIXTEEN 180
SEVENTEEN 185

EIGHTEEN	191
NINETEEN	200
TWENTY	212
TWENTY-ONE	215
TWENTY-TWO	228
TWENTY-THREE	233
TWENTY-FOUR	245
TWENTY-FIVE	254
TWENTY-SIX	259
TWENTY-SEVEN	272
Acknowledgements	279
About The Author	281

INTRODUCTION

Naina, a shy teenager, believes that falling in love leads to breakups, pain and heartbreak, and is determined to stay away from all of it.
Amar, the new boy at school, is attracted to Naina the moment he sees her and is slowly falling in love, even if she doesn't feel the same way.
Can they come together and fall in love?
And can their love survive the return of an ex-girlfriend? Or worse, a near-fatal accident to someone close to them?
Because, it can take months to fall in love, but just one moment to tear it all apart.

This charming, coming-of-age novel by debut author, Kavery Madapa, is set in a boarding school in the 1980's and is a nostalgic look at what it means to grow up, fall in love and discover who you really are.

ONE

I chose to sit in the shade of a large rock, so if I fell asleep while revising, I wouldn't have the sun on me. However, the sun has moved since then, and I jerk awake to find I'm gently baking in the heat of its rays. The huge golden orb is right above me and it is very, very hot. Sitting up, I move back into the shade, away from the glare and instantly feel much better. Revising geometry portions for mid-terms, on a hot Sunday afternoon guaranteed a quick doze between theorems!

I look down at the familiar scene below me. My school is in the middle of a large valley. I have the best view of it; a line of red roofed buildings that end at the edge of a sports field. The valley is surrounded by small hills or hillocks, depending on who you ask, with rocks of all sizes distributed haphazardly as if thrown by a petulant child.

Higher up the hill I spot some goats; bells on their collars making a sweet sound. The goatherd guides them over the rocks then chooses a flat rock to sit on. Pulling a flute from his bag he begins playing a popular song. A lone eagle comes into view gliding effortlessly as it scours the valley for any prey then drifts away on a current of warm air.

On this Sunday, the whole valley is in a soporific haze or perhaps it's just me that's feeling sleepy. I spot a lizard coming towards me and suddenly I am no longer sleepy. Lizards of any size look menacing to me, and this one is large. Plus, it's flicking its tongue out as it advances.

'Shoo, shoo,' I yell at the reptile, clapping my hands loudly.

'Go away, shoo.' The startled reptile quickly changes course, disappearing under a rock.

'Naina, do you have to make so much noise?' grumbles my best friend Neha, who also dozed off. She sits up, pushing her long, straight hair away from her face. Rubbing her eyes, she looks accusingly at me. 'I was in the middle of a lovely dream.'

'Let me guess,' I say smiling at her, 'Your handsome prince was about to kiss you?'

Neha opens her mouth to answer but she is interrupted by a loud bell. It is for Sunday lunch. We both are on our feet immediately. Hostel life ensures we are always hungry and missing lunch is not an option.

'Ok, Naina,' says Neha pushing her feet into her shoes. 'You know the drill. Five minutes is all we have.'

We have had a lot of practice doing this mad dash down the hill since it is our favourite place to study. Looking down we spot a trickle of students from our hostel begin the short journey to the dining hall.

Books in hand, we start the descent, with Neha taking the lead. I follow her, keeping a small distance between us. Knowing which rocks can take our weight and which to avoid, we hurry down a narrow path that has formed in the scrubland.

The ground is hard, but our shoes still send up small puffs of red dust. Staying clear of thorny bushes and loose stones, we make good time, reaching the bottom of the hill in a rush.

We pause to catch our breath, dust our clothes, then we are off again.

Breathless, we join the other hungry boarders on their way to lunch. Neha gives me a thumbs up as we split up.

I fall in step with Jyoti, whom we all call Jo, and Priya, who share a room with Neha and me. Like us they are in the tenth standard and are revising a complicated theorem for tomorrow's paper.

I look over at Neha who is talking to our hostel warden, Anita Ma'am. Our warden picks a small twig from Neha's hair and points back to the path we came from. Neha looks sheepish but not too worried. Anita Ma'am is also our Maths teacher, and she has a soft spot for Neha, a Maths whiz.

Entering the dining hall, we sit at our usual table. Once everyone is seated, a bell sounds to start a minute's silence before the food is served. We look at our empty plates, willing the seconds to go faster so we can eat.

One Sunday not so long ago, a student started singing the Indian national anthem on a dare from another boy. As the melodious chant started, we all sat in stunned silence, then stood up and belted out the rest of the national anthem as expected of us. The boy got a strict 'talking to' from his hostel warden but was something of a hero for a while.

The original song choice was Pink Floyd's *Another Brick in the Wall,* which would not have gone down well… at all!

The sound of three hundred students and hostel wardens talking at the same time makes a racket, but we are used to it. The food is strictly vegetarian and usually tasty; however, Sunday lunches are the exception. Today's lunch is nondescript *parathas-* a flatbread- (which no self-respecting cook would own up to making) with a potato curry and some mysterious vegetable no one can identify. Even the cooks need a day off.

We tuck into the meal anyway, finishing with a bowl of thick yoghurt, the saving grace of the meal.

From across the table, Reena, another classmate, is trying to get my attention. I am sure she has some news she wants to share. Reena always gets wind of news before anyone else. How does she do it?

'Guess what?' she asks during a lull in the chatter around us. 'We are getting two new students in our batch! And they are joining this weekend. Isn't that exciting news?'

She has a lot more to say but a stern look from our warden and a reminder to finish her lunch means any further discussion will have to wait.

Those of us who hear the news are taken aback and discuss it quietly amongst ourselves. New students in our batch? That is exciting. Why are they joining a new school at this time of the year?

It is the middle of September with mid-term exams underway. The Big Exam, the ICSE is only months away! This is our first major board exam and will decide the fate of all of us. Changing schools in the tenth standard is not a usual occurrence.

After lunch, we have a 'quiet' period which means lying down to read or rest. I have permission to go to the main assembly hall for a practice session. I am part of a group that leads morning assembly three times a week, so we have singing sessions often. After revising or trying to revise geometry all morning, I am looking forward to a singing session with the group.

I remind Anita Ma'am where I am going and exit the hostel through its tall wooden doors.

Our hostel is one of the newer ones built to accommodate the growing number of students since the school was started on a small scale, as an experiment, years ago.

The first two months of school seemed too long and most of us were homesick and miserable. That was back in 1980 when most students in my batch joined in the fifth standard.

The road to the assembly hall is flanked by rows of flame trees on both sides, some of which are still in flower. Nearby a rose garden vies for attention with a hedge of hydrangeas. Not for the first time I wish I could capture it all in a drawing or sketch. But my drawing skills are stuck in the stick figure stage, sadly.

At 2.45 on a Sunday afternoon there is no one else around, just the September heat bouncing off everything. The end of the road gives on to a lawn with a small path running through it.

Heading down this path, I stumble on a pair of long legs in blue jeans and sneakers. A couple more steps and I discover the legs belong to a boy with long hair dressed in a white t-shirt.

He is stretched out on the grassy lawn, gazing with total concentration at a butterfly a few inches from his face.

I don't recognize him, which is strange. In a school this small, everyone knows everyone. He turns to look at me and I notice his long, brown hair flops over his forehead. Another sign this guy is not a student at this school. All male students receive a standard short haircut every month. Long hair is a big no-no.

'Are you alright?' I ask, hoping he is not hurt.

The butterfly takes off and the boy lifts himself off the grass, standing in one fluid motion. He is slightly taller than my five feet eight inches and seems all arms and legs. But he has an ease about him like he would be comfortable in most situations.

'Hi, I'm Samir, but you can call me Sam,' he says with a big grin, as if we have known each other for a while. His wide set light brown eyes are fringed with long lashes. He offers me his hand and I give it a limp shake.

'I'm Naina. And you can call me.... err...Naina,' I say rather lamely. That did not sound cool at all. Trying to recover, I quickly ask, 'Are you visiting Waterview High?'

'Nope, I joined yesterday. Put my stuff in the Senior Hostel, and got my Admission number too,' he replies, referring to a number given to each student when they join. 'I'm in Class 10A.'

'Oh, you're in my class then,' I say realizing Samir must be one of the new students Reena spoke of at lunch. I wonder who the other one is.

Looking around, he says, 'Don't you just love this place? Look at all the flowers and trees here. And the insects, too.'

'Yeah, flowers and trees are nice, but I hate insects,' I say with a shudder. 'And reptiles of any sort.' Noticing a large book in his hand I ask, 'Are you catching up on the school syllabus already?'

If he is, the teachers will love him.

He grins. 'No, this is my sketchbook. Want to have a look?'

I nod. I notice his long, slender fingers as he shows me the first page of a large drawing pad. It's covered with pencil sketches of flowers and trees in minute detail. Amongst all this, he's added a few lady birds, a dragonfly, and some butterflies.

I gaze at this cornucopia with more than a little envy. Turning the page, he reveals a sketch of the scene in front of us, the flame trees, the garden on the edge of the lawn and even the iconic U-shaped sundial.

'Wow,' I blurt out, 'You are very good. Pinto Sir, our Arts teacher, will be happy to have you in his class.'

Samir grins. I notice a dimple appears on his right cheek when he smiles.

'The Arts teachers usually like me, it's the Maths and Physics teachers who find me difficult to teach.'

I glance at my watch. Shoot, I only have five minutes before the practice session starts.

'I have to go, or I'll be late,' I say as I start walking away. 'But I will see you in class tomorrow, Samir. I hope you like it here.'

'I'm sure I will,' he replies. 'Plus, I can tell we are going to be friends, Naina,' he says confidently. As I turn to look back, I notice he's stretched out on the grass again.

* *

'Should we wake her up? It's almost time.'

'No, it's ok if she gets another five minutes of sleep, Jo.'

'I think she should wake up now.'

I want to put my pillow over my head and ignore the whispers, instead I roll over with a yawn so my roommates can stop worrying about me.

'Oh, great, Naina. You'd better get ready,' Jo looks worried. 'We don't have much time.'

'Don't worry,' I say flinging back the sheet. 'There's lots of time till the exam. It's only after breakfast, isn't it?'

'Yes, but we thought you may want to revise some more,' Priya says pulling a floral top over her head to match the dark blue trousers she is wearing. The great thing about our school, is there are no uniforms, but that also means finding something that's clean and wrinkle-free to wear every day. Still, it beats wearing a boring uniform any day.

'No more studying for me,' I inform Priya firmly.

I have found there is a point at which my brain rebels at any more revision. It is best to retain what I have already learned instead of cramming any more in.

Neha walks in looking rested and happy. Anything Maths-related comes easily to her. She cannot wait to say goodbye to

English and History next year, while I cannot wait to drop Maths and Physics.

'Ok roomies,' she begins with a big smile. 'Here is the plan of action for today. We complete today's exam, and that's us done with mid-terms.' She does a little two-step in the middle of our room. 'This means it's time for a midnight feast tomorrow. Ta-da.' She finishes her little speech with a flourish.

'What? That's not possible, Neha,' Jo exclaims.

'We could get caught. Besides, now that we are seniors, we should be more…responsible,' Priya says doubtfully.

'Neha, I don't think that's a good idea at all,' I add my bit too, but Neha waves away our concerns.

'Listen, every term we have at least one midnight feast,' She squints at her reflection in the mirror then turns away satisfied. 'We've been so busy with mid-terms we forgot to have one; what better time to do it?'

Once the idea is out there, it takes on a life of its own. At breakfast, girls from other rooms excitedly tell us they've been waiting for this term's midnight feast. Having one is a tradition handed down by our seniors who grew up on a diet of Enid Blyton books, like we did. Blyton's books that are set in boarding schools feature midnight feasts and midnight walks much like the ones we have.

*   *

Outside our classrooms a group of boys and girls are swapping last minute tips and answers for the geometry paper. Forty nervous students sound very noisy.

I catch sight of Reena and go over to talk to her.

'Hi, I met one of the new students you mentioned,' I say but she looks blankly at me, her mind clearly on the upcoming exam.

Suddenly she gets what I am talking about.

'Oh yes, there are two of them. They are both in our batch,' Reena continues over the din of our excited classmates. 'They are ....'

Behind us the classroom doors open and my batchmates surge towards them in a mini stampede.

'They are what?' I ask puzzled. 'What did you say?'

Reena starts walking towards her classroom saying something I can't quite catch.

In the confusion someone bumps against my arm and a small leather pouch is knocked from my hands. It sails above me in a graceful arc as I watch in dismay. The pouch contains a Parker pen from my parents, sharpened pencils I will need for the exam and all my geometry tools.

I run towards it hoping to catch it before it falls and bang into something that stops my progress. Scratch that, I run into *someone.*

'Oof,' I say, winded from the impact.

'Watch where you're going,' a voice says in exasperation.

Trying to locate the voice I look up in time to see a long arm reaching high above me. The arm catches my bag. I follow it all the way down to find it belongs to a tall guy dressed all in black, shirt, trousers, and shoes. I massage my shoulder wondering if that was muscle or a brick wall, I just ran into.

Up close I take in the brown hair, light brown eyes, and wide mouth. Now where have I seen a face like that recently?

'Samir?' I ask, before I can stop myself.

In that instant I notice he is taller and broader than Samir but with the same brown eyes. These are now fixed on me in what?

Exasperation? Irritation? Pain? It's hard to tell this close. But he's not happy.

'Sorry, I thought you were Samir,' I blurt out. 'But you're not.'

'No, I'm not' he agrees seriously. 'Last time I checked.'

How rude. Then it dawns on me. A pair of twins have joined our batch! That's what Reena was saying. This is Samir's twin. I read somewhere twins don't like to be mistaken for each other.

Nice one, Naina! Off to a great start.

'Naina, Naina,' I can hear someone calling my name from our classroom.

'Do you mind?' says the guy with a definite frown on his face. 'You're still standing on my shoe.'

'Oops, sorry,' I apologise and back off. I look down at his shoes which are not as polished as they might have been fifteen seconds before.

'Naina, *come on*, the exam is about to start,' Jo's panicked voice brings me back to reality. Snatching the bag and its precious contents from Samir's twin I manage to say, 'Thanks a lot' before hurrying into the classroom with seconds to spare.

TWO

The next day our entire batch is treated to an outdoor class. We are glad to be outside, after a week of being cooped up writing mid-term exams and file out of the school building in high spirits. Both sections have English today, so TK Sir, our English teacher, decides a joint session makes sense.

'Hey Naina, wait up,' I hear a shout from behind as Samir catches up with Neha and me. I am a bit nervous when I introduce them to each other since Neha and I have been a tight unit for so long. But his easy banter puts her at ease quickly.

'Are you happy to be done with mid-terms?' Samir asks. We both nod emphatically yes.

'Now we can plan other things,' I say happily thinking of tonight's midnight feast. I notice Neha shaking her head and I quickly change the subject. Better not to say too much about our plans for tonight.

'Tell me Samir, how come your hair is still long?' I ask. 'I thought all the guys had to have short hair.'

'The barber is away from school this week, so I am safe till then,' he grins. 'Next week my brother and I will have the same haircut as every guy here.'

'Your brother has joined too?' asks Neha casually though it's been a hot topic amongst us the last few days.

'Yeah, we both joined over the weekend,' he confirms.

'Actually,' I pause and clear my throat. 'I think I met your brother yesterday.'

'Tall guy who looks like me?' asks Samir and I nod.

'Um, yeah. I met him just before the exam yesterday,' I confirm. 'He caught my bag and saved it from being trampled by our classmates.'

I omit the part where I might have ruined his shoes by standing on them for a few seconds.

Samir laughs, 'That sounds like Amar. He is an ace bowler and fielder. He's trying out for the cricket team this evening.'

That explains how he caught my bag so easily.

'Are you from Bombay?' I ask Samir. When he nods a yes, I add. 'So am I. Here's to all the Bombayites at school,' I tell him as we exchange a high five.

'Wait a minute,' Neha says, frowning. 'Two more Bombayites in our batch? I need more support for Delhi. Who else is from Delhi?'

Scanning the students around us, then calls out to Rahul who is walking ahead with Amar.

'Rahul, I need some help, please,' she tells him. 'Is Bombay or Delhi the better city?'

'Oh, Delhi any day. We've got the Qutub Minar, Connaught Place, Rashtrapathi Bhavan,' he says counting the landmarks on his fingers.

'*Boring*,' I say with emphasis. 'Bombay has the Taj Hotel, Gateway of India, Victoria Terminus and, and?' I look at Samir for help.

'Marine Drive and Hanging Gardens. Plus, you can see Amitabh Bachchan or Hema Malini if you are lucky,' Samir declares. 'Or

Kapil Dev or Ravi Shastri.'

'Hey, you can see the President or the Prime Minister in Delhi, if you are lucky,' says Neha gamely but even she knows it's a lost cause. We all burst out laughing.

The rivalry between Delhites and Bombayites will never end, and that's the fun of it.

By now our group of forty odd students has reached our destination. It's a huge banyan tree with granite benches and tables set up in a semi-circle. TK Sir perches on a large bench facing this semi-circle.

'Ok, settle down everyone,' he begins and waits till we are all seated. TK is a great teacher, very supportive and a great inspiration to lovers of the English language and literature like me. Neha considers our Maths teachers to be great inspirations too but while I like Anita Ma'am's style of teaching, our other teacher, Jayakumar Sir, does not inspire me at all. To each their own!

'Some of you may have met the two new students,' TK says looking around at us. 'I'd like to introduce Amar and Samir Malhotra from Bombay. Boys, can you please stand up and introduce yourselves?'

A wave of whispers starts when the twins stand up. Most of us have studied together for years and know each other well by now. So, any new students always get a lot of attention. Though the twins are a short distance from each other the resemblance is obvious, yet they are very different. The same strong features look striking on both.

'Hi, everyone,' Amar says with a small wave. 'I'm Amar and this is Samir. We are from Bombay. And yes, we are twins. But I'm older by five minutes.'

'*Only* five minutes,' Samir says dramatically. Everyone laughs.

We can tell this is an old argument between them.

Amar grins and continues, 'My interests are cricket and music. I've brought my guitar with me as well.'

Samir quickly lists his interests as anything to do with art and painting. Having seen his sketchbook, I'm not surprised. He is seriously talented.

He adds, 'You'll rarely see me near a sports field unless Amar is playing cricket.'

'At least now we have a real set of twins,' says someone from behind us.

Neha looks behind with a frown. Five years ago, when we both joined school, we were called The Twins since we spent so much time together, had similar names and wore our long hair in a ponytail. Then at thirteen I shot up to five feet seven inches leaving Neha behind at five feet three inches. She says she is waiting for her height to catch up to mine while I am waiting for my curves (if any) to catch up with me.

'I hope you will welcome Amar and Samir,' TK continues in a more serious tone. 'Joining a new school is not easy as you know. I am counting on all of you to make the transition easy for them which includes not giving them a hard time.'

I look across at the twins, wondering how they are settling in so far. I was one of a large group of new students when I joined. It made it easier that so many of us were going through the same experiences together. We bonded over those hard times and became firm friends forever. I'm glad Samir and Amar have each other to lean on.

An hour and a half later our class ends. I glance at my watch to check if it really is twelve-thirty while a rumble from my stomach confirms it is time for lunch. To my mind time appears to fly when we are studying English but drags in subjects, I don't like much.

While we gather up our books and pens before leaving, TK Sir reminds us that a book review of Thomas Hardy's *Far from the Madding Crowd* is due next week. We were given a month to do it. Having forgotten all about it, I need to pick up a copy from the library.

'To end the class today, the word I want you to spell is *chiaroscuro*,' says TK pronouncing it perfectly. Every week he challenges us to spell a word. I notice some classmates looking at me, waiting for the correct answer. I love spelling words and I have got most correct in the past. Now they are leaving it to me by default.

I see a raised hand on the other side of the class.

'Yes, Amar,' TK says encouragingly. 'Can you spell *chiaroscuro*?'

Amar spells the word correctly and we all clap. He's good at sports, plays the guitar and can spell correctly? Who said life is fair?

As we pass the school building, I duck into the library for a copy of the book, urging Neha and Samir to go on ahead. I recall reading the book in my Thomas Hardy phase some years ago, but having a copy on hand will certainly help while writing a review.

I'm in luck. There's just one copy left on the shelf. I grab it in relief and hurry over to the desk. Anita Ma'am does not like us to be late for meals.

'Hello, dear,' says Lalitha Ma'am, the librarian. 'Haven't seen you in a while. Mid-term exams, no? What are you borrowing today?'

Seeing the novel in my hand, her face falls. 'Oh *beta*, I promised the last copy to that nice boy over there. He's a new student and is filling out a new library card form.'

Looking in the direction she is pointing to, I see Amar sitting at a table filling out a form. Just my luck. I'm surprised he is doing the book review since he and Samir only joined this week.

Conceding defeat, I hand the book over to Lalitha Ma'am and head for the door. I'll have to see if any of my roomies have finished the review and borrow their copy.

'Naina, Naina, just a minute,' the librarian calls out. I turn around to see Lalitha Ma'am gesturing for me to come back. I return to the desk reluctantly.

'Amar, have the two of you met?' she asks him.

'No' I say.

'Yes,' says Amar.

Lalitha Ma'am looks at both of us, confused.

'We bumped into each other,' Amar clarifies with a straight face. I do an internal eye roll. Accurate, but he could do better than that.

'Amar has very kindly agreed to share the last copy of the book with you,' Ma'am says beaming, happy to have solved the problem.

'That's alright,' I say to her. 'I'll borrow a copy from one of my roommates.'

Amar holds the book out to me, but I assure him I don't need it. I'm pretty sure Jo would have finished with her copy by now.

'Fine. But you still owe me a pair of shoes. Since you ruined my best pair,' he tells me seriously.

The librarian and I glance at him in surprise. I remember stepping on his shoes by accident, when we first met, but surely, they are still wearable.

'Naina, you spoilt his formal shoes?' Lalitha Ma'am asks in alarm.

'Why did you do that? How will he manage till the end of term?'

Glancing at Amar, I detect the ghost of a smile. He's enjoying this.

'I didn't do it on purpose, Ma'am. We were going in for an exam and there was a large crowd. I didn't see him and by mistake I …' my voice trails away when I notice a big smile on Amar's face.

'It's ok, Ma'am. I was just kidding,' Amar clarifies with a wide grin. 'My shoes have since recovered.'

'Ok, ok, now both of you must hurry to the dining hall for lunch, 'Lalitha Ma'am says. Glancing at the clock, she points to the door of the library. 'Go, go. You mustn't be late.'

We hurry out of the library together while a familiar feeling of dread washes over me. The prospect of walking a hundred odd meters to the dining hall with Amar for company is both daunting and alarming. I'm nervous and shy around people I don't know well. I can't handle a situation like this.

At a point where the roads intersect, I stop and point to the path on the left, 'I have to go back to the hostel first, so I'll go this way.'

'Sure?' he asks, giving me a curious look. I wonder if he can read my mind and knows I'm intimidated by walking with him.

'I'm sure,' I confirm with a weak nod.

Once he is out of sight, I break into a run. I'll have to take the long way to the dining hall, so I had better hurry. Moreover, I'm so hungry. And I'm *so* late for lunch.

*   *

That night, we all gather in the largest dormitory of the hostel after the lights are turned off at ten o'clock. The curtains have been pulled back to allow moonlight in through large windows. The scene is set for our midnight feast.

Sitting in a semi-circle we take stock of the spread of before us. There are chocolate biscuits, walnut brownies, a spicy cornflakes mixture, peanuts, Tang and Bournvita. Technically the last two don't qualify as food, but in the absence of anything else that is edible, they are part of our midnight feast. Twenty hungry boarders can make all this disappear in no time.

'Are you sure Anita Ma'am went to sleep?' I ask Reena who is overseeing that part tonight.

'Yes,' she whispers. 'All the lights in her room are off. She doesn't stay up this late.'

I give her a thumbs up.

'What's this?' asks Priya pointing to a large plastic bag.

'That's two bags of gold fingers,' answers Neha. 'Arjun and his friends went to Third Mile village today.'

Gold fingers are long, yellow, and crispy snacks, hence the name. Third Mile village is a handy distance of three miles from our school but has a long name we can't quite pronounce.

Arjun and Neha have been in an on-off relationship for the last three years. He is a senior in the eleventh standard and is besotted with her. She is crazy about him too but from time to time she breaks off the relationship for various reasons. Last year it was to give Arjun a chance to do well in the ICSE. This year she feels she needs a break so she can concentrate on the same exam.

'Are you two back together?' I ask her a bit puzzled.

'Not really,' whispers Neha. 'But I told him we were running short of food, so he picked these up.'

'Ok,' I say like I understand but honestly, I don't. They have been down this road before so Arjun must be hoping they will get back to dating again soon. I hope so too.

We polish off every bit of food and move onto the next part of the midnight feast. Swapping ghost stories! Not the best thing to do when we are sitting in the dark, but that's part of the thrill. We are soon deep into a story about ghosts that inhabit an old house nearby, unexplained screams and sounds in the night, accompanied by dancing skeletons and floating buckets of blood. It's such a scary tale, we try our best not to scream at the best parts. Shivers run down our spines as we gather closer, smiling nervously at each other in the moonlight.

Suddenly, we hear the unmistakable sound of a door opening. A few seconds and a couple of squeaks later the door closes. Now this is a sound we know very well.

'Oh no,' Reena whispers, confirming our fears. 'That's Anita Ma'am's door. She must have woken up.'

'Quick, let's hide everything,' says Neha in a panic.

For a moment we all freeze, till Priya starts gathering wrappers and remnants of snacks, together. Someone throws a bed cover over the food. Those of us from other rooms hide behind beds while the girls whose room this is, clamber on to their beds pulling the covers over them. We have about a minute to do all this.

Light from our warden's torch sweeps over windows and doors. We have locked the two doors from the inside, so we are safe. Jo and I chose the same bed to hide behind. Fingers to our lips, we huddle together pulling our shawls over us.

Jo is a giggler and once she starts, it's difficult to stop her. Now she lets out a nervous giggle and claps a palm over her mouth. I hope she doesn't have a giggling fit. There couldn't be a worse time for it.

In my mind I run through all the rules we are breaking right now: -

1) *Staying up after ten p.m.*

2) *Being in another dormitory.*

3) *Eating after lights out.*

Best not to think of what will happen if we get caught. After what seems like an eternity, we hear our warden's room door open and close again.

We all relax visibly.

A while later, after checking that the coast is clear, the four of us creep back to our room. While Neha draws back the curtains, to let the moonlight in, I retrieve a thermos of hot water and a tin of Cadburys Drinking Chocolate from the dressing table.

'Best time for a mug of hot chocolate,' I declare. Neha and I begged our warden for some hot water, minutes before lights out.

Sitting in bed, cradling our mugs of hot chocolate we declare the night's activities a great success.

'What did you think of the twins, the new guys?' asks Priya changing the subject. 'I think they are cute. And they are from Bombay. I like Bombay guys.'

Priya is prone to developing crushes on guys extremely fast. She gets over them quickly too. Meanwhile, Satish a classmate has been quietly in love with her for years. So far, she has not reciprocated his feelings, but we and Satish live in hope.

When I shake my head and smile at Priya, she declares, 'Some of us have crushes, Naina. Not all of us can go through school like you. No dating. No boyfriends. Nothing to come in the way of your grades and activities.'

I've heard all this before, and while not a hundred percent correct, is mostly true. Neha gives me a small smile. She's the only one who knows the reason for my reluctance in dating anyone or falling in love.

'C'mon Priya,' says Neha quietly. 'That's not fair. Whether Naina chooses to date or not is entirely up to her.'

'Ok, ok,' Priya says, putting her hands up. 'Sorry, that was mean of me. I've never understood why you keep guys so far away, Naina. Did something happen to you?'

'Yes,' I tell her slowly. 'Something happened two years ago which haunts me to this day.' However, I don't elaborate, reluctant to spoil tonight with memories I've kept locked away for so long.

Jo fights back a yawn, which sets all of us yawning. We settle down for the night, tired but happy.

'Naina, pretty please will you sing a song for us?' asks Jo. 'It'll be a great way to end tonight.'

'What song should I sing, Jo?' I ask fighting back another yawn.

'You know my favourite song, Naina,' she says happily pulling a blanket over herself and snuggling down in bed.

I take a deep breath and launch into '*Fernando*', by Abba.

THREE

A group of us are lounging on the steps leading to the assembly hall. We're meeting to decide what our batch is doing for the inter-class competition. It's an annual function and every batch in the senior school can put up two items.

'I can't believe it's already the end of September,' says Neha shaking her head in disbelief. 'This term is flying by.'

'What sort of items do we put up?' queries Samir who is sitting with Neha and me. 'Songs, short plays, things like that?'

'Skits are a big favourite here,' I reply.

'And songs,' adds Neha. 'Naina usually sings a solo. So that's one item done. If we agree on one more, that's it for our batch.'

'Someone might want to do something else, Neha,' I say. 'Let's ask everyone and then decide.'

Neha laughs saying, 'You're not getting out of doing a solo, Naina. It's become a tradition. Ok, let's take a vote.'

She walks down the steps and stands in front of us. I envy her confidence and wish some of it rubbed off on me. But five years of knowing her has not made me any more confident.

'Alright, guys and girls, if all those interested in taking part are here, let's begin,' Neha says. 'Any ideas on what we should do for the inter-class competition that's in a week's time?'

'Can we wait a few more minutes?' asks Rahul. 'Amar wanted to attend this meeting too, but he has to finish cricket practice first.'

'Did he have any suggestions?' asks Neha.

'Hang on,' Samir says sitting up suddenly. 'I just remembered. Amar suggested doing *Bohemian Rhapsody* by Queen.'

'Sing *Bohemian Rhapsody*?' I ask doubtfully. 'That would be way too difficult.' Though the song ranks high (number one) on my ride or die list of songs, I would never attempt singing it.

'We don't have to sing it, just enact it,' says Amar joining our group. 'The way it's written is like an opera or a short play. It'll be great to act it out and do a fellow Indian, Freddy Mercury, proud.'

He must have stopped off to have a shower since he's now in a white T-shirt and jeans and his hair appears damp. He has a quiet confidence about him that gets the group's attention.

'Oh,' I say uncertainly, trying to wrap my head around the idea. He sets a cassette player down on the steps and pushes play. The opening line of the iconic song begins. Listening to it I see how we can present it in a dramatic way. Amar is right, the song has been written like a three-act tragedy. Why didn't I see that before?

'What do you think?' asks Amar as the song ends. 'Do you think we can pull this off?'

The response is unanimous, everyone is keen to try a dramatic version. We now have a decision on one item. Neha is thrilled. It usually takes us a long time to decide on anything.

'Great,' says Neha. 'That's decided. What's the second item for us?'

'A solo by Naina, of course,' says Rahul with a grin. 'Naina, do you have a new song to sing this year?'

I look up and see fifteen pairs of eyes on me. Now would be a good time for the earth to open and swallow me whole. Despite being a member of the choir and dance troupe, being in the limelight doesn't come naturally to me.

'Why don't you decide on a song and let us know?' Samir asks helpfully.

'Sanjay used to accompany me on the guitar, but he left last year.' I reply. Hopefully this is my ticket out of doing a solo this year. 'Perhaps someone else would like to do something this year.'

'Amar has a guitar; he can accompany you,' Samir remarks with a grin. I glare at him, but he's looking at his twin brother and misses it. Amar looks at me and I'm sure, he is not keen on any of this.

'Sure,' he says quietly. 'I'm sure we can decide on a song.'

'Great,' say Neha and Samir together.

'That was really easy, folks,' Neha declares. 'Let's start working on the details.'

She's come prepared with chart paper, pencils, markers, and a ruler. She's in her happy place. Propping the paper over a blackboard we start working on a dramatic rendition of the famous song.

Everyone seems happy except for me. I confess to being nervous at having to work with Amar. He seems like a nice guy but from previous experience I know I'm a poor judge of character when it comes to guys. I learnt that the hard way when I was thirteen.

 Moreover, Amar is smart, witty and easy on the eyes. Just the kind of guy who'll make me forget my rules of not getting involved with anyone.

Running through my options of how to solve this problem, I hit on the perfect solution. What if I just tell him I can sing without any accompaniment? That sounds reasonable. I'm sure he'll be relieved, and I won't have anything more to do with him. Besides, he must have better things to do.

Genius idea! I congratulate myself, cheering up immediately. I'm so focused on how to avoid working with Amar, the rules of the competition slip my mind completely.

'Lucky you,' says Priya walking up to me. 'You get to work with Amar. I would love to be in your shoes. Just looking into his brown eyes would be enough for me.' She sighs dejectedly.

I smile weakly in reply and consider coming clean with my latest plan. However, I decide not to say anything till I've put the plan into action first.

Looking around I spot Amar on the steps tuning his guitar.

I approach him saying casually, 'Hi Amar, I thought we should have a chat about the song.'

'Hi. It's Naina, right?' Amar looks questioningly at me. I nod in reply. I notice his eyes are more hazel than brown in colour. No wonder Priya was sighing over them.

'Listen,' I say in a rush. 'You don't have to play the guitar for me. I can manage without one. I'm sure you have better things to do.'

'Sorry, I missed most of that,' Amar says smiling up at me. I must admit he does have a nice smile.

I repeat what I said hoping I don't sound too rude.

'Did you say you don't need me to play the guitar for you?' he queries.

'That's correct.'

'So, let me get this straight,' he says slowly, sounding more puzzled than relieved. 'You don't want to work with me on this song?'

'Yes.' I say again.

'Despite Neha saying we should?' I nod again.

'And correct me if I'm wrong, but the last time we met, you took the long route from the library to the dining hall rather than walk with me?' Amar asks his eyes now dark and inscrutable.

Uh, oh. Busted!

'Technically it's not the long route,' I point out. 'Because I had to stop off at our hostel first.' *'Liar'* a small voice inside of me says. I try and ignore it.

'Hey guys,' Samir says flopping down on the steps beside Amar. 'How's it all coming along?'

Instead of answering, Amar turns and looks at me. His expression is hard to read. Somehow this whole exercise has not turned out the way I'd hoped.

I swallow, 'It's a work in progress.'

'Oh good,' Samir says happily. 'I knew it was a great idea.'

* *

'Wasn't it nice of Amar to offer to play the guitar for you?' asks Neha on the way back to the hostel after practice is over.

'Oh yeah,' I say vaguely not wanting to confess what I've done. I need to figure this out in my head, first. I have a feeling I've forgotten something, but I don't know what it is just yet.

Neha, however, senses something is wrong.

'Did you both decide on a song?' She frowns, looking hard at me.

'We decided it's better if I sing on my own rather than get Amar to accompany me on the guitar,' I say in a rush. 'I'm sure he would rather do other stuff.'

'Amar said he'd rather do other stuff?' Neha asks disbelievingly.

'Not in so many words but that's the idea I got,' I say stalling, not meeting her eyes. Neha knows I'm a terrible liar.

'Naina, *all* songs have to be accompanied by some instrument like a guitar or a piano,' Neha points out. 'It's one of the rules of the competition. I thought you knew that.'

'Oh no, I totally forgot,' I say in dismay, realizing this is what I overlooked when I came up with my brilliant plan. 'What do I do now, Neha?'

'I think you'd better start from the beginning,' she answers. 'Then we'll see what we can do.'

By the time I finish the long version we've reached our hostel. Neha seems at a loss for words. Almost nothing renders her speechless. I flop down on my bed and let out a long sigh.

'Naina, we need someone to play the guitar for you. And since it's a competition it's got to be someone in our batch,' Neha says finally. 'You have to convince Amar, since no one else plays the guitar.'

'I can't Neha, I told him very clearly I didn't need him,' I say putting a pillow over my head, wishing this whole problem would just go away.

'Well, my friend, you do need him,' she says. 'And the sooner you convince him, the better. I'm sure you two can work together for the sake of the competition.'

'If I ask Amar, will it involve some begging or groveling on my part?' I ask in a small voice.

'It depends on Amar,' Neha says thoughtfully. 'But prepare to grovel, anyway,' she says with a wicked grin.

I groan out loud. Did I get up on the wrong side of my bed just today or every day this week?

*   *

It's the weekend again. Gentle winds drift over us. Overhead, clouds are playing tag with each other in the sky. The grassy slope we are lying on is soft and cushiony.

Life is good.

'So, today's plan is to steal some mangoes from the orchard?' Samir begins tentatively.

The slope we are stretched on is close to a mango orchard located within the school grounds.

'Well, *steal* is a strong word,' I say reluctantly. 'The orchard's there and we are here. It seems alright to take a few fruits, given how hungry we are.'

'And they are fine with that? The guys who guard the orchard?' Samir persists.

'Hmm... they might not be that okay with it,' Neha says cautiously. 'I mean there's a bit of yelling and stuff. But so far no one's complained.'

'Or if they have, we haven't heard about it,' I say.

By now we can see Samir's ready to call the whole thing off. Which seems a shame given our mission this weekend is to show him all the fun stuff we do at school.

'Why don't you be our lookout person?' Neha says, noticing Samir's reluctance in this endeavour. 'That way if you see someone coming you can warn us, so we don't get caught.'

'Alright, that sounds better,' Samir sounds relieved.

We've been helping ourselves to fruit from these orchards for so long that the line between stealing and not stealing has blurred over the years. Besides, when it's a Sunday and the only meal to look forward to is an unexciting one, lines blur very fast!

'What time do we go in?' Samir asks.

'Eleven thirty is their lunchbreak. So that's the best time. We've got some time to kill before that,' I say looking at my watch.

'No worries,' Samir says. 'I could lie on this slope for a while. Perfect day.'

I agree with him.

'Samir, did you and Amar do your mid-terms at your old school?' I ask him, voicing a question I've been mulling over.

'Yep, at the start of September. It made sense to finish them before joining Waterview High,' he answers.

'You're probably wondering why we joined so late in the term,' he continues. 'Our younger brother was diagnosed with a tumor at the start of the year. My parents have been so busy with his treatment it made sense for us to join a boarding school to complete our ICSE.'

'Oh no, Samir, so sorry to hear that,' I say sitting up.

'Samir, we had no idea,' Neha says sitting up too. 'Sorry about your brother.'

'Hey, that's alright,' he says. 'Sometimes life delivers a curveball, right? It's been hard watching him go through chemo sessions. But the latest tests have been good, so we are hoping for the best.'

After hearing this I feel awful about refusing Amar's help. I wish I could meet him right now and apologize.

'How are your parents coping?' I ask. 'Do they have family to help them?'

'Yeah, our grandparents have been super helpful. Besides, we're glad we chose to join this school.'

'You like it here?' Neha asks.

He nods. 'Yeah. Amar and I can just be ourselves. Rather than the twins whose brother has cancer. Plus, the art department's great. And there's lots to do here like the annual play and all the competitions.'

'Samir, speaking of competitions, we need your help with the inter-class competition,' I say, grateful for a chance to broach the topic.

'Not we, *you* need his help,' says Neha correcting me with a glare.

'Ok, ok I need his help,' I say.

I give him a quick recap of the exchange between Amar and myself.

'I need to ask him if he'll play the guitar,' I say at the end. 'Do you think he will?'

'Yeah, he will,' he says in an offhand way. 'He likes you, so he will.'

'Really? How do you know?' I feel a prickle of alarm working its way up my spine. I'm still wary of anyone who shows an interest in me. Whenever someone does, visions of me as a hurt and rejected thirteen-year-old surface again. As much as I like what I've seen of Amar so far, I'd rather he was not interested in me.

'I know the signs. Whenever your name comes up, his tone gets very casual,' Samir says with a grin. 'Like he doesn't care, when I know he does.'

'Uh oh, wrong thing to say to Naina,' Neha says shaking her

head. 'Abort, abort,' she says making slashing gestures against her neck.

'What? Why?' Samir says puzzled. 'Isn't Naina happy that Amar likes her?'

'Naina doesn't do romance,' Neha says. 'Or boyfriends, or dating. She doesn't want to get involved with anyone. She even has rules for all of that.'

Samir looks at me and I shake my head and shrug instead of saying anything.

'You don't date?' he asks.

'No,' I confirm.

'That's sad, Naina,' Samir says pensively. 'Like a wise man said, isn't it better to have loved and lost than never to have loved at all?'

'I believe that an owner of a lonely heart is much better than an owner of a broken heart,' I counter. 'Which also happens to be a favourite song of mine.'

'What about you?' he turns to Neha.

'Umm…well,' Neha tries to find the right words.

'She and Arjun are a couple,' I explain. 'On and off. Right now, they are off. In a month or a week, they may be on again. It's hard to say.'

I lean close to Samir and stage-whisper, 'He is her penguin. You know, her mate for life. She just doesn't know it yet.'

Neha laughs at that. 'That's kind of true.'

Pulling a piece of paper and a pen from his pocket, Samir asks me, 'When's your birthday?'

'Fourth of March,' I say.

'When's yours, Neha?' he turns towards her.

'Eighth of July. And yours?'

'Sixteenth of November. I knew it,' he says triumphantly showing us the piece of paper with our birthdays written on it.

'Sorry,' I say quite mystified. 'Knew what?'

'Fourth, eighth and sixteenth. See the pattern there?'

'Okay,' Neha says. 'I get the pattern of numbers, but so what?'

'In addition, we are all water signs. Pisces, Cancer, and Scorpio. We were meant to meet. And become friends,' he declares. 'Like the Three Musketeers.'

'Oh great. Since Amar and you have the same birthday, does that mean I can be *his* friend, too?' I say with a glint in my eye.

Samir laughs loudly. 'Now, you'll have to clarify that with my brother. Somehow, I don't think he'll agree.'

Checking her watch Neha notes, 'Hey guys, it's almost eleven thirty. We'd better go.'

Leaving the verdant incline reluctantly, we head towards the orchard. Just outside the grove we pause to find a large tree from which Samir can keep watch.

'Wait here for us,' says Neha. 'And if you see anyone coming, whistle loudly.'

'Why isn't there a fence?' Samir asks, looking around the grove. 'Shouldn't there be a fence to keep us out?'

'If there's no fence it means they don't mind us visiting. See, I told you it's okay,' Neha declares. And with that dodgy logic, the two of us enter the mango grove.

Neha and I select three ripe mangoes, while I pick a raw one. If you add salt to raw mango slices it makes an instant pickle. Yum!

We perch on a low hanging branch that over the years has become a convenient swing. Bobbing up and down on the branch, we lift our faces to catch the sunlight as it filters through the branches above. If only life were this simple, ripe mangoes, warm sunlight and a clear blue sky above.

All at once, I spot a flash of colour to my left. A guy in a bright red shirt is striding quickly through the trees.

'Neha, someone's coming,' I warn her. 'Look, he's over there.'

'What? Where?' she asks looking around and spotting him immediately. 'Oh no. Let's run.'

Both of us take flight while keeping a tight hold on the fruit we have plucked.

Seeing us, the guy breaks into a run yelling out to us.

'That does not sound good,' I yell to Neha as we reach the spot where Samir is waiting for us.

'Samir. Samir, there's a guy after us,' Neha yells. 'Run, run.'

Samir emerges from behind the tree looking scared.

The guard is now closing in on us.

Seeing the guard, Samir waves and yells at him. The guard slows down unsure if Samir is going to put up a fight. Instead, Samir takes out his wallet and extracts a couple of notes, waving them at the guy.

'Wait, wait, I've got money,' he yells. Showing the notes to the guy, he carefully places the notes on the ground and walks away. The guard stops and counts the notes. Satisfied, he leaves, smiling and waving as he walks away.

'Why did you give him money?' Neha asks him breathlessly when we reach the safety of the road.

'So that he'd stop chasing us,' says Samir reasonably. 'Besides, now that we've paid for the fruit, they can't complain about us.'

'I hope they don't expect to get paid every time,' I say in a worried tone. 'But thanks anyway.'

The mangoes are warm and delicious. We tear the skin of the fruit with our teeth and devour the soft flesh inside. Finishing the fruit in minutes, we chase the rivulets of juice that drip down our arms. After a quick clean up at a tap on the side of the road, it's time for lunch.

On the way to the dining hall, we introduce Samir to our favourite walking rhymes, starting with this one-

'A farmer got drunk and packed up his trunk and left, left, left, his wife and 49 children in a starving condition...'

We're so busy matching our feet to the rhyme, we don't hear someone yelling out to us.

'Hey, freshie,' someone yells. 'Hey, stop, we need to talk to you.'

The three of us finally stop to figure out where the sound is coming from.

Ah, of course. It's the A2Z Bullies.

Every school has bullies aka thugs or tormentors. We have Aadesh, Appu and Zoravar or the A2Z Bullies.

Aadesh is tall and skinny with a perpetually angry (hangry?) expression, Appu is large with a potbelly hanging over his jeans and Zoravar is short and thick set with a gummy smile.

'Freshie,' Aadesh says addressing Samir. 'You have to stop when we call you.'

'Says who?' asks Neha stepping in front of Samir.

Aadesh looks a bit peeved on seeing Neha and me. We've had a few run-ins with these guys and have never backed down.

'Neha, you stay out of this,' Zoravar says with a gummy grin that hides his true intent. 'You don't have 'Freshie Month' in the girl's hostel. We do and the rule is we can get to know the freshies.'

'Really?' I ask. 'Does TK Sir know this rule? If not, we can let him know.'

'Hey, hey,' Appu says, moving his large bulk to join the conversation. He raises his hands. 'Why are we all getting so serious? We're just trying to be friendly. That's all.'

'There's better ways of being friendly than yelling at him,' declares Neha. 'And if you try anything, we'll tell TK Sir and the headmaster. I promise.'

'Now, now, Neha, Naina,' Zoravar says with a smarmy look that would make Kaa the snake, proud. 'You don't want to be called a sneak or a tattletale now, do you?'

Neha and I look at each other while considering his question.

'If you don't mind being called a bully or a thug,' I tell him. 'I don't mind being called a sneak.'

'C'mon,' Neha tells Samir as the three of us turn away. 'Ignore them. But if they bully you, let us know.'

'You can't protect him all the time, you know,' Appu yells out, as we walk away. 'We'll get him on his own, one day.'

As tempting as it is to end this exchange with a rude hand gesture, Neha and I refrain from doing that. The three of us carry on walking.

FOUR

'Girls approaching,' yells a boy as soon as he spots us on the road to the senior boy's hostel.

'Females coming to the hostel,' yells another boy running towards the large grey building to warn the hostel inmates. Then more accurately he yells, 'Girls reaching in ten seconds. Ten seconds, guys.'

'Dames approaching the hostel,' this cry comes from within the hostel, and we hear an echo of it repeated a couple of times inside the building.

'Dames? Really?' I ask Neha in mock seriousness. 'That is so 1920's. I'm insulted.'

We both chuckle at this elaborate security system. All we are doing is visiting the senior boy's hostel, but from the cries we just heard you'd be forgiven for thinking we were an advancing army.

Anytime a girl visits the boy's hostel, a lookout yells a warning to the other boys. Neha and I have been to this hostel many times over the years as her brother Aditya or Adi for short, was at school till last year. We get the same over-the-top greeting every time. When pressed, Adi said it was a warning to the other boys not to emerge clad only in shorts or less.

Eww! In that case they can keep their security system.

The building in front of us was built at the same time as our hostel and sports a similar façade of grey granite blocks. The boy's hostel has large balconies and open walkways while ours has a solid frontage, and all corridors open onto a courtyard. The front of our hostel has a pretty garden with a hedge running around it. In contrast the front of the boy's hostel is dry and sandy. Just two cacti plants have managed to survive.

We wave out to Samir when we spot him on one of the balconies. He knows about our visit today.

'Hey Samir,' Neha calls out to him. 'Can you tell Amar we're here to see him? And please tell TK Sir we are here to see Amar about the competition,' she adds.

TK Sir is the senior boys hostel warden in addition to being our English teacher.

'Also, let Sir know we got permission from Anita Ma'am to visit your hostel,' I add. Samir yells ok and disappears inside.

All this might seem excessive to someone new, but as students we know that despite being a co-ed boarding school (or perhaps because of it) teachers do not encourage visits to each other's hostels. Which seems logical if you are a teacher or a warden but not so much to us students.

Neha nudges me as Amar emerges from the hostel. The standard short haircut given to all male students, suits him nicely. He is wearing denim shorts and a rumpled *Metallica* t-shirt.

'He looks good even in a wrinkled t-shirt. Now that is hard to achieve,' notes Neha in a low whisper as he comes towards us. 'Perhaps there *is* something about Bombay boys.'

'Hi Neha, Naina,' says Amar as he joins us. 'What's up? Samir said you wanted to talk to me. Must be something important to risk coming to our hostel,' he adds with a laugh.

'My brother Aditya was in school till last year, so we are used to it,' Neha explains. 'Amar, the reason we are here is to ask a big favour of you.' She smiles brilliantly up at him.

'Sounds serious, but I'll help if I can.'

'Well, it's about the inter-class competition. As per the rules, every song needs to be accompanied by a guitar or piano. And in our batch, you are the only one who plays the guitar.'

'You want me to play the guitar for Naina's solo?' asks Amar before she can finish.

Neha turns and gives me a *now-would-be-a-good-time-to-say-something* look.

'Yes,' I agree, but my voice comes out as a whisper. Clearing my throat, I try again. 'Yes, please. I need you to accompany me on the guitar.'

I glance at him quickly, hoping he can't see that I'm nervous he might refuse my request. I get the full force of those light brown eyes and it triggers a funny, weightless feeling in my stomach. The feeling you get while standing on the edge of a precipice. His expression doesn't give much away but I'm sure he'd like to say a lot more. He can't have forgotten I was a bit rude the last time we met.

Instead, he says, 'Sure, not a problem. We have a practice session tomorrow, right?'

'Yes,' I say nodding in relief. Wow, this is way easier than I expected. I was worried for no reason. I give Neha a triumphant smile. See? Not much grovelling needed!

And contrary to what Samir said, Amar doesn't seem interested in me at all. That's another bullet dodged.

'So, we'll see you tomorrow, then,' I say hastily, wanting to wrap it all up.

Done and dusted!

'On one condition' he says with a small pause. I glance at him in alarm. 'I need a favour from you. It's folk dancing night tonight, isn't it?'

'Yes,' I agree cautiously. 'The second Sunday of every month is folk dancing night for senior students.'

'Great. So tonight, how about you teach me a couple of dances?' he asks. 'That sounds fair, don't you think?'

'It's not that exciting,' I tell him trying to sound very casual. 'Just some slow folk dances. Quite boring really. Nothing like a disco or a party,' I add in desperation, hoping he'll change his mind.

'No problem,' Amar says. Now there is a definite twinkle in his eyes. He knows what I am trying to do.

'And everyone has to dress formally,' I say in a last attempt to ward him off. I pause to take a breath.

'I think I can manage that, Naina,' he says gravely, waiting for me to try another tactic. I have run out of excuses. I look at Neha for help. She doesn't say anything but is looking very amused by this exchange.

'Right, so that's settled,' she says jumping in suddenly. 'See you at seven thirty tonight, Amar.'

'I'll be there,' Amar assures us as he turns to go back to the hostel.

'That was very smoothly done,' Neha nods in appreciation on the way back to our hostel. 'Very smooth.'

'Him or me?' I ask, though I know the answer already.

'Him,' she confirms. 'Samir's right, he likes you.'

'I could have done with some help from you Neha,' I tell her, but she shakes her head at me.

'I helped convince him to play the guitar, didn't I? The rest of it was beyond my scope as a friend,' she says with a wide grin. 'But, very entertaining. He has you figured out, Naina.'

'But you're my *best* friend,' I protest to her.

'I am, and a best friend should know when to step aside,' she says with a sly smile and a wink. 'Relax, Naina, it's no big deal. Just some boring folk dances like you said.'

*   *

I'd be lying if I said we don't look forward to folk dancing night every month. I know fifteen-year-olds in Bombay are doing more exciting things on a weekend. But for us this is exciting. We get a chance to dress up, go dancing and stay out till nine thirty.

By seven that evening we are raring to go. Priya, Neha, and I are checking out what each other is wearing while applying a last layer of lip gloss. The three of us are wearing colourful and festive midi skirts with cotton tops. Some of the dances have slow, graceful movements and it's better to wear something loose to dance in. Jyothi's not joining us tonight. She looks quite tired, so we urge her to have a hot mug of Bournvita and take it easy.

'You will miss Naina's big date tonight,' Neha tells her. 'But don't worry. We'll tell you all about it tomorrow.'

'It's not a date,' I say for the umpteenth time, but no one listens to me. My roomies are so excited a guy has managed to pin me down to a date. Which it isn't of course.

'Ok,' counters Priya laughing. 'It's a non-date. But please let me have at least one dance with Amar, Mr Hot New Guy.'

'Just go and have fun,' declares Jo. 'And think of me when you are doing the chicken dance.'

We agree to her request with a laugh. Jo is not much of a dancer, preferring to watch from the side. The only song that gets her on the floor is the infamous chicken dance which is played at least once each time.

As we join the other girls on the way to the hall, I am a bit nervous. While I'm happy it's folk dancing night, I'm also nervous about dancing with Amar. Maybe he was just teasing and won't attend after all. But what if he does?

Once we arrive at the hall, I forget everything else and join the large group of girls and boys who are already there. The benches that usually fill the hall have been pushed to the side creating a large space for dancing.

Music and dancing, what more can one ask for on a Sunday night? Sure, the music they play is not fast or current, but I don't mind. And by the looks of it, this group doesn't either.

'Can I have the first dance with you, fair maiden?' asks a familiar voice and I turn to see Samir. My eyes widen as I take in the vision before me.

'It's meant to be formal dress,' I say pointing to his colourful ensemble.

'I am formally dressed,' he protests with a wide goofy grin. 'This is my version of formal.'

Over dark trousers and a shirt he is wearing a silver-coloured bomber jacket with the word *'Disco'* in multicoloured letters over his left pocket.

'And the best part is this,' he declares, turning to show me the back of the jacket where the word *'DISCO'* covers most of it. I also notice the back of his trimmed hair has a row of silver stars painted on. 'Business in the front, party in the back. What do you think?'

'How did you create such neat stars on your hair?' I ask in wonder.

'A stencil and a spray can of silver paint,' he says. 'Don't worry, it washes out easily.'

'You look amazing. I'm a little jealous, to be honest,' I say with a half laugh. 'What if we have an actual Disco night someday?'

'I have more stuff like this,' he says with another wide grin. I believe him.

The large speakers in the hall suddenly come alive with static noise signalling the start of the first dance. Samir takes my hand, and we join the rest of the students on the floor. The first song is a popular Jewish folk song. This version starts off slow, making it easy for me to show Samir the steps. Gradually the tempo of the song gets faster and faster leaving us breathless but happy when it ends.

'Wow,' says Samir clapping with the rest of us and trying to catch his breath at the same time. 'When they said folk dancing, I thought I'd be snoozing through the dances. But this is a good workout.' He abandons his jacket on a chair.

'It is,' I agree as the next number starts playing. It's *Isle of Capri*, for which we need to form two large circles. The dance requires us to dip and sway to the catchy tune, changing partners till we are back to our original partner. I am quite out of breath after it.

Neha claims Samir as her partner, and I decide to take a break.

Caught up in watching the dance, I jump when a deep voice says 'Hi, Naina, mind if I join you?'

Amar dressed in a cream shirt and black trouser is standing nearby. He certainly cleans up well. He moves closer and I catch a whiff of a fresh citrus, woody scent. 'Sorry, did I startle you?'

'Hi,' I reply as my stomach takes a familiar dive again. 'I wondered if you'd make it tonight or not.'

'Hoping I would, or I wouldn't?' he asks with a chuckle.

'It wouldn't matter if you had or not,' I say in what I hope is a nonchalant tone.

'Really?' he asks with a smile. 'I didn't want to come here only to see you leave. Because the last few times we've met, you've always been in a hurry to leave, no scratch that, to run away from me.'

'That sounds very dramatic, don't you think?' I ask, trying to defend myself.

'The first time you ruined my shoes and ran, the second time you chose the longer route and ran, the third time, you....' He counts each instance off on his fingers and I interrupt him hurriedly.

'Ok, ok,' I say. 'It may have seemed like that, but I wasn't running away from you.'

'Oh good,' he says with a wide grin. 'Glad we cleared that up. You're looking lovely tonight'.

'Thank you,' I reply, caught off guard by the compliment. 'You, too,' I say without thinking this through.

'Lovely, me?' he shoots back as I should have known he would.

'Better than you did this afternoon,' I amend.

'I'll take that as a compliment,' he says solemnly.

As a new song starts, I take a deep breath and decide to take the plunge.

'Shall we dance?'

'I thought you'd never ask,' he replies.

We join our friends on the floor accompanied by lots of clapping from Samir, Neha, and Priya. Thanks guys. I was hoping we'd blend in with the crowd, clearly that's not an option.

For my luck this dance requires us to dance as a couple. I show Amar the steps keeping as much distance as I can, between us.

'I don't bite, you know,' he says disarmingly.

'Sorry?' I say trying not to lose my concentration.

'I'm no expert at this,' he says. 'But I'm sure we can fit a whole other person between us.'

He's right of course. Once the music starts, I have no option but to move closer.

Dancing with him is easier than I expected. He picks up the steps quickly and I realise we move well together.

My heart is still beating fast. I remind myself that we are just dancing, nothing more. Between dances I steal a look at him which he notices.

'Better? Not too scary dancing with me?' he deadpans.

'I'm not scared of you,' I tell him. 'I'm just awkward sometimes.'

I find it difficult to look at his face, so I settle for a point below his chin.

After a few dances we switch partners with Samir and Neha. Midway through the next dance, Samir pulls a cassette from his trouser pocket and shows it to me.

'I was hoping to play a few songs from this tonight. Do you think it's possible?'

'We'll have to ask for permission,' I say looking around to see who is in charge tonight. Every folk dancing night, there are two teachers on hand to see things go smoothly. Tonight, it's the turn of our Hindi teacher and his wife.

'Hello Naina, how come you are not dancing?' Sharma Sir asks as we approach him and his wife.

'Hello Sharma Sir, can we play a few of our own songs in the last ten minutes tonight?' I ask with what I hope is a winning smile. He looks at his wife. She gives him a small nod. She knows me well as she coaches us in classical music. He agrees to our request. We thank them both happily and make our way to the guy manning the sound system. Occasionally it helps to have a good reputation, I decide.

Samir rewinds the cassette and waits for the last dance to end.

'What songs are you going to play?' I ask, worried they may not go down well.

'Don't worry,' he says confidently. 'You'll like them, I promise.'

He taps the microphone and says, 'Hi everyone. For the last ten minutes of tonight's session, we have permission to play some pop songs. Here goes, hope you like them.'

The song starts and I recognise the title track of *Footloose*, a movie I saw over the summer holidays. Happily, most of the crowd stays on the floor for the next two songs as well. As the last song ends, we all wish we could dance for a while longer. However, rules are rules.

Collecting our jackets and wraps we say our goodbyes and head for the stairs. It must have rained earlier since the night feels much cooler now. I put on the jean jacket I brought with me and walk briskly with Neha and Priya towards our hostel.

'Naina, just a minute,' I almost miss the voice from behind amidst the sound of our chatter. Turning, I see Amar behind us. 'Do you have a minute?' he asks.

I fall behind to talk to him as my roomies carry on. All at once I am nervous about why he wants to talk to me. I kept my side of the deal tonight and taught him two of the dances. That makes us even, right?

'Hey' I say as he starts walking with me. My mind goes into overdrive. Do I have to walk with him all the way to the crossroads? What does he want to ask me? What does this mean? Is this about him liking me? Does he want to ask if we can start dating, be a couple or something along those lines? All these thoughts swirl around in my head. I decide that if he asks me, I will just have to gently and firmly say 'No'.

'I wanted to ask you…' Amar begins but I interrupt him before he can finish.

'Amar,' I say in a rush. 'I need to tell you that I can't do it. I really can't. It's nothing to do with you. It's just that I'm so busy with the all the stuff I take part in, plus preparing for the board exam. It's not possible for us to date. So, it's best we remain friends.'

I end my spiel when I realise, he has gone very quiet and very still, while looking straight ahead.

'You can't do what exactly?' he asks once the words stop tumbling from my mouth.

'Err, umm…you were going to ask if we could be more than… Wait, what were you going to ask me?' I realise, I don't have a clue.

'I was going to ask if I could bring some cassettes tomorrow so we could choose a song for you,' he says. 'What did you think I was going to say?'

Right then I feel like the biggest fool this side of the equator. I feel my cheeks go pink then red. Thankfully it's too dark for him to see how embarrassed I am.

'Oh, that's fine. We can choose a song tomorrow,' I mumble in reply hoping he didn't get the gist of what I said earlier.

'Wait, what did you say about us remaining friends?' he asks suddenly.

I shake my head, willing myself to keep quiet and hoping I won't succumb to verbal diarrhoea again.

'I think you've guessed that I like you, Naina,' he says once he realises, I'm not going to say anything. 'But I have no idea if you feel the same way.'

If I open my mouth now, the truth he wants to hear will come tumbling out. The fact that I really like him too. That I like the way he looks at me. The way he teases me when I'm being too serious. The way he says my name, like no one else has said it before. That I'm scared liking him will turn my world upside down and change it forever and I don't know if I can handle that. Instead, I say nothing, nothing at all. I pull my denim jacket closer. I'm suddenly cold.

'Are you going to stay quiet till we reach the crossroads?' he asks when I don't reply.

'That's the plan,' I admit. I glance at him from the side. I can't tell what he is thinking.

'It's alright for you,' I say finally. 'All this comes easily to you.'

'Meaning what, exactly?'

'You're from Bombay. You've had a lot of practice. At flirting, girlfriends, the whole thing.'

'And you haven't?'

'No.'

'How come?' he sounds curious. 'You're from Bombay too.

Haven't you dated there? Or here?'

'I'm a 'Bombay girl' only in name,' I say with air quotes. 'All my growing up was done here. And no, I haven't dated. I don't plan to till after the board exams.'

'So romance is off the agenda till after the exams. What if you meet someone before that? What if you fall in love?'

I shake my head resolutely. 'I won't. Romance is great in books and novels. In real life it's messy. And painful. Someone's heart always gets broken.'

'Life is messy, Naina. And sometimes painful. That's the whole point of it,' he says reasonably. 'It's a roller coaster ride.'

'I have to go,' I say as we reach the crossroads.

Ahead of me I see Neha and Priya waiting for me under a lamplight. Another lamplight behind Amar keeps his face in the dark. I can't make out his expression.

'Saved by the crossroads again,' he says ruefully. He takes a step towards me, saying, 'So you want to be just friends?'

'Yes, I'd prefer that,' I say though my voice sounds unsure even to my ears.

'I already have friends, but if that's what you want, then fine,' he replies. Reaching out he moves a lock of hair away from my face. 'I hope you're right about what you want.'

'Good night, Amar,' I manage to say.

'Good night, Naina,' he says, leaning closer. I want to move away but I can't. My feet seem to be rooted to the ground. I close my eyes and feel something soft touch my forehead.

Then he's gone and only a faint woody, citrus fragrance suggests he was ever around.

I jerk loose from the spot and take the stairs two at a time. I can feel a sob making its way up my throat. Neha and Priya stop talking when they see me running down the path towards them.

'Was that a non-kiss for the non-date?' Priya asks but on seeing my face she hugs me tight and asks, 'Oh Naina, what happened?'

I'm saved from saying anything since Anita Ma'am is calling us from the door of the hostel. As we hurry in, she closes the door.

FIVE

A few hours later I wake up with a start. The little clock with luminous hands on the dressing table tells me it is two o'clock. Must have been a bad dream that woke me up. Moonlight streams in through our window. Now that I am awake, I might as well go to the loo. Grabbing a small torch and a cardigan, I make for the door of our room. It's ajar which means one of my roomies is already outside. I glance at the other beds, but I can't tell who it is.

Once outside I quickly put my cardigan on. The nights get quite cold closer to winter. I hear a muffled sob and spot someone sitting on the stairs leading to up to the first floor of the hostel.

'Priya? Jo?' I whisper. 'Neha?'

'It's Jo,' comes the reply.

'Jo, what's the matter?' I ask in alarm as I sit beside her. 'Are you felling unwell?'

She sniffs softly,' I'm ok Naina. I couldn't sleep so I came out here. I didn't want to disturb all of you. Did I wake you?'

'No, I needed to go to the loo,' I assure her. 'What is it, Jo? You've been out of sorts lately.' I give her a quick hug. She feels thinner somehow. 'You've lost weight too.'

She nods. 'It's about my sister, Chitra. I'm worried about her.'

'Is she alright?' I ask. 'She must have started her degree by now.'

She nods again.

Jyothi and her sister Chitra are from America. They joined our school in their teens because their parents felt they were missing out on Indian culture and were growing up too American. Jo is the reason we start each term with a large supply of Tang and yummy American chocolates and sweets. Along with issues of *Seventeen* magazine. Chitra completed the twelfth standard exam last year and returned to America.

'She met a guy at a party last year and they started dating. My parents don't approve of him as he is American and white,' Jo explains. 'They asked her to stop seeing him, but she refuses. Now she's threatening to leave home and stay with her boyfriend.'

'Ok,' I say slowly trying to decide where the problem is. 'She's over eighteen, so she can do that, right?'

'Yeah, but my parents are paying for her to go to university, so she has to listen to them,' Jo says, as she starts sobbing quietly. 'If she gets a scholarship to cover her fees and living expenses, she'll leave home. So…my family might be split in two and I can't do anything about it.'

'I'm so sorry Jo, I had no idea what you were going through,' I tell her. 'I should have asked if you were ok.'

Jo always looks out for us, and I feel guilty for not asking her why she hasn't been herself lately.

'Naina, Jo, what are you doing here?' asks Neha from the foot of the stairs.

Jo and I give a start on seeing Neha. She climbs up to where we are sitting.

'I was worried when I got up and found both of you gone,' says Neha. Crossing her arms over her t-shirt, she shivers a bit. 'Wow, it's cold out here, guys. Let's go back inside.'

'That's true,' I say. 'It has gotten quite cold. You two go ahead, I still need to go to the loo.'

Back in our room, the four of us discuss Chitra's dilemma while keeping warm under blankets and quilts.

'Is Chitra ready to leave home to be with her boyfriend?' asks Priya.

'Yes, she is pretty serious about him but is scared of leaving my parents and our home,' answers Jo.

'Don't know if I could do that,' Priya says.

'What about you Neha?' asks Jo. 'If you had to choose between Arjun and your parents, who would you choose?'

Gosh,' Neha answers in a subdued tone. 'I hope I never have to choose.'

I listen quietly. *If falling in love can break up a family and cause so much pain, is it worth it?*

'Naina?' Jo looks at me.

'I don't think I could leave home and not go back,' I say slowly. 'It sounds so…final. I wish we could help you in some way, Jo.'

Looking at the three of us she says, 'Actually I think you already did. Just talking it over with all of you has helped a lot.'

'We must tell each other what we are going through,' I say. 'It's why we became roomies right? Because we liked and trusted each other.'

I wonder if life will ever get that difficult for us. Is this what it means to grow up and become an adult?

'Naina, you never told us what happened between Amar and you last night,' Priya suddenly says.

'Nothing happened,' I say reluctantly.

I hadn't said much on our return to the hostel, and my roommates didn't ask me about it.

'He wanted to bring some music for me to listen to.'

'And that upset you?' Neha probes.

I sigh, 'He said he liked me,' I take a deep breath. 'And…and since I don't have feelings like that for him, I… I told him we should be friends instead. End of story.' My voice sounds scratchy and uneven to me. 'Besides, you know my rules about dating anyone.'

'Oh Naina, I thought you liked him.'

'What did he say?'

'Poor Amar. Was he surprised?'

I knew it would lead to more questions. I wish I hadn't said anything at all. That would be ironic after my spiel about being good roomies and sharing everything.

'Hang on, if *you* don't have feelings for Amar, why were you so upset last night?' Priya asks seriously.

'I don't know,' I admit to Priya. After a pause, I add, 'Actually I do. I think this is a good time to tell you and Jo why I'm so reluctant to date or get involved with anyone.'

I glance over at Neha who nods encouragingly. Till now she was the only one who knew why I behave the way I do.

It was the summer I turned thirteen. Like every other teen, I was going through a roller coaster of emotions. Insecurities and anxieties plagued me daily. Was I too tall? Too skinny? Not pretty enough? Not sophisticated enough. When would I look grown up? When would someone be interested in me?

I was home for the holidays. It would be two and a half months till we were back at school. Every summer we planned a lot of activities which included a few weeks away from the heat of Bombay. This summer however, my parents were busy with the wedding of my cousin which was a week away. Neel, my brother, was busy with college as usual.

Left on my own, I was a little bored.

One morning, I sat in my parents' bedroom watching my mum get ready for a full day of wedding planning. My dad had promised to help me with a school project after work; till then I was on my own.

As I crossed the hall, the phone rang. I had a large bowl of ice cream in one hand and an *Asterix* comic in the other. The last thing I wanted to do was answer the phone. I knew it wouldn't be for me, anyway.

'Naina, can you answer the phone?' my mum said on her way out of the front door. 'If it's for me, please take a message. See you later, sweetie.'

The door closed behind her.

'Hello,' I said, trying to sound grown up. 'This is the Kumar residence.'

'Well, hello,' a male voice said. 'What luck. I'm looking for Neel who I'm told is part of the Kumar residence. Could I speak to him?'

The voice was smooth and velvety with a distinct American accent. He sounded grown up and very sure of himself.

'I'm sorry, Neel's not at home,' I answered politely, checking the bowl to see how my ice-cream was doing. 'I can give him a message when he returns.'

'That's too bad,' the guy on the other side said. 'But since he's not around, I'm happy to talk to you.'

Like most girls I'd been told not to talk to strangers, many times. Without missing a beat, I replied, 'Sorry, but I don't talk to strangers.'

This was answered with a chuckle. 'See, I'm not a stranger. I'm Meena Auntie's nephew. I'm here to attend my cousin's wedding.'

Meena Aunty was my mother's older sister whose daughter was getting married at the end of the week.

'Oh,' I replied, not sure what to say next. 'Ok, if you give me your name and number, I'll ask Neel to call you.'

'My name's Rael, and this is my number,' he replied, giving me his contact number. 'What's your name? It's only fair I know who I'm speaking to.'

'My name is Naina,' I said reluctantly, still hoping to end the conversation so I could get to my ice-cream and comic book.

'That's a lovely name to go with a lovely voice,' came the smooth reply. 'Are you as pretty as your name?'

At thirteen I was new to the world of flattery and insincere words. Besides no one really looked at me as anything more than a kid. So, his attempt at a compliment fell flat.

'Sorry I don't know what you mean,' I told him truthfully.

'Never mind,' Rael replied. 'It was nice talking to you, Naina.'

I left a message for Neel and forgot about the phone call.

The next day, the phone rang around the same time. It was Rael again, still waiting for Neel to return his call.

'I left your name and number on Neel's desk.' I assured Rael politely. 'I'll leave another reminder for him to call you.'

'That's alright,' Rael said smoothly. 'At least I get to talk to you again. How are you spending your holidays?'

That was the start of a week of phone calls and long conversations. Rael called every day around the same time, having figured out that I was on my own. While the maids went about their work, he and I chatted on the phone.

It was flattering to have someone who spoke to me like I was a grown up. He never asked how old I was, so I never told him. I instinctively knew the rest of my family would not approve so I didn't tell anyone about these calls. Besides, it felt good to have a secret of my own. It made me feel important.

On the day of the wedding, I was giddy with excitement. I was finally going to meet Rael in person. In the car, I asked Neel if he'd spoken to Rael since he'd left a couple of messages.

'No, I never got around to it,' Neel replied. 'It doesn't matter anyhow.'

I didn't have a chance to find out what he meant because we had reached the wedding venue by then. Rael turned out to be a twenty-five-year-old guy in a badly fitting suit, with an obvious squint, and a nervous tic in his shoulder. He was shocked to see how young I was, and I was dismayed to find out I was just one of many girls, he had been calling and chatting up that week.

I never mentioned this episode to anyone in my family, too mortified by how easily I was taken in by a creepy guy with a great voice on the phone. Clearly, I was a bad of judge of character and I was not ready for any of this. That's when I set these rules to save myself from future heartbreak.

> 1. Don't get involved with or date anyone till after school.
>
> 2. Save yourself the pain of rejection, breaking up and

> *heartbreak.*
>
> 3. *Concentrate on important things like studying, the choir and dramatics.*

When I finish, Priya and Jo rush to my defense. 'It could have happened to anyone, Neha,' Priya points out. 'This guy sounds like a real jerk.'

'True,' Jo agrees. 'Sounds like he does this sort of thing a lot. Lucky for you, this was over the phone and not in person.'

'But it proved how little I know of guys. And that I wasn't ready to get involved. After that, I've steered clear of guys and dating,' I explain.

'Amar doesn't look the sort to act that way,' Neha says thoughtfully. 'He seems more mature than that.'

I look at her doubtfully. I wish I could believe her, but few things in life come with a guarantee.

* *

I'm in a strange mood the next day. On the one hand I'm dreading attending the rehearsal yet strangely I can't wait for classes to be over. The last class appears to go on forever. By the end of it, I've worked myself into a panic. What if I turn up and Amar doesn't? What if he turns up and is rude and dismissive to me? Or he refuses to work with me?

The last scenario would be totally understandable. Teenage egos are fragile, delicate things as I know all too well. I run out of any more possible scenarios. Instead, I keep turning the same ones over and over in my mind.

Then a germ of an idea forms in my head. What if I fall sick and can't attend the rehearsal? That seems like the solution to all my problems.

'Can't wait for today's rehearsal,' Neha says breathlessly joining me on the way back to the hostel. 'We have to cover so much in five days.'

'Yeah, about that,' I start hesitantly. 'I'm not feeling too well.'

'Naina don't even try that,' Neha turns to me. 'You can't skip today's rehearsal. We only have five days to prepare.'

'What if he's not there?' I stop and ask worriedly. 'Or what if he is but he won't talk to me?'

'Who?' the blank look on her face shows she's forgotten all about my predicament.

'Amar.'

'Oh, he'll be there,' she continues walking.

'Wait,' I catch up with her, pulling on her arm to get her attention. 'How do you know? Did he tell you?'

'We had a quick catch up about *Bohemian Rhapsody* after class, so I'm positive he'll be there. Feeling better?' she asks with a smile.

Feeling better is not possible right now but I link my arm through hers as we carry on walking.

When we reach the assembly hall after a quick shower, it's reassuring to see the number of students already there.

'Naina, you're just the person I was waiting for,' Samir greets me cheerfully. 'Amar and I had a blast going through our collection of cassettes last night. We've chosen a few we think you'll like. C'mon, I'll show them to you.'

I follow him to the far corner of the hall where a cassette player sits amidst stacks and stacks of tapes.

'That looks like a lot of tapes,' I exclaim. 'I thought you narrowed it down to a few?'

'Oh shoot, I'm sure the ones we chose for you, are here somewhere. Wait, here's Amar,' Samir sounds relieved. 'He'll know where those cassettes are.'

'Hey Naina,' Amar greets me casually. He's dressed in a black t-shirt and jeans, but somehow makes that classic combination look good. My heart starts beating faster as I recall the last time we met. I'm finding it difficult to look directly at him, wondering just how this is going to go.

He reaches behind the cassette player and hands me a bunch of tapes with a smile. And just like that, I know we're going to be fine. His voice and behaviour are so normal, no one would guess the gist of our last conversation. And going by Samir's manner, Amar hasn't told him either.

I can relax. It's going to be okay. After all it's not like we dated, or anything. For the next hour, we work through the choices till we have just two songs, *Angel of the Morning* by Juice Newton and *Diamonds and Rust* by Joan Baez.

'I suggest you listen to them on your own and decide which song you prefer,' Amar says handing the two tapes to me. 'Then we'll work on it, tomorrow.' He also hands me a Sony Walkman, 'This will help with the harder parts of the song.'

I take the Walkman reluctantly, turning it over to find a small sticker with Amar's name fixed to the underside. It feels so intimate, somehow, holding the device he probably uses every day and every night. Besides, I don't feel comfortable accepting anything from him.

'Relax, Naina,' he says, noticing my reluctance. His tone is mildly teasing, 'I'm only lending it to you for the next few days.'

'I knew that of course,' I tell him, quickly. 'What'll you use instead?'

'I'll borrow Samir's, if I need to,' he assures me.

I'm saved from saying anything else by Neha and Rahul, who come over to see how we're getting on. While the two guys are talking, Neha looks at me briefly with raised eyebrows. I give her a small nod. All good so far. But today is only day one.

After dinner, I claim my favourite armchair in the common room, the one that faces a large window. I place the Walkman in my lap and take a cassette out of its cover. Amar's name is written in bold, black ink on the small, white label. His cursive writing is confident and assured.

An image of him sitting on the steps, strumming his guitar comes to mind. A smart, funny guy who loves music and plays the guitar. It's what any girl would want in a boyfriend. Not me, of course given my reluctance to fall in love and my rules, but some other girl willing to take a chance. With a sigh, I slot the cassette in and start listening.

* *

'Do you know how to read music?' Amar scans the paper on which I've written the words of *Diamonds and Rust,* the song I chose last night.

'No, I never got the chance to, before I joined school. Besides, here we are trained in Indian classical music.'

'How do you balance the two worlds of Indian and Western music?' he sounds curious. 'The two are pretty different, aren't they?'

'For me a good melody is what matters,' I point out. 'Whether it's Western or Indian music, doesn't matter.'

'Never thought of it that way,' Amar says with a nod. 'Once you learn to play the guitar or piano, it's easy to read Western music.'

Seeing the doubt on my face, he offers, 'I could teach you if you want. It's not that hard.'

I turn his offer over in my mind. Is this a ruse to get close to me? But Amar goes back to studying the lyrics, so I decide he's just being helpful and …. nice. That's a surprise. It makes me feel bad for turning him down. I almost wish he was rude and stand-offish; that would be understandable. And easier to deal with.

Before we start, Amar points out the basic notes he's added above the words of the song and explains what each one means. When we get to the end of the page, we reach out simultaneously to turn it over. Our hands touch, the shock of the contact making me pull away quickly.

'Static electricity,' Amar observes. It wasn't, but I don't correct him.

He strums the opening notes while a familiar tingle goes through me. I get goose bumps the first time I sing any song. Some get me tingly every time I sing them; this song is going to be one of them. When I'm singing, I don't think about anything else. For a few minutes nothing exists, but the song and the guitar.

I reach the last line, my voice fading away while Amar ends with a flourish.

'That sounded good for a first attempt,' he says appreciatively.

'It did,' I agree with him. 'I practised a lot, last night. I'm guessing you did too.'

He grins, 'Yes, I did.'

'I'm surprised you listen to Joan Baez,' I continue. 'I thought Metallica and Pink Floyd would be more your kind of music.'

'Isn't that stereotyping?' Amar asks seriously.

'Sorry,' I say lifting my hands in mock surrender. 'I didn't mean to be judgemental.'

'Actually, you're right. I picked up a few of my mum's tapes by mistake,' Amar admits with a grin.

'But the tapes had your name on them.'

'First rule of hostel life; put your name on *everything* you own, or it will disappear,' Amar says ruefully. I chuckle at that. It feels good sharing a joke with him.

It's only when I notice the rest of our group packing up, that I realize the hour and a half has sped by so quickly. We all head for the dining hall, excited and happy. Neha and Samir are thrilled with the progress they made today. I look around for Amar, curious to see if he'll shift his interest from me to someone else. Reena and Priya are chatting to him as we go in for dinner, but he doesn't seem particularly interested in either.

'You've got to stop staring at him, Naina,' Neha teases, taking a seat next to me at the long table. 'For someone who is *not* interested in him you seem way too interested in him.'

'I don't know what you're talking about,' I protest.

'I noticed you checking Amar out on the way to the dining hall,' she points a fork at me accusingly. 'You have to agree that you did.'

'I was only checking to see if he'd taken all the stuff he brought with him,' I insist. But Neha just winks at me.

* *

The next day, I fret over what to wear, before deciding on a light blue tunic and jeans. Amar is already there when I reach the hall. He is tuning his guitar, his long, slim fingers sliding gently over the strings; his head cocked to one side. I notice his brown t-shirt is a perfect foil for his eyes. He is so engrossed; it gives me a chance to study him. Would he have been a good boyfriend? I'll never know. Now that we are working together, I'm starting to like him a little. Or a lot more than I thought I would. Perhaps I rejected him too quickly, but I had to stick to my rules.

'Naina. Naina,' I snap back to reality with a start. Amar smiles, 'You were looking so serious just now. Is everything ok?'

Since I can't tell him I was thinking about *him*, I offer a shaky smile instead. If only we'd met at another time in my life, things may have been different.

We run through the song twice and then once more to work out some kinks. Taking a break, we chat about growing up in Bombay, the things we miss about the city and the things we don't. The schools, friends and family we left behind to study here. Talking to Amar is easy and enjoyable. Can dating someone be this simple? When do things get complicated?

Neha comes over and asks us to have a look at what they've done so far. Walking with Amar towards the front of the hall, I recall how apprehensive I was about these rehearsals three days ago. When he joins Samir in front of the stage, I realize with a pang of sadness there are only two more rehearsals left. Only two more days of spending time with Amar. Is he feeling the same way? Or is it just me? How did I go from not wanting to meet him, to looking forward to doing just that?

As the song begins, I'm blown away by how good the dramatic version is. Freddie Mercury once called *Bohemian Rhapsody* a 'mock opera' and the dance moves choreographed by Samir and Priya play on that. They are a good blend of modern dance steps with some elements of ballet added to it. My classmates clad in black leotards, run through the whole song collapsing in a dramatic heap on the stage as the last notes of the song play out. Those of us who are watching, clap madly.

'How is it?' Neha asks me apprehensively. 'Tell me the truth so we can make changes if necessary.'

'Only a couple of things need to be improved, Neha,' I assure her. 'Other than that, it's perfect. I don't know how you did all this, so quickly.'

'Really?' The grin on her face is ecstatic. 'You're sure of that?'

'Yes. I'm sure,' I say giving her a hug. 'Once the lighting is sorted, we'll see it at its best.'

As it turns out, Thursday is the last day that Amar and I get to spend time together. On Friday, we rehearse the two entries together to check we're keeping within the time allotted to us. Amar and I barely have time to exchange a few words before we run through it all again and again. As happy as I am the rehearsals are a success I'm disappointed it's all ending tomorrow.

That night I sit dejectedly on my bed, turning Amar's Walkman over in my hands. I run a finger over the label with his name on it. After the competition, I won't have a chance or excuse to talk to Amar. What am I going to do? Because we are in different sections, we may meet once a week if a teacher combines both sections for a class but other than that, the future looks bleak.

'Hey, you,' Neha bounces onto my bed. 'Why the long face? Cheer up. After tomorrow, you won't have to meet or talk to Amar. Your life can go back to what it was before.'

My life before I got to know and like Amar. I can barely recall it. I quickly go over my no-dating rules in my head hoping they will work like they usually do. As Neha leaves to brush her teeth before lights out, it occurs to me that if she knew what I was thinking right then, she'd have the biggest laugh of her life. And say, 'I told you so!'

SIX

The morning of the inter-class competition, I'm up early. I haven't figured out a solution to my problem. But rather than lying around in bed, moping, I get up and get dressed. I have an urge to see the sunrise and I know just the place to see it from.

I leave a note for my roommates telling them where I am going, then head upstairs to the first floor of the hostel where the eleventh and twelfth standard girls stay. Being a Saturday, no one else is up. I head to a place that Neha and I stumbled upon last year. It is an overhang that sits right under the roof at the front of the building. Few girls know about it and fewer still can swing up to reach it.

Once there I spread a thin quilt on the cold, concrete floor. Then I carefully set out the letter paper and pen I've brought with me. It's been ages since I wrote to Mimi, my friend back in Bombay. So much has happened, that I need to tell her about.

By now the sun's rays are peeping over the hills in front of me. As an audience of one, I am thrilled to be watching it. With the valley now bathed in a warm glow, I begin my letter. I finish one sheet and I'm about to start on the next when I hear a car approaching. Few cars are seen around here since our school is so far from any major city or town. I peek over the rim of the ledge to get a better view of the vehicle.

A white Ambassador reaches our hostel and parks outside. Must be parents here to visit their daughter. I wonder who the lucky girl is?

A lady inside the car glances at her watch but does not get out. The doors of the hostel are still closed, as it's so early.

From the other side of the car a man gets out. He looks so familiar that I crane my neck to get a better look.

From the close-cropped hair to the aquiline nose, I recognize my dad! In shock and surprise, I grab my things and swing down from the ledge, going down the stairs two at a time.

What are my parents doing here? And how come they never told me of this visit? No mention of it by letter or at our monthly phone call.

Anita Ma'am hears me fumbling with the bolts on the front door and comes out of her room.

'Naina, what's the matter?' she joins me at the front door, looking worried.

'My parents are here,' I tell her excitedly hardly able to get the words out. 'They're outside. I didn't know they were coming to visit me.'

With her help I get the doors open and hurry down the short flight of stairs. My dad sees me coming so he is ready when I launch myself at him. It's a good thing he is tall else I might have knocked him down in my excitement.

'Naina,' he says when I finally ease my grip on him. 'Sorry, we couldn't tell you in advance that we were coming.'

'It's ok,' I say bravely trying to fight back tears. 'I'm just glad you're here.'

'Let me get a good look at you,' my dad says. 'Have you grown taller?'

'Only a little,' I reply, my voice still a bit shaky. I feel shy suddenly, even though they are my parents.

My mom gets out of the taxi, and I launch myself at her though with a bit more restraint. As usual she is immaculately dressed in a pale peach shalwar set. She used to be a model before she got married and retains that poise and composure even now.

'Naina, so good to see you,' she says when I let go of her. 'Dad had an urgent meeting in Madras, so I decided to join him. That's why we didn't mention it in our letter last week.'

'It's fine,' I say happily. 'I don't mind surprises like this.'

My mom hugs me tightly while looking closely at me. People say I resemble her because we both have dark wavy hair, large eyes, and a wide mouth. But on her, the same features make more of an impact. I am used to being a diluted version of my mother.

'Have you lost some weight?' she asks. 'You seem a bit thinner. And a bit taller.'

'I'm five feet eight inches now,' I tell my mom proudly. 'That's why I look thinner. Where's Neel?' I ask looking around for my brother.

'He's preparing for the SAT exams so he couldn't make it,' my mum explains. 'But he's waiting to see you back in Bombay over the holidays.'

Anytime parents come to school, the student becomes a mini celebrity for a while. And that's how it is with me this weekend. Telling my parents, I'll meet them after class I return to the hostel. Everyone on our floor now knows my parents are in town and I get a lot of grins and a few envious glances. As much as we enjoy being at school the thrill of family visiting, never goes away.

The usual two hours of class every Saturday go by slowly. Wanting to spend time with my folks, I keep glancing at my watch, willing the hands to move faster.

'I'll have lunch with my mum and dad and meet you at the rehearsal,' I tell Neha. She nods, her hands full of props, papers and pins.

'It's looking really good, Neha' I tell her since she looks a bit worried. 'You don't have to worry about our entries.'

'It's not that,' she answers with a frown. 'I'm hoping we can move all the stuff we need over to the hall before practice.'

'Why don't we ask Samir or Rahul to help us?' I suggest.

'That's a great idea,' Neha says with a laugh. 'Don't know why I didn't think of it myself. Listen, go have lunch with your parents. We'll see you later.'

I give her a quick hug saying, 'We're going to win this, I know we will.'

Later that evening my dad drives the three of us to the hall. The building is ablaze with lights and looks quite full. Since this competition is for the senior school, only students from the eight to the twelfth grade will be attending.

'I wish Neel were here too,' my mum says as we reach the auditorium.

'Yeah, that would have been great,' I agree although knowing my brother, he and his friends must be planning a huge party at our apartment tonight. I grin at the thought.

I find chairs for my parents and ask Jo to keep an eye on them. Several of my teachers are here tonight and I know my parents will want to catch up with them later.

Backstage, everyone is dressed and ready. As the main character in this version of *Bohemian Rhapsody*, Samir is dressed in black tights and a long black shirt. Neha is applying white paint to his face. I go over to help.

'Let me do that Neha,' I say to her. 'I'm sure you want to check a few things before you go on stage.'

'Thanks,' she replies handing over the brush to me.

'Aha,' I tell Samir waving the brush in front of him. 'Your face is now in my hands.'

He grins. 'What did you think of the rehearsal yesterday? You left soon after, so I didn't get a chance to ask you.'

'It looked good. The dances you choreographed are dramatic and will make an impact.'

'Are your parents attending tonight's show?' he asks.

'You bet,' I say as I finish painting his face. 'They are excited to see what we are putting up. Hey, any idea where Amar is?'

'He said he'd be near the large speakers in case you were looking for him,' Samir replies. 'How's it going with the two of you?' he asks wiggling his eyebrows which are now white. 'Any chance you'll take pity on my brother?'

Shaking my head I say, 'It's not like that you know, Samir. We're friends.'

'Oh no, the old 'just friends' spiel,' he replies dramatically. 'Poor Amar.'

I stick my tongue out at him. 'Break a leg. I'll catch up with you later.'

I find Amar chatting to Gigi, a student in the ninth standard. She looks thrilled to be chatting with him. I feel a pang of envy and something else I can't put my finger on. Maybe, regret that I can't talk to him the same way.

Amar turns and sees me. 'Hey,' he lifts his hand in a small wave.

'Hey,' I as my heart rate quickens.

Gigi says bye and goes to join her classmates.

'All set?' Amar asks in a neutral tone, his face turned away from the light.

I nod. 'Going on stage is always exciting,' I say. 'The lights, the audience and hopefully the applause.'

'Yep,' he agrees. 'It's quite a heady feeling.'

'Amar, I wanted to thank you for…everything,' I try to gauge his expression but it's difficult in the dim light.

'Everything?' he asks.

'For helping me choose a song, for the practice sessions….' My voice trails away.

'I agreed to help you. I'm keeping my promise,' he shrugs. 'It's not a big deal. Besides, that's what friends do, right?'

'Right,' I say. 'Of course.' I almost forgot that's what we are.

There's isn't time to say anything else as moments later the lights go off, and the show starts. First on stage is the eighth standard with a spoof on our teachers. It gets a lot of laughs once we figure out which teachers they are mimicking. The ninth grade presents an Oriya dance which is quite well done.

Then it's time for our batch's enactment of *Bohemian Rhapsody*. When my classmates finish the number the applause is deafening. Samir and gang finally exit the stage. Giving Neha a quick high five, I follow Amar onto the stage.

It's the first time in years that my parents have seen me on stage. In the darkness everything but the sound of Amar's guitar fades away. It goes off without a hitch and we leave the stage to much clapping and whistles.

I smile at Amar.

'Thank you. I couldn't have done this without you,' I say.

He shrugs again, 'Not a problem. See you around, Naina.'

And with that he's gone.

I join my parents in the audience and watch the rest of the classes go through their items.

No prizes are awarded but the top three batches will be announced. After the last batch exits the stage, we are positive we stand a chance.

When the results are announced our batch is one of the top three. We all lose it right there, jumping up and down, yelling and congratulating each other. We're thrilled at how well we worked together.

It's only later that I notice Amar wasn't part of the celebration.

* *

One of the perks of my parents visiting me is I get to wake up late for once. We're staying at one of the guesthouses on campus so I can afford to laze around. There are four guesthouses at school. Each has two bedrooms, bathrooms, a living area, and a small kitchenette. After breakfast we sit in the quadrangle with our mugs of tea and coffee. A father and son staying in another guesthouse come out to meet us. They are here to check out the school before applying for admission for the ten-year-old boy.

Leaving my dad to keep them company, my mum and I stroll towards the stream that runs near the guesthouses.

'Do you recall your own interview in 1980?' asks my mum. 'All those years ago?'

'Yes.' I say with a laugh. 'Feels like it was just yesterday.'

'I know. How time flies,' my mum says wistfully. 'You were only ten years old, but you were so set on joining once you heard about the school and all that it offered.'

I nod thinking back to when I came with my dad for admission to Waterview High.

'That's the first time I met Neha, you know,' I say. 'We became friends and then best friends.'

'Speaking of friends,' my mum says linking her arm through mine. We match our steps as we continue walking. 'As a teenager in a co-ed school there's going to be a time when you meet someone special. When that time comes, I hope you'll talk to me about it.'

Wait, what?

'What do you mean?' I say warily, wondering where this is going.

'Well, if you have someone you are interested in or you like, I hope you come to me for advice.'

I swallow and point out casually, 'But this is such an important year, mum. I need to concentrate on getting good grades in the ICSE.'

We reach a stone bridge that spans the stream. Leaning against it my mum says thoughtfully, 'Naina, honey, there will always be an exam. This time it's the ICSE, next time it will be the final for the eleventh standard then the twelfth and so on. You can't keep your life on hold forever. If there's one thing we aren't worried about, it's your grades,' mum goes on. 'Every teacher we spoke to, said you're doing well.'

'But my grades are not as good as Neel's,' I say. 'They never are.'

'Sure, but he wants to be an engineer, so he needs those grades,' says my mum. 'Writing has always been your forte. Besides, you take part in so many activities here, it all balances out. Don't be so hard on yourself.'

'Oh,' I say. 'I never thought of it like that.'

'Does that mean there is someone?' my mother looks at me with interest.

'You know the guy who played the guitar for me last night?'

'Did he join school during this term?' Mum wonders. 'I didn't think I had seen him before.'

I tell her about the twins and why they joined school months before the ICSE.

'Oh no, the poor boys,' she shakes her head. 'Dealing with cancer so young must be awful.'

Looking down at the flowing water she asks, 'Do you like him?'

'Yes, I do. I like Amar,' I say realising it's the first time I've said that out loud. 'But I told him I didn't.' I tell her about the last conversation I had with him.

'And he still agreed to accompany you on the guitar? That's something. Not many, if any, guys would do that. It's quite mature of him.'

'I know,' I say slowly. 'I was surprised too. I think it says a lot about him. I need to tell Amar that I like him. Tell me mum, did you date anyone in school or college?'

'Oh yes,' she laughs. 'I went for the exciting, badly behaved guys. Exciting but not very intelligent. I did the whole kiss-a-lot-of-frogs-before-meeting-my-prince thing.'

I laugh at that. Somehow, I never pictured my well-behaved mum going for exciting guys.

'Speaking of guys,' I say as my dad walks down the path towards us. 'Here's dad.'

'Let's keep what we discussed between us, Naina,' my mum says hurriedly as my dad comes closer. 'You know your dad's views on this topic.'

'Yes,' I chuckle. 'The guy worthy of dating his daughter hasn't been born yet.'

My mum laughs at that.

*   *

My folks leave after lunch that day. As their taxi disappears down the road, a trace of the old homesickness returns. I know, I know. Feeling homesick after five years in hostel sounds strange but there it is. Leaving the guesthouse, I head in the direction of my hostel. I promised Anita Ma'am I'd be back by two-thirty; I have half an hour to myself.

After meandering along for a while, I reach a grove of trees. I want to check on a nest we spotted a few days ago. I figure the eggs must have hatched by now. A narrow path runs between two hedges, and I head down that quietly so I don't disturb the birds.

Nearing the tree in which the nest is, I notice a guy standing there. He turns around on hearing me approach. It's Amar. At once, I feel a lightness in my chest, followed by elation. There's so much I need to tell Amar. About how I feel about him. I'm sure he'll be happy to learn I'm attracted to him too.

He puts a finger to his lips as I join him. We watch silently as four hungry little chicks yell loudly for food. The parents, make endless trips, to and from the nest gathering bugs and worms for them.

We back away from the nest a while later

'I'm glad all the chicks survived,' I say happily to Amar.

As I pass a hedge, a twig catches the sleeve of my cotton shirt and pulls at it. My shoulder suddenly feels bare and exposed.

'Ouch,' I say trying to extricate my shirt from the thorny twig. Instead, a few more thorns get caught in my sleeve.

'Hang on,' Amar says. 'Just stand still and I'll take a look.'

He unhooks the thorns from my sleeve one by one. I pull my shirt back over my shoulder and turn to thank him.

He's so close to me; I can almost see myself in his light brown eyes. The dense, thick forest feels like it's closing in on us. Amar's faded denim shirt and jeans appear to have a faint green tinge because of the canopy of trees above.

'Amar,' I say faintly. 'Thank you.'

Forgetting that he knows nothing about my decision or my change of heart, I put my hand out to touch him. My fingers graze his collar and then the top buttons of his shirt, but he doesn't move. When my hand travels up to his mouth and my finger brushes his lower lip, he looks puzzled and confused.

He backs away from me, slowly. The movement tugs me out of my reverie. Turning, I hurry down the path till I reach the open road.

Why on earth did I do that without telling him my feelings have changed. Me making a move on him must be a huge surprise to him.

'Naina, wait,' Amar calls out once we are clear of the narrow path. 'Naina, slow down.'

He catches my arm, and I am forced to stop and face him. My face feels hot and flushed.

'What just happened back there?' he says, his voice sounding rough. 'Is this your idea of a joke? You said we could only be friends and now this?'

'I'm sorry, ok?' I flinch from the roughness of his voice. 'I don't know what came over me. I'm sorry.'

'That's it? That's all you have to say?' he asks. 'I spent an entire week being a friend like you asked. When did that change?'

'I'm not sure. Sometime during the past week.'

'This past week? You hurried away after each rehearsal like you couldn't stand being near me,' Amar persists. 'Was that some elaborate act?'

'It wasn't an act,' I say reluctantly. 'I was trying to hide my feelings from you. You said you had feelings for me. Well, I have feelings for you too, Amar.

I see the disbelief on his face.

'I don't expect you to believe me,' I assure him.

He runs his hand through his hair saying, 'You're right. It's hard to believe that after our last conversation.' He paces up and down the road in front of me.

'I told you I haven't had much practice at this,' I remind him.

Glancing at my watch, I notice the time and suck in my breath. I only have ten minutes to reach my hostel.

'Oh no, I've got to run, Amar. Sorry. I promised Anita Ma'am, I'd be back by two thirty.'

'Come on,' Amar says immediately. 'If we hurry, you can reach in time.'

He starts walking. I want to say more. I need to explain why I acted the way I did. But right now, getting back to the hostel is the most important thing.

'Are you coming?' he asks glancing back at me.

I nod. We break into a sprint, reaching the back wall of my hostel with minutes to spare. I stand in front of him rather awkwardly, hoping he'll say something, anything, to ease the tension, but he doesn't.

Finally, I manage to say, 'Thanks. Look, I'm sorry for.... you know…back there. Can we talk sometime?'

'I think you'd better go in,' he says, no change in his expression.

Just before entering the hostel, I turn around hoping he's still there, but he isn't.

*   *

I don't see Amar the next day or the day after that.

'Has Amar been coming to class?' I ask Neha that evening.

'Yep. Haven't you seen him?' she asks. 'I thought you two must have cleared things up by now.'

After I told Neha what happened, she assured me he just needs time to work things out but I'm not so sure. And besides going to their classroom to talk to him, there's no other way I can meet him.

'No, I haven't seen him since Sunday. Perhaps he's still mad at me.'

'That's strange,' Neha says. 'He likes you and you like him. End of story. Maybe we'll see him after dinner tonight.'

But after dinner that night, when I join Neha, Samir, and Arjun outside the dining hall, I don't see Amar anywhere.

'Two words, Naina,' Samir says excitedly when he sees me. 'Fireflies.'

'That's one word, Samir,' I tell him with a laugh.

'Ok, how about, fireflies tonight?'

'Wait I'm lost,' I protest. 'What's this about? Is 'fireflies', code for something?'

'Do you remember the place where we saw those fireflies two years ago?' Arjun asks me.

'Yeah, I do. Why?'

'Last night I went there with a couple of guys and the fireflies are back. In fact, there are more than what we saw two years ago,' Arjun explains. 'Neha wants to go there tonight.'

'Shh, lower your voice,' cautions Neha checking to see if a teacher is passing by. 'Are you in, Naina?'

'Yes please,' I say in delight. 'Samir you're in too, right?'

'Oh yes,' Samir says. 'I've never seen fireflies out in the open.'

'Do you think Amar will join us?' Neha's casual tone belies the importance of the question. I send her a silent 'thank you'.

'I'll see if he is keen,' Samir says after a pause. 'He's been in a funny mood lately.'

I glance down at my shoes so Samir can't see my face. If Amar knows I'm part of the Firefly Brigade tonight, will he agree to come?

SEVEN

After lights out, we wait patiently as the rooms on the first floor go dark one by one. Those rooms overlook the garden wall we need to climb over. Around twelve o'clock, the last room's lights go off and it is finally time for us to leave.

Jo locks the room door behind us as we leave. Priya, Neha, and I clad in dark jumpers, jeans and sneakers reach the garden wall undetected. The wall is made of granite blocks with handy spaces at regular intervals right through its height of seven feet. The downside is, it ends where Anita Ma'am's room begins. If she or the upstairs warden happen to look out of their bathroom window, it's game over for us.

Once we are over the wall, we take a moment to adjust to the darkness of the campus. With only a few lamps and moonlight as our guide, we start walking, sticking to the side of the road.

So far so good.

'Did Arjun say anything about the guards?' Priya whispers referring to the two men who patrol the school campus after dark.

'Last night the tall guard was on duty so we're hoping it'll be the lazy one tonight,' Neha whispers back.

Thinking about the two guards, I suppress a giggle. They are another reason our midnight walks are so interesting.

They could not be more different from each other. The tall one has limitless energy. He runs down roads and jumps over hedges, appearing out of the darkness, suddenly. His circuit of the campus is so erratic, it's hard to plan a route when he is on duty.

But the best part is his antics. He should have been an actor. The first time we saw him, he was standing in the middle of the dark, empty road brandishing his wooden stick at imaginary enemies. We had to stop and duck behind a tree. As we watched, his switched on his torch and waved it, like it was a lightsabre. With sweeping motions, he swung it from left to right and back again. He was using it to cut the bad guys in half!

Dropping the torch, he punched non-existent enemies, while yelling dialogues from the latest Bollywood movie. 'Take that and that,' he yelled. 'You rat, you pig, you dog. I will hunt you down. I will kill you, then I will kill your father, your brother and everyone in your family.'

This was almost better than the walk itself. The only time Jo accompanied us on a midnight walk, this guard was on duty. Jo went into a fit of giggles, that set all of us giggling and laughing. This led to hiccups that were so bad we had to retreat to the school building to recover.

In contrast to the first one, the other guard is tubby and rather lazy. He leans more towards sentimental dialogues with an imaginary lover.

'Oh, my beloved, you're my Laila, I'm your Majnu,' he croons to a rose bush or a flame tree nearby. 'Say you'll be mine forever. My darling, oh my darling please come to me.'

Often, he breaks into sad songs which sound terrible since he can't hold a tune, but his sorrow would impress even Romeo if he was around.

We all agree that the lazy guard is better than the energetic one, as his slow progress is easier to deal with.

At the end of the road, we spot three figures in dark clothing waiting for us.

Is one of them Amar?

'Hi guys,' says Priya softly.

The boys greet us in whispers. One of them is taller than the rest, so there's a chance it's Amar.

'We need to hurry,' Arjun tells us as he and Neha start walking in front. 'We must get there before the guard starts his round of the campus.'

'Hey, Samir' I say falling in step with him.

We discuss *The Glass Menagerie*, the school play being put up this year. Both of us are keen to take part in it, but with the coming exams it won't be possible.

I'm grateful that my relationship with Samir is simple and straight forward. Not complicated with texts and subtexts, like it is with Amar.

Priya and Amar are behind us as we make our way down the path. I can hear her teasing him about being serious all the time. He laughs and replies. I strain to hear his reply, but I can't quite catch it.

The track we are on ends at the side of a stream. Several flat stones have been placed in the water and serve as steppingstones for us. The guys go ahead to test them. On the other side, rough steps have been cut into the steep mud slope.

Neha and Priya ascend these with the help of Arjun.

'Thanks Arjun,' I say taking his hand as I clamber up the steep steps.

'Amar,' a familiar voice corrects me.

'Oh, hi,' I say thrown by this.

'All good?' he asks in a neutral tone.

'Yeah, you?'

'Nothing to complain about. We'd better catch up with the rest,' he says gesturing to the others.

'Are you still angry with me?' I ask.

Might as well address the issue head on.

'No. Should I be?' Amar asks.

'Haven't seen you since…Sunday so I thought you….'

'I saw you.'

'Really, where?' I ask in surprise.

'On the way to dinner last night,' he answers.

Oh. Was he looking out for me or just happened to see me? I wish I could ask him, but I don't have the guts to.

'We're here,' he says cutting short any further conversation between us.

We climb to the top of the slope and gasp at the scene in front of us. A bank of trees across from where we are, is lit with the glow of a million fireflies. The lights go on and off like a synchronised display. It is a living, breathing, work of art.

The six of us stand in stunned silence at this spectacle. I've been here before but, I'm still speechless.

'It's magical,' says Priya shaking her head in wonder. 'We could never create something like this.'

'Yes. And no,' I say a little breathless.

I look over at Amar to find him looking at me. 'It's beautiful, isn't it?' I ask. He nods.

After a while we move over to a small platform made of bamboo and rope that's used as a lookout by the farmers.

'Far out,' Samir says, the wonder in his voice still evident. 'We should have a class field trip out here so everyone can see this.'

'Yeah,' I agree. 'I wish we could do something like that.'

Perched on the roughly tied bamboo poles, I can just make out Amar standing off to one side. Our earlier conversation was cut short, so I don't know if he's avoiding me.

The conversation turns to school and exams as it usually does.

In a bid to change the topic, Arjun starts telling us Knock Knock jokes. He knows a lot of them. We're so caught up in these catchy jokes, we forget to keep a lookout for the guard.

'Hey guys, I can see a light moving there,' Amar says suddenly. 'Can anyone else see it? Over there,' he says pointing off to the left of where we're sitting.

'Where?' asks Neha, as we fall silent.

Moving through a line of trees is a light that's approaching us. The pattern it makes in the dark, suggests the light is from a torch.

'C'mon,' Arjun says urgently. 'I thought this might happen. Let's hide in the old banyan tree.'

We follow Arjun down a path between two fields till we reach the banyan tree. It's the oldest and largest one on campus with impressive clusters of aerial roots. A few roots are so wide, two or even three of us can hide in them.

I enter the base of a thick root. I'm sure it will make a good hiding place.

Once inside, I realise I'm not alone.

'Is that you, Priya?' I ask the shadowy figure I can barely make out.

'No, it's Amar,' he says.

I groan inwardly knowing one of us will have to find another place to hide in. That will have to be me because he was here first.

'Oh,' I say. 'Fine, I'll leave.'

'Wait, don't go,' he whispers. 'Please.'

'Are you sure?' I ask in a low voice; mindful the guard may be nearby.

'This place is big enough for two,' Amar replies.

'Is it?' I ask. 'The last time we were in a small space you moved away so fast, my head spun.'

Amar moves into the centre of a pale shaft of moonlight shining through a crack in the root.

He's so close to me.

If I reach out, I can touch him, but I don't.

'Is this close enough for you, Naina?'

'You haven't answered my question.' I point out.

He sighs. 'You insisted we could only be friends and I tried to do that the entire week. It wasn't easy but I thought I'd succeeded. Then last Sunday you did a180 degree turn and…. you took me by surprise, Naina. I thought you were teasing me. I thought it might be an elaborate ruse. I didn't know if it was real or not.'

'That was, *is*, real,' I say quietly. 'I like you. I have liked you for a while.'

He is close enough for me to feel his breath on my face.

'Naina Kumar,' he says in a teasing tone I have missed these last few days. 'Are you saying you and I feel the same way? At last?'

'Yes,' I say softly and then bravely enquire, 'Is that okay?'

He chuckles and moves closer. 'It's more than okay.'

I feel his hand on my waist and move towards him slowly.

My heart starts beating faster and my stomach takes a deep dive. I feel light-headed from how close he is.

I smell a familiar minty toothpaste. Is it mine or his? He leans even closer, and I feel the pressure of his lips on mine.

My first kiss.

Ah. Now I understand what the fuss is all about. I get the whole time-stops-when-we-are-together thing.

As first kisses go it's perfect. More than perfect.

From far away I can hear someone calling our names. Amar slowly ends the kiss. My hand brushes his chest and I realise his heart is beating as fast as mine.

'Your heart's beating so fast,' I say a bit lamely.

'It is,' Amar agrees. 'Now you know the effect you have on me.'

'Amar, Naina,' Samir calls out again. 'Where are you guys? We're leaving.'

'Are you, ok?' Amar asks me.

'Yes.' He takes my hand as we join the others.

On our way back to the platform I ask, 'Did the guard pass by?'

'Yeah, but he didn't see us. He just moved on,' says Neha. 'Didn't you hear him?'

'Umm….no,' I say reluctantly. 'Which guard was it?'

'The tubby one,' says Arjun. 'You must have heard him singing.'

'I think they were too busy, to hear anything,' laughs Samir. Wagging a finger at us he says, 'Naughty Amar and Naina.'

In the dark I feel four pairs of eyes on us.

I start laughing and the rest of them join in.

'Aww, look, my bestie is all grown up. That's so cute,' Neha says hugging me tightly. 'Welcome to the world of dating.'

We stop for one last look at the fireflies in all their orchestrated splendour. Arjun has his arm around Neha. She snuggles closer to him. Looking back at me, she grins. They are back together and I'm happy for them.

Amar stands near me. I lean against him feeling his warmth. He puts both arms around me.. The moonlight picks out the lines of his face. This is all so new to me that I close my eyes wanting to remember everything.

This turned out to be a perfect night after all.

The next morning, I spot a small bouquet of wildflowers on my desk. Settling into my chair, I glance at it quickly. The flowers have been fastened with ribbon and a small twist of paper.

'Morning Naina,' says Samir from his seat next to mine. 'Do you like the bouquet?'

'It's from Amar, isn't it?'

'I can neither confirm nor deny that' he claims laughing.

I untwist the paper from the flowers and smooth it out. It's a drawing of a large, red heart with an arrow pierced through it and is signed by Amar.

'Cute, right?' asks Samir.

I grin. 'A little cheesy but cute.'

Placing the flowers and paper carefully in my desk I ask Samir, 'How many such bunches of flowers has he given? I wonder.'

Samir shakes his head, 'I'll say this, Naina, he's never had to work so hard to get a girl.'

While I'm deciding if that answers my question or not, our Maths teacher Jayakumar Sir enters and begins his lecture.

While our teacher drones on, my mind wanders back to last night. We sat up late to fill Jo in on our midnight walk. My roomies were thrilled that Amar and I had kissed. Almost more thrilled than me. Okay, maybe not because I'm still on cloud nine.

'Naina, does this mean you're no longer reluctant to date and fall in love?' Jo asked. 'Or do you still have doubts?'

'A few,' I said slowly. 'Dating has its downside, you know. I've seen this firsthand. Two years ago, my brother Neel broke up with his girlfriend, Richa,' I began. 'They were great together till he decided she was too clingy. I was at home that day. She ran down the corridor sobbing so loudly I thought she was in pain, you know like actual, physical pain.'

Priya pointed out. 'All's fair in love and war.'

'I guess,' I said. 'These holidays he broke up with another girl and the same scene played out. It was like déjà vu. I told him - please break up with your girlfriends when I'm not around.'

'Naina, when you fall for someone, there's a fifty percent chance you will break up,' Neha reminded me. 'All relationships end sometime.'

'Exactly,' I said. 'I don't want to be that girl crying and running through someone's house.'

Priya said sombrely, 'We're all going to get there someday.'

I'm pulled back to the present when Jayakumar Sir assigns a problem for us to work out. Back to the joys of trigonometry.

After morning classes are done, Amar waits for me outside our classroom.

'Hi,' he says. 'Did you get the flowers I left on your desk?'

'Thanks,' I smile. 'Cute but cheesy.'

He laughs, 'It's the best I could do. My drawing skills are nothing compared to Samir's. Lunch?'

'Yes,' I say.

Walking next to Amar, I realise it's the first time I've walked down this road with a guy. A guy and girl walking together at school is a sign they're dating.

From behind us I hear the faint sound of a song. As it gets closer and closer, my heart sinks. I know the sound of this ditty very well.

'Amar and Naina sitting in a tree, k-i-s-s-i-n-g'.

'Amar and Naina sitting in a tree, k-i-s-s-i-n-g'.

Neha and Priya are skipping along, singing this familiar rhyme. It's so loud and clear, no one can mistake who it's about. They come up to Amar and me and then carry on skipping their way to the dining hall.

I feel myself go red from my cheeks down to my toes. I glance across at Amar who looks very amused by it.

'Sorry,' I apologise. 'They've been waiting a while to do this.'

'I don't mind,' he says laughing. 'But you're blushing.'

'I've done similar stuff to Neha and some others, so I can't complain.'

'There goes your plan to keep this discreet,' Amar quips. Seeing my surprise, he goes on, 'I know you'd rather keep this quiet.'

'Not forever,' I assure him. 'Just till I get used to it myself. How's cricket practice going?'

'Good. The team from our sister school near Calcutta is supposed to be very good,' he answers. 'Have you seen them play?'

'They were here two years ago. They've got a couple of strong batsmen and bowlers,' I say. 'Rahul said our team is pretty good now that you've joined.'

'Will you be watching the game?' he asks. 'Should be a good one.'

I nod. 'I'll definitely be watching.'

* *

'It feels really strange going with you to Lovers Spot,' Neha says as we leave the dining hall on Friday evening.

The place we are headed to is a stone wall in front of a line of flame trees on the edge of the sports field. There aren't any lights here, making it the perfect spot for couples to hang out. It's also the best place to keep an eye out for our warden as she heads back to our hostel after dinner.

Neha knows this place well, but for me this is a first.

Arjun and Amar are waiting for us when we reach there.

'Is this where we're having our first date?' Amar asks after we've chosen a spot on the wall.

'I know right?' I reply. 'If we were in Bombay, this wouldn't be something we'd do.'

Leaning against the smooth trunk of a tree, we let our legs hang over the wall.

'We'll be in Bombay this time next month,' I say by way of conversation. 'This term seems to have whizzed by.'

'I know, I know. It's because of me,' Amar says grinning at me. 'What can I say? I have that effect sometimes.'

'No way,' I reply laughing. 'Maybe a little bit because of you. And Samir. Speaking of Bombay, tell me how many bunches of flowers have you made till date?'

'Seriously? None.'

'C'mon, that can't be true,' I insist.

'I've never put together flowers for anyone, Naina. If I needed a bouquet, I went out and bought one.'

'Oh, right,' I say. 'That's not what I was asking.'

'I know,' Amar says softly. Looking at me he continues, 'Why don't you ask me what you really want to know?'

'Okay, Amar Malhotra, how many girlfriends have you had?'

'Two.'

'That's all?' I sound disappointed.

'Well, ma'am, I'm sorry you're disappointed,' he laughs. 'I'm fifteen. What did you expect?'

'And do you have a type?'

Leaning back on his elbows he says, 'Looking at you, I'd say smart and pretty but with an attitude,' he says.

'Attitude, me?' I sound surprised.

'Naina I've spent almost two months trying to win you over. I think that says it all, don't you?'

'It's because I didn't know what I wanted. I wasn't trying to give you a hard time, honestly,' I tell him.

'I know. That's why I figured I had a chance.'

'Ok, let's change the topic,' I say. 'What are your passions?'

'That's easy. Music and cricket. What's yours?'

'Books, music, and writing. Oh, and acting and dance. If you had to choose between music or cricket, what would you pick?'

'That's a hard choice,' he says. 'Cricket, I guess. Could you choose between books and music?'

'No,' I say after a pause. 'Can't live without either.'

'Naina, Amar,' Neha's whisper-shout reaches us.

'Hey guys, I can see Anita Ma'am going back to the hostel,' Neha continues. 'We'd better head back too.'

'Can we do this again sometime?' I ask Amar as we both stand up and stretch, while leaning against each other.

'Well, I don't know,' he says in a mock drawl. 'I'm trying to impress a girl and I need to spend more time with her.'

Seeing my expression, he grins, pulling me into a hug.

'I'm kidding. You're the one I'm trying to impress,' he says.

'I'd say you've succeeded. Good night, Amar,' I say. Standing on my toes I kiss him tentatively at first then with more confidence. If he's surprised, he doesn't show it but pulls me closer. We reluctantly break apart and leave. I may be getting the hang of

KAVERY MADAPA

this.

EIGHT

The game between our team and the team from Riverview started early this morning. We missed two hours of play while we attended extra class. Closer to the exams, classes on Saturday will get more frequent.

Our team chose to bat first, and the score is now 220 for 7 which is a decent score. Amar has not gone into bat yet.

'Hi,' he says grabbing a chair for me to sit on. 'How was class?'

'Good. I'll go over what we covered later. How are we doing?'

'Not too bad. Rahul's on the field now. He's scored 50 runs, the best so far.'

'Are they a good team?' I ask him.

'They are. They have good strategies.'

'Being close to Calcutta, they play against a lot of outside teams. More opportunities to improve.'

'I'll be batting next,' Amar observes. 'If any of the current batsmen get out.'

'I've never been a cricket groupie before,' I say with a grin. 'It's exciting.'

'Fingers crossed, it'll be exciting,' says Amar.

Five minutes later Shiva who is batting with Rahul, is caught LBW and exits the field. Amar squeezes my hand, smiles, and walks onto the field. I wish him luck as he leaves. I can feel my heart beating fast and I'm not even playing!

Amar and Rahul make a good team. They have practised together a lot, and it shows. They quickly push the score up to 250 runs.

After a few minutes I get up and start walking. Neha joins me.

'What's up with you?' she asks. 'You seem a bit tense.'

'I am,' I say. 'Watching Amar bat makes me anxious.'

'Relax, it's only a game. Just don't tell the guys I said that' Neha says with a grin. 'How is it all going? With Amar, I mean.'

'Great,' I answer. 'He's a nice guy. I made the right decision. How's it being back with Arjun, again?'

She laughs. 'We've lost count of the number of times we've broken up. But I feel better being with him than not being with him,' she answers after a pause. 'You know?'

I nod. 'I'm happy you two are back together. Neha, I get why people fall in love. Sometimes I feel so happy and light when I'm with Amar, I'm scared I'll float away,' I tell her.

'Yeah, that's the highs of being in love,' Neha agrees.

'But the lows can be really bad,' I remind her. 'And that's what I'm scared of.'

'I forgot to ask, what made you decide to go ahead with Amar?'

I consider her question. 'This will sound weird, but he was decent enough to keep his promise to accompany me even after I turned him down.'

'Yeah, that was surprising,' agrees Neha. 'Most guys would've left you on your own. High and dry.'

We hear a few cheers and a few groans. Rahul starts walking off the field. The score sits at 285 for 9 wickets.

Soon after, Amar is bowled out and as the tenth batsman, the game is over for our team.

The score is 310, all out.

Day two of the match starts off well for our team when two wickets fall early in the day. Watching Amar bowl, I see why Samir was so confident. He's clearly in the zone and is laser focussed while bowling.

Standing on the side of the sports field I am still a bundle of nerves.

'Naina, come sit with me for a moment,' Samir calls out.

I join him under a tree where he's set up shop. He's got his sketchbook, a few pencils, and some charcoal sticks with him. Two more sketchbooks with a few loose sheets of paper are on the ground near him.

'What's up?' I ask sitting down beside him. I lean against the broad trunk of the tree. 'You look busy. And calm. Unlike me.'

He shrugs. 'I've watched Amar play many times so I'm not a nervous wreck like you. Listen, I need to finish this sketch of you, but it's hard with you moving around so much. What do you think?'

He holds out a loose sheet of paper. It's a charcoal sketch of me standing on the edge of the field. In the close-up I'm looking over my shoulder with the wind whipping my hair over my face. I look mysterious, like a heroine in a book.

'Wow, I look exciting and mysterious,' I say with a gasp. 'You are so good at this.'

Samir laughs, attempting a mini bow while sitting. 'Thank you. You are exciting and mysterious. Just ask my twin.'

'I think he's figured me out by now,' I chuckle. 'Samir, you have got to do this professionally someday. Is that your plan?'

'Yep,' he says flipping the page over. 'I can't think of anything that makes me happier. This one's of Amar.'

He's caught Amar at the end of his run just as he's about to release the ball to the batsman. I catch my breath at the way Samir has caught his twin brother in motion.

'Wow,' I say exhaling slowly. 'You can feel the speed of his delivery.'

'Okay missy, stop drooling,' he admonishes me. 'You can have this sketch.'

I laugh, 'I'm not drooling, but would you blame me if I was? No worries, I'll take it from you later.'

As I look back at the field it's clear the visiting team is in trouble. The score is now 120 for 6. With only a few wickets left, our team has a real chance of winning. A tea break is called, and both teams go into a huddle on opposite sides of the field.

When play resumes it's as if our team has decided to win this match no matter what it takes. Amar and Shiva are bowling with something close to recklessness. It seems to be paying off.

A few wickets later, the visiting team is all out for 255.

Our team erupts in excitement. Players take off their caps, throwing them in the air. There's lots of fist pumping, yells, cheers, and full-on hugs. The field starts filling with students and teachers all cheering and congratulating the team. Even the team from Riverview is congratulating our players. Neha, Samir, and I get into a group hug that ends with a lot of screaming.

It's a manic scene for sure. In the distance I can see Amar being carried aloft by his teammates in a celebratory lap through the grounds.

'Look, he's coming this way,' Neha says pointing as he leaves the field. We all start waving and yelling out his name, so he can locate us in the crowd. With a huge grin he exits the field, running towards us. He gives Samir and Neha a quick hug, but his eyes are on me. He is bright eyed and full of a jittery excitement that comes with winning. I recognise that feeling. I get like that after being on stage.

'Congrats, Amar,' I say holding my hand out to shake his. He takes it but his hand keeps moving till it reaches my shoulder. His other hand reaches around my waist. Before I realise what's happening, Amar is dipping me back low. I lift my left leg to keep my balance as I bend backwards from my waist.

He bends forward lower and lower, till his lips touch mine in a kiss!

Amar sets me back on my feet and everything around me appears to be spinning. In any other place I'd have been thrilled to be kissed in such a romantic way. Who wouldn't? But on a field full of students, teachers, and my classmates, not so much. I put my palms over my cheeks to contain the full-on heat rush I'm having.

'Oh, shoot,' Amar says as realises too late that close to a hundred people have just witnessed the kiss. 'I'm sorry.'

I'm about to turn and exit the scene, like I would usually do. Instead, with a small, albeit shaky smile I reach up and kiss him on the cheek. He releases me slowly, too shocked by my response.

'Congrats,' I repeat, hoping I look calmer than I feel. 'That was a great game.'

'Are we good?' Amar asks me quietly.

I smile more confidently at him. 'It's time I stopped running. The fact is we're dating. Most people know that already and those who don't, do now.'

NINE

A neat line of steel trunks snakes its way down the corridor to the front door of our hostel. A name and admission number are painted in white on two sides of each trunk. Every trunk is filled with clothes that have we have outgrown and washed so often; our mothers will never recognise them. None of these clothes will return with us next term. Except for a treasured pair of Levi jeans or a pair of lucky sneakers. Instead, our trunks will be filled with a new set of clothes and shoes for our last and final term at school.

Random pieces of paper and plastic lie on the ground along with an abandoned hanky and a lone sock. In the courtyard, the washing lines are bare of their usual complement of clothes and clothes pins. Buckets and mugs are stacked in colourful, gravity-defying stacks against a wall.

In our rooms, beds have been stripped bare and look forlorn. Mattresses lie in neat piles on the side of the rooms. Our cupboards are clean but empty.

It's a Saturday morning and the term is officially over.

Ahead of us is one and a half months of holidays. Which would sound great but for the piles of homework and revising we need to do during the same holidays.

The last week at school was jam packed with extra classes as our poor teachers raced to complete the syllabus. Finally on Friday evening after one long session before dinner, we were done. Brain fry, anyone?

Depending on where we live, each of us has been assigned to a group for the trip back home. Neha is in the Delhi group while Jo and Priya are in the Madras group. I'm in the Bombay group which goes to Bangalore by bus before boarding a train to Bombay.

Addresses and phone numbers are exchanged, rash promises are made to write as soon as we reach. But we all know it'll be at least a week before we contact each other.

Soon it's time for one last goodbye. Neha's group is the first to leave. As part of the Delhi group, she has a two-day journey ahead of her. We all hug her quickly.

'I'm going to call in a day or two so you can fill me in on the gossip,' she says with a grin.

'Arjun will fill you in before I can,' I point out. He's in the Bombay group too.

'Nah, guys don't provide enough detail,' she counters. 'Take care, Naina. See you in Delhi in a few weeks.'

Each holiday one of us visits the other and this time round it's my turn to stay with Neha for a week in Delhi.

After lunch, our trunks are picked up by a minivan. Those of us in the Bombay and Bangalore groups start the short walk to where the buses are waiting for us. Reena is my usual travelling companion on these journeys. Waving goodbye to our hostel wardens, we notice the relief on their faces; another term over with no major disaster.

I smile when I see Samir, Amar, and Arjun near the buses. They are discussing the best route the buses should take, the best buses on Indian roads and how long it would take them to drive the same route if they had the chance. Regular boy stuff!

A young girl approaches us, a card in her hand. I know her as

Diya, a fifth standard student. I've seen her around campus.

'Hi, Amar' she addresses him shyly. 'I made this for you.' She hands Amar a handmade card.

'For me?' he asks in surprise as he takes it from her. 'Can I open it now?'

She nods seriously. He sits on a stone bench, so he is at her level and opens the envelope. The front of the card has a couple of line drawings of Amar bowling. Inside the card says-

Thank you for winning the match for the school. Love Diya

'Thanks a lot, Diya,' Amar tells her in a serious tone. 'I'll be sure to keep this with me.'

She shakes his hand and leaves. Amar grins sheepishly at us and stows the card safely in his backpack.

Samir remarks to me. 'That's your competition. A fifth standard student with a crush on Amar.'

'I recall having a crush on my seniors,' I admit with a smile. Noticing a bunch of books in Samir's hands, I ask. 'What are those?'

'I found these at the bottom of my trunk,' Samir says holding the books out to me. 'They're full of puzzles; great to have on long journeys. Hey, why don't we sit together on the bus and work on a couple of these?'

'Sounds good,' I say. Turning to Amar I continue, 'I'll sit with you during the second half, if that's okay?'

'Sure,' he agrees.

'Hmm…' Samir grins. 'Since the boyfriend has given permission, we can go ahead.'

'Samir, stop trying to create drama where there isn't any,' I admonish him. 'You know I don't need permission.'

'Okay, okay,' he says holding his hands up and grinning. 'It's tempting though. Trouble in Paradise and all that.'

'It took us long enough to reach Paradise,' Amar says wryly.

The bus drivers hop on to the waiting buses and sound the horns. It's our cue to climb aboard. The four of us fill a row with Samir and me on one side and Arjun and Amar on the other. Each group has two teachers in charge to ensure students reach home safely. Sharma Sir and Jayakumar Sir are our escorts on this trip. Looking after forty odd students for a day and a half is not easy, I realise suddenly.

As the buses pass familiar landmarks like the auditorium, the school building, and the swimming pool, we yell out 'Goodbye' to each one. The last goodbye is for the stone arch that serves as the entrance to the school campus.

The landscape we are driving through is mostly scrubland interspersed with large rocks. This is what our campus looked like before the school took it over.

Once we reach the open road, the singing begins. We kick off with favourite songs like *Five hundred miles* and *Country Roads* then continue with *She'll be coming around the mountain*. Half an hour later we have run out of songs and energy. Sharma Sir's wife, Meera hands out packets of biscuits and oranges. Everyone tucks into the snacks happily.

Choosing a book from the pile between Samir and myself I tell him, 'I didn't think you were a fan of puzzles.'

'I like them for long journeys,' he answers. 'Is this the first time you've been away from school this term?'

'We had a daytrip to visit an ancient temple and a waterfall. That was before you and Amar joined. After that we've been busy finishing the syllabus.'

'Glad I wasn't around for the visit to the waterfall,' Samir says with a shudder. 'I hate pools and waterfalls.'

'Seriously?' I ask him. 'Don't you swim?'

'No. I can't swim because I hate water,' he says with vehemence. 'On swim days I help out at the art department instead.'

'Oh,' I say intrigued. 'I love the weekly swim day at school. Maybe you had a bad time in a pool when you were a kid. What about swimming in the sea? Like say at Juhu Beach?'

'Oh God, no,' Samir says. 'Dad used to take us there earlier, but we don't go there anymore.'

'Let's change the subject,' I say since he is clearly upset. 'How's your younger brother doing?'

'Dev is much better,' he says flashing me a grateful smile. 'He'll be at home when we reach tomorrow. He's out of danger and things look hopeful.'

'I'm glad, Samir,' I say thankfully. 'Hey, can I ask you a personal question?'

'Sure, what do you want to know?' he says with a wide grin that brings out his dimples. 'It's about Amar, isn't it? Ask away and I will spill my guts.'

I shake my head and laugh. 'Nope, it's not about Amar. If it was, I would ask him myself. This is about you.'

'Oh, that sounds serious,' Samir quips.

'It's just that I wondered if you had feelings for any girl at school or in Bombay. You've never mentioned anyone. But if it's too personal…'

'I'm not into girls,' Samir says cutting in. 'At least I don't think I am.'

'Not into girls. Older girls then?' I ask trying to understand what he means.

'Not into females, I meant,' he says slowly looking straight at me.

'Oh,' I say doubtfully. 'You mean....?'

'Right,' he says with a grin. 'But it's very confusing so for now I'm going to stay single.'

'Okay,' I say as I digest this piece of information.

'Are you shocked or surprised?' he asks.

'Neither' I say after a pause. 'Just wondering how I never picked up on it. I should have known, don't you think?'

'It never came up in conversation, so I never mentioned it.'

'Anyhow,' he says picking up two puzzle books and giving me a wide grin. 'Let's see who's the first to finish ten pages of one of these.'

'Game on,' I say accepting the challenge.

Halfway through our journey we get a much-needed loo stop at a restaurant with a few shops nearby. Climbing out of the bus we are hit by the noise and dust of a busy highway. Being at school for four months we've gotten used to the silence of the valley.

'Hey, stranger. I got this for you,' Amar says handing me a bar of chocolate. I turn the bar over taking in the familiar gold wrapper with five shiny stars on it.

'A 5 Star chocolate,' I say in delight. 'Thanks. Seems like ages since I had one.'

'Hey, that chocolate should be for me,' Samir protests joining us. 'She lost the puzzle challenge. I won, so I get the chocolate.'

Laughing I say, 'Winning by cheating does not count, my friend.'

'Do I look like I would cheat?' he asks Amar and me with an innocent look.

'Leave me out of this,' Amar says laughing. 'But if you play Monopoly with Samir, don't make him the banker.'

'Why am I not surprised you cheat at Monopoly?' I tell Samir as we board the bus.

'And at Cluedo,' adds Amar with a wicked look at his twin.

'How can you cheat at Cluedo?' I ask Samir. 'It's not possible.'

'Only one way to find out,' he says with a grin as we take our seats. 'We'll have to have a game someday.'

A light rain starts to fall as the buses near Bangalore. Traffic gets heavier as cars and trucks clog the road. The driver slows down to avoid the dozens of autos and bikes weaving in and out of the two-lane highway. The windows of the bus are now closed to keep the noise and pollution out.

At the next traffic light, the driver of the other bus sounds a double toot of his horn. We yell out goodbye and wave furiously as the Bangalore group bus takes the road leading into the city. They will be home well before dinner tonight.

I stretch my legs under the seat in front of me. It feels good sitting next to Amar. I lean my head against his shoulder. He takes my hand in his, lacing his fingers through mine. Somehow this feels more intimate than just holding hands. The whole bus is bathed in a 'golden hour' glow as the sun sets behind the distant hills. We spot Sharma Sir coming down the aisle and both of us straighten up and sit a little apart.

'This journey will be the longest time we've spent together,' Amar remarks to me.

He's right. We rarely have a chance to spend more than half an hour together at school. There's always a class or a practice session to go to. Or an extra tutorial to attend. Or a teacher or student nearby.

'I need to give you my phone number,' Amar reminds me.

'Oh yeah. Just a minute,' I say retrieving my address book from my duffle bag. He adds his number and address under A.

'Don't forget Samir and I are having a party on the sixteenth of November for our sixteenth birthday,' he reminds me.

'I need to figure out a way to attend it,' I say. 'My dad is a typical Indian dad as far as parties are concerned. I'll have to ask Neel, my brother, to help me.'

'He can come too if he wants,' Amar says. 'If he doesn't mind hanging out with us.'

I laugh thinking of Neel. 'He's eighteen but he's always up for a good party. I've never really hung out with him, you know? To him and his friends, I'm the kid sister.'

Amar chuckles saying, 'Yeah, at eighteen, fifteen-year-olds seem way too young. I have a cousin like that. But as we've grown older the gap seems to get smaller. Can I call you at home? Or is that a bad idea?'

'Umm…' I weigh up the risks in my head before replying. 'It may be better for me to call you after my dad leaves for work.'

'Okay, that makes sense. Do they know about me?' he asks with a smile.

'I kind of told my mum when they visited school last month. But my dad doesn't know yet.'

'He'll probably think I'm a bad influence on you. Or not good enough for you, or something like that,' Amar chuckles. 'Dads don't like guys who date their daughters.'

'Hey,' I protest. 'Mums don't like girls who date their sons.'

'True,' Amar agrees.

'Parents,' we say together and laugh.

*   *

It's grown dark by the time we reach the station. We are greeted by the controlled chaos of a city terminus. Though the city is nowhere as large as Bombay it seems to be in a mad race to catch up. After our luggage is stowed away in our carriage, we board the train. The ladies' compartment is usually booked for us but over the years Reena and I have found it's better to take berths in the general area.

As soon as we settle into our compartment the train jerks forward. A couple of long whistles later it starts and we're on our way. Most of the coach has been booked for our group so it's easy to find everyone. Something about a train journey makes me feel hungry and I'm already looking forward to dinner.

Stowing our duffle bags on the topmost berth, Reena and I look around for the rest of our friends. Amar and Arjun are helping the teachers tally the luggage to ensure everything has been loaded on the train. I carry on till I come upon Samir sitting on a lower bunk looking miserable and a little lost.

'What's up?' I ask sitting next to him. 'You don't look happy.'

'When they said we had to travel by train I assumed it meant in the air-conditioned coach, not in the general coach,' he says in a sad tone.

I look around seeing it through Samir's eyes. Our coach is full of students, teachers, trunks, and bags of all sizes. People are walking around stepping over trunks and suitcases. In addition, random vendors are trying to sell coffee, tea, and snacks. It's quite a lot to take in for the first time. Most of us have done this journey so many times we know exactly what to expect.

I start laughing then check myself and say, 'You know I've grown so used to travelling like this, I've forgotten there is an AC coach. Listen, with all of us here, the journey won't feel that long.'

'If you say so,' Samir answers in the same monotone.

'Once everyone settles down let's have a game of cards. I'll even let you cheat,' I offer with a grin. 'Do you know Rummy?'

'Yes, I do' Samir answers cheering up a little. 'Arjun's got a pack of playing cards. Good idea Naina.'

With help from Amar and Arjun we create a makeshift table out of two steel trunks. Because we are still technically 'at school' we can't play for money but settle for sweets instead.

A group of us start playing just as the dinner service begins. By now we are ravenous as our last full meal was lunch at school. Though dinner is a full meal with chapattis-a type of flatbread-and rice, Samir buys some bread rolls, a tub of jam and a packet of Amul butter. In the past he has found the food on trains very spicy.

With dinner over, Amar passes around some chocolates and hard-boiled sweets he picked up at the station.

The teachers can finally relax since everyone is safely on board. Sharma Sir even agrees to play a few card games with us. Meera Ma'am, his wife takes out a half-finished scarf that she is knitting.

I join Amar on the seats across the aisle. These have a lot of leg room, perfect for long legs like ours.

I gaze out of the window at the passing towns and stations as they whiz past. Vignettes of village life forever etched in my memory. A truck lumbers down a dusty road leaving a cloud of dust behind. A dog runs after it barking. The remains of a fire send up a thick plume of smoke. A street lit by a single lamp illuminates a family of three on a cycle.

'Hey,' Amar says with a smile. 'Penny for your thoughts? You look like you're far away.'

I grin at him. 'Sorry. Being on a train always makes me a bit pensive or moody. I'm not sure which.'

'That's random,' he says with a laugh. 'Train journeys remind me of certain movies. Like those old Hollywood westerns or some Bollywood movies with train sequences.'

'True,' I say snapping out of my pensive mood. 'There are a few like that.'

'Let me show you something cool,' he says getting up and walking towards one end of the coach. At the other end, the train attendants are collecting and stacking the dinner trays ready to offload them at the next station.

Stopping at the door of our coach, Amar unlocks and opens it.

The countryside rushes past in a blur of trees, bushes and lampposts, but a huge, orange moon hangs low, looking close enough for us to reach out and touch it. I catch my breath.

'Wow. That's amazing,' I say joining Amar at the door. He places one arm on either side of the door so it's safe for me to stand next to him. Just to be safe, I hold on tightly to the handle on the side of the door. The way Amar looks at me is so intense I feel I could melt away right there. We close and lock the door behind us.

'Is that all you wanted to show me?' I ask Amar.

'Well now that you mention it……' he says putting his arms around me. The noise of the train falls away. I lean back in his arms looking at a face I've come to know so well. Straight eyebrows, dreamy brown eyes, and a generous mouth. He traces the angle of my cheekbone before kissing me. I slide my hands around his waist and into his back pockets. We fit together so perfectly, like nothing can come between us.

TEN

By evening the next day, we're ready for the journey to be over. The day has been a busy one starting with coffee and tea in the wee hours of the morning. With the whole day before us we went through every type of entertainment we could think of. Starting with *Antakshari*- a singing game- after breakfast, various card games, Samir's books of puzzles, Hangman, and so on till we ran out of energy.

As much as we enjoy the company of our schoolmates, we are desperate for a meal that does not come in an aluminium tray and is not vegetarian.

At Lonavala most of us disembark to purchase some iconic peanut bars. Amar, Reena, Arjun, and I wander around the station looking for something to do. Since it's a weekend there's a carnival of sorts near the station. We end up at a stall where for a small price you can throw rings around stuffed toys. Arjun and Amar win a stuffed dolphin and monkey and gift them to Reena and me. I hope the monkey will fit into my duffle bag, so I won't have to explain how I got it to my parents.

'Not the sort of gift I was planning on giving you,' Amar says looking at the brown and cream coloured stuffed monkey. 'He looks a bit manic; don't you think?'

I laugh, 'Yeah, he does. But he's also kind of ugly-cute.' I sigh and say, 'Another two hours and we'll be in Bombay. Can't wait to see my folks. Do you know who's coming to pick you and Samir from the station?'

'My dad for sure,' Amar replies. 'Not sure if mom can make it. Depends on how Dev is doing.' He suddenly turns his face away from me.

A glance at him tells me he is very upset. 'I'm sorry, Amar. I didn't want to make you sad.' I want so badly to put my arms around him and comfort him. But we are on the platform in full view of dozens of people.

Back on the train the mood is now upbeat because we are so close to home.

'Naina, I need your phone number,' Samir tells me. His address book is open, while he waits for my answer, pen in hand.

'Hey, wait a minute,' Amar protests. 'I don't have her number so why would she give it to you?'

'Because I'm her best friend and you're her boyfriend,' Samir says in a matter-of-fact way.

'Guys,' I tell them. 'I'm not giving either of you, my number. I'll call you when the coast is clear, that is after my dad goes to work. If my dad picks up the phone, I'll have a lot of explaining to do.'

'That's inconvenient,' Samir grumbles. 'What do I put next to your name?'

'Put TBA' I say with a grin. 'To be announced.'

* *

Later that evening the train pulls into the station, then crawls sluggishly towards the barriers with loud creaks and groans. I'm standing with Amar by the window looking out at the platform.

'I'll call after a couple of days,' I promise Amar. 'I need a day or two to recover. I'm sure you'll be busy too.'

'I will,' he agrees. 'I want to help my parents with Dev's

treatments.'

Scanning the crowd for familiar faces, I realise this is a bad place to be in. My parents will be able to see us clearly.

'Look, I'd better collect my bag and other stuff,' I tell him. 'My parents will be somewhere in that crowd. I hope everything works out well for all of you.'

'This is it then?' he asks looking intently at me. 'Let me memorise your face, Naina.'

I nod. 'I'm doing the same,' I assure him.

He holds out his hand, I squeeze it tightly and turn away before my emotions take over.

There's a general clamour as goodbyes are exchanged. The train groans to a final stop. We're home!

The first person I see once I exit the train, is my brother, Neel. Letting go of my bag, I reach up to hug him.

'Hi shorty,' he says with a big grin. 'Welcome back.'

'Neel,' I protest. 'I'm five feet eight now. Technically, I'm no longer short.'

'I'm over six feet so technically, you still are,' he points out, taking my bag. 'Mum and dad are over there. You carry on Naina; I'll get a porter for your luggage.'

I hurry over and greet my parents. All of us are talking and laughing at the same time. Looking at my family I get a warm, fuzzy feeling; I'm so lucky we are together again.

'Naina, have a good holiday,' Samir calls out as he passes by. I turn and see that he and Amar are accompanied by a tall, good-looking man who must be their father.

'Thanks Samir. Same to you and Amar,' I say sneaking a quick smile at Amar. They both wave, smile and are immediately swallowed up by the crowd. I notice their mum didn't make it to the station after all. I hope that's not a bad sign.

I send up a silent prayer: *Please let things work out for them. Please.*

'Who was that?' my dad asks as we make our way through the crowd to the car park.

'That was one of my classmates,' I answer.

'I've never seen him before,' my dad points out.

'They've just joined,' I say quickly, hoping my dad will drop the subject.

'They?'

'They're twins, Dad. They joined school this term.'

Thankfully we reach our car by this time. Neel pays the porter and stows my luggage in the boot.

'Hey bro,' I tell Neel, getting into the back seat with my mum. 'Is it safe for you to drive?'

'It is. I got my license a while ago,' he grins at me in the rear-view mirror. 'You have to keep up with what's happening here, squirt.'

The car inches forward through the crowd of people. I move over to my mum and lay my head on her shoulder. She takes my hand in hers.

Sleep threatens to overtake me as my eyelids close. I need to stay awake for dinner. Mum has made her famous chicken curry for dinner.

'I think I know that man,' dad says out of the blue.

'Which man?' mum asks.

'The guy who was with Naina's classmates,' my dad explains.

'I'm sure I've met him years ago.'

Despite being sleepy I open my eyes in alarm.

My dad has met Amar and Samir's dad? What? How?

In the rear-view mirror Neel catches my eye and raises one eyebrow questioningly.

That question will have to wait till tomorrow. I shrug, yawn and fall asleep.

ELEVEN

Over the next day and a half, I drift in and out of sleep. My room door is closed most of the time except for when our dog, Twinkle joins me for a nap. I manage to get up for meals and to have long showers with no danger of hot water ever running out.

At some point my steel trunk and duffle bag are unpacked and emptied of their contents. Mum insists on getting all my clothes and linen washed, though they've been washed at school.

Two days after I arrived, I'm finally ready to face the world again.

I sit up in bed and take stock of my room taking in my desk, dressing table and my cupboard. My eyes fall on a spectacular brown and white mess on one side of my double bed. Twinkle has somehow got hold of the stuffed monkey and reduced it to a hundred small pieces.

'Naughty dog,' I tell her. 'That was a gift from Amar. Look what you've done to it.'

She grins back at me not sorry in the least. *Rest In Pieces, monkey.*

The clock on my desk tells me it's just after ten o'clock. Since it's a Wednesday my dad must be at work. It's a good time to call Amar and Samir.

But first I need to find something to wear. The inside of my cupboard is decorated with posters of Barbra Streisand, The Police and Abba, along with posters of Joni Mitchell, Bob Dylan, and Def Leppard. I grin at the wide variety of artists I am paying tribute to. It's taken me a while to collect these posters; some from old issues of JS magazines and others that I begged for and acquired from Neel.

I root around the sparse contents of my cupboard and decide on an old t-shirt and a pair of jeans. The jeans feel funny on me. A look in the mirror confirms my worst fears. The jeans sit well above my ankles. If our apartment got flooded right now, my jeans would not get wet at all!

That's what happens when you gain an inch and a half over four months. I change into a faded wrap skirt instead.

At first glance our apartment seems empty. I wander around till I find my mum and Mary, our live-in cook in the kitchen.

'Naina? Good, you're up,' my mum says looking up from her cookery book. 'Are you hungry? I'm making some brownies.'

'I'm still digesting the omelette I had at eight o'clock, mum.'

'If you're up to it, we can go shopping,' mum offers. 'You've outgrown most of your clothes. And the ones you brought back are faded and threadbare.'

'Alright,' I say. 'Can we leave in half an hour? I need to make a couple of calls.'

I flop down on the leather bean bag and dial the number Amar wrote in my address book.

'Hello,' says a familiar voice. 'Samir speaking.'

'Hi Samir, this is Naina. How are you?' I say, my face breaking into a grin.

'Naina, Hi. We wondered what happened to you. Are you okay?'

'Yeah, I'm fine. I was taking it easy the last couple of days.'

'Listen, when do we see you?' Samir asks. 'Seems like ages since we met. So much to catch up on. Uh, oh here comes Amar. I guess the boyfriend is more important than the friend. Ok bye.'

'We must meet soon,' I say to Samir. There's a scuffling sound from the other side.

'Hey Naina,' Amar's smooth voice comes over the line. 'How are you?'

I sigh happily into the receiver. He sounds good even over Bombay's dodgy telephone lines.

'Hi, Amar, good to hear your voice. How's your family?'

'All good here. I was waiting for you to call. Guessing your dad is at work?' he chuckles.

'Yes, he is. And mum' in the kitchen,' I tell him.

'I've missed you,' Amar says. My heart skips a beat and any doubts I had melt away. I've missed him too. 'When can I come over and see you?'

I rack my brain for a good time to meet him and come up with the best plan I can think of. 'I take our dog Twinkle for a walk every evening around four-thirty. I can meet you somewhere here.'

'Where do you stay?' Amar asks me. 'I can drive over.'

'We're on Carmichel Road, just over from Peddar Road,' I say. 'It's a long way from Cuffe Parade, isn't it? You said that's where you live.'

'Don't worry about that,' Amar assures me. 'It's not that far. Shall we say tomorrow around four-thirty?'

'Yes, please,' I say. 'But are you allowed to drive?'

'If I'm accompanied by someone with a license, I'm good,' Amar says. 'See you tomorrow.'

I put the receiver back in its cradle. He said he missed me. Nothing can top that. My day just became perfect. I hug my knees to my chest and laugh happily.

The heavenly smell of brownies wafts out of the kitchen. The bliss of being at home!

'Ready to go?' my mum says coming out of the kitchen. 'Naina, you said you'd be ready, but you're aren't!'

'Give me ten minutes,' I answer hurrying to my room.

What does someone who has outgrown most of her clothes wear to go shopping?

*   *

The flyer in my hand is for a couple of sales on Warden Road so that's where we are headed to. Although my mum drives, getting a parking spot in this area is difficult so Keshav our driver is with us today.

'You need a few nice tops, jeans and a couple of shalwar sets,' my mum says looking down at her list. 'Do you want anything else?'

'Something dressy as well,' I say thinking of the party Amar mentioned.

My mum looks at me in surprise. 'You never buy anything dressy, Naina. Every time I ask, you say you don't need it. What's up?'

'You remember the guy I told you about in school?' I ask her slowly. She nods. 'He and his brother are having a party next week. They're turning sixteen.'

'Oh,' my mum says digesting this information. 'You'll have to convince your dad to let you go, you know that.'

'If Neel comes too, Dad will agree, won't he?' I query looking at her.

'In theory, yes,' mum says. 'I'd be happier if Neel was with you. But you need to ask him.'

'Yeah, that's the hard part,' I say doubtfully. 'Think he'll agree?'

My mum smiles. 'Play the kid sister/older brother card and I think he'll agree.'

I laugh, 'I can do that.'

An hour and a half later the boot of our car is full of bags. We've got everything on mum's list and then some. We're about to call it a day when mum spots a pop-up shop with a great window display.

'C'mon Naina let's make this our last stop,' my mum, the indefatigable shopper declares.

'Okay,' I say though I'm keen to go home and try out the stuff we've bought.

There's a large crowd inside the shop so, it must be a popular one. Mum nudges me towards a rack of formal dresses and jackets.

'This will look good on you,' she says taking a cream-coloured dress off the rack. 'Why don't you try it? It'll be perfect for the party.'

The changing rooms appear to be full, so I prepare myself for a long wait. Just then a door opens, and a girl exits. As she passes me, I realise I've seen her before. Back then she was crying her heart out after my brother broke up with her.

'Hi,' I say. 'Richa?'

She stops and looks blankly at me. 'Sorry,' she says. 'Have me met before? I'm terrible with faces.'

'I'm Neel's sister, Naina,' I inform her. I see her make the connection and wonder if she would rather not have met me, given her history with Neel.

'Neel, of course. He's a nice guy,' she says with a lovely smile. 'How is he? It's been ages since we met.'

'He's fine,' I say. 'Busy studying for entrance exams for colleges in the US.'

'Oh yeah, I remember him mentioning that. Say a big 'Hi' to him, Naina,' she says warmly. 'Nice meeting you.'

With a wave she wanders off.

I enter the changing room mystified. She was so upset when my brother broke up with her, but she still thinks he's a nice guy. How is that possible? Is it because she's a nice, forgiving sort of person? Would I be this happy talking about a guy who broke up with me? Doubtful.

When I put the cream dress on, I know it's the one. It's a sleeveless dress with a cowl neckline. It fits me perfectly. It even comes with a sheer wrap in case I need it.

'I like this dress a lot,' I tell my mum when she enters the changing room with a few more dresses for me to try out. 'What do you think?'

'It's perfect for the party,' she agrees. 'Naina, there's a bit of a queue at the counter. Will you pay for the dress? I'll go outside and let Keshav know we're ready to go home.'

Handing me some cash, she leaves the shop. I join the queue which gets shorter when a large group of girls pay and leave. I hand over the cash thinking shopping is not that hard after all.

Bag in hand, I walk down the long corridor towards the front door.

A couple of guys enter the shop loudly discussing a game of

cricket that's being played today. Seeing me on my own they stop in front of me.

'Hi,' one of the guys says giving me a big, flirty smile. 'How come we haven't met before? I would have noticed a pretty girl like you.'

He's cute in an obvious kind of way. Nice hair, nice smile. Polo t-shirt with a pair of sunglasses hanging down the front of it. Faded jeans, sneakers and lots of cologne. A Bombay guy for sure.

I roll my eyes. Can't he come up with better lines?

Next, I give him a glare. It's one I've perfected over the years. One needs an arsenal of glares in this city, so you're not taken advantage of.

'Excuse me,' I try and walk past them.

'Hey, at least say 'Hello' to us,' the second guy insists. Putting a hand over his heart, he pauses and asks dramatically. 'Tell me, where have you been all my life?'

They both need to find better lines. The first guy changes tactics, humming a popular song and singing, *'Does your mother know that you're out?'*

I recognise the line immediately and start smiling despite trying hard not to. Is this the latest thing? Using an Abba song to flirt?

Behind the two guys I spot mum coming back to look for me. Oopsie!

'Actually, my mother does know that I'm out,' I tell the chatty guy pointing to mum. He turns around, his face falling when he sees her. His breath comes out in a rush of air.

'Sorry aunty,' he stammers. 'We were only being friendly. We didn't mean any harm. Sorry.'

'That's fine,' my mum says. 'But would *your mother* want to know what you're doing?'

The boys don't stop to answer. They turn and disappear inside the shop. I'm guessing they won't be using that line again today!

'Do you know them?' mum asks when we're outside.

'No. I don't,' I assure her. 'They were just being silly. Probably came to collect their moms or sisters.'

After lunch I wander into Neel's room. As usual it's a mess. Or what he calls an organised mess since he insists, he has a system. He swears he knows where everything is, though it doesn't look like it.

'Hey, sis,' he says. 'What's up?'

'Do you have a minute?' I ask him hopefully. Between classes at college, entrance exams for US colleges and his busy social life, it's hard finding time to chat with him.

'Sure,' he says dropping into a chair by his desk.

'I met a friend of yours today,' I tell him sitting down on a couch. 'Richa. She was shopping like we were.'

He frowns as he tries to place the name.

'You used to date her about two years ago,' I say helpfully.

'Oh right. Yep, I remember her,' he says. 'How is she?'

'She's fine. She said to say 'Hi' to you. *Bhaiya*, how do you do it?'

'Do what?' he asks sounding puzzled.

'Date girls, then break up with them. You break their hearts. Yet they still remember you as a nice guy.'

'Because I am a nice guy,' Neel says laughing.

'What I mean is what is your funda on dating?' I ask.

'Funda? Sounds like a slang word from your school,' he quips smiling. 'Listen, I don't know if you are ready for a lesson on dating. How old are you?'

'Fifteen, so I'm definitely ready,' I tell him flatly. 'Besides there's someone I like a lot, hence the questions.'

'Oh, shorty,' he says in surprise. 'I'm impressed. Maybe I can't call you 'shorty' anymore. Who is he?'

'First, tell me what *Dating Neel 101* is, then we'll talk about me,' I say grabbing a cushion and making myself comfortable.

'Ok,' he says leaning back in the chair. 'When I start dating a girl the first thing, I tell her is I'm not interested in getting serious, because I'm going to the US, and I need to concentrate on the entrance exams. Plus, long-distance relationships are out since I don't know how long I'll be gone. And I don't know when I'll return. Etc, etc. The girl agrees and we start dating.'

'So far, so good,' I say.

'Yeah. A few months into dating, most girls get serious, then they want a commitment and then... you know things go downhill after that,' Neel shrugs and shakes his head. 'I remind them this was never going to be a serious thing like I told them at the start. That's when we break up.'

'That's when I see them running down the corridor, sobbing their hearts out,' I add.

'Yes,' Neel agrees sadly. 'I never mean to hurt them, Naina. But I can't commit to anything. Not at this point. It wouldn't make sense.'

'So basically, your system is flawed,' I say with a grin.

'Ha, very funny,' Neel says with no humour. 'Okay maybe it's a work in progress. I always call them after we break up to see how they're doing. I'm not that heartless you know.'

'Hmm…' I say mulling over that.

'Okay, your turn now. Who is this guy? And is he worthy of dating my kid sister,' Neel says giving me what he thinks is a tough look.

I give him the short version of how Amar and I met and started dating.

'Not bad,' Neel nods approvingly. 'At least he kept trying till he won you over. Full marks for that. So where do I come in?'

'The twins are having a sixteenth birthday party and I need you to come along too. Dad will agree to let me go if you're there.'

'I'll be near Cuffe Parade that night, so it should be alright,' Neel says after thinking it over. 'I'll tell dad about the party and ask him for permission for you to come too. Is that okay?'

'Yes, that's perfect Neel *bhaiya*, thanks,' I say excitedly jumping up.

'On one condition,' Neel says. 'No calling me *bhaiya* when we are out. Just Neel is fine.'

'Done,' I say getting up and giving him a hug. 'Maybe you are a nice guy after all.'

TWELVE

The next evening, I leave the house after four o'clock led by Twinkle on a leash. Years ago, when we first asked our parents for a dog, the condition was that Neel and I had to take her out for a walk every day. Although she started out as company for Neel and me, she quickly became the third child of my parents. Or their favourite child as we often tease them.

Everyone knows Twinkle. She is a silky terrier and like dogs of her breed, she is very vocal. People know she is out for a walk from her high-pitched bark and the sight of large dogs running away from her. She is a force to reckon with.

I enjoy walking around our neighbourhood. Our road is lined with tall apartment buildings on either side which give way to old houses and villas set inside gardens down short driveways. It's the less crowded part of the city with enough greenery to forget you're in Bombay. This is an area I'm familiar with since my old school is one road away.

I spot a tall guy leaning against a white car. Amar. Classmate. Cricket hero. Newly minted boyfriend. Looking smashing, waiting for me. We grin at each other.

'Hi,' I greet him, my grin threatening to jump off my face.

Twinkle jerks the leash out of my hand, making straight for Amar. Too late I realise I don't know if he likes dogs or not. He bends down and she jumps right into his arms. She licks him enthusiastically wagging her tail all the time.

'She likes you,' I say in surprise, joining him. 'She's very picky, you know.'

'Have I got her approval?' he asks laughing.

'Yes,' I say. 'And let me tell you it's not easy getting it. We have friends who she still doesn't like. After years and years of meeting them.'

'One family member down, three more to go,' Amar quips. He puts her down and I take hold of her leash again.

'Sorry about that,' I tell him. 'I didn't ask if you liked dogs or not.'

'We have a golden retriever called Misha,' he says. He gives me a big smile. 'Hey, it's good to see you. Feels like a long time but it's only been a few days.'

'It does,' I agree. 'How did you get here?'

'I came here with our driver, Vikas,' Amar says gesturing to a guy in white, standing next to the Contessa. 'I need to have someone with a license if I'm driving.'

'Hello Madam,' Vikas says approaching me. 'If you don't mind, I can take your dog for a walk. Then you have time to talk to Sir.'

'Oh,' I say surprised by his offer. 'Are you sure? Twinkle can be hard to handle.'

'I take Misha for a walk every day,' he says. 'She is a big dog. I can manage.'

'Just be careful, please,' I say handing the leash to him. 'She is very precious to us.'

He gives me a smile. Twinkle trots off without a backward glance at me. So many dogs to bark at, so little time. Not a chance that she's going to miss me.

We lean against the car, our shoulders touching.

'You look good,' Amar says. 'I missed you.'

'I missed you too,' I say in a near-whisper, still self-conscious saying things like that.

'Feels good to be home, doesn't it?'

'It does. How is Dev?'

'So much better. The operation was a success. He's recovering well,' he says the relief evident in his voice. 'With us in boarding school, my parents could concentrate on Dev's treatment and now, recovery.'

'I'm glad.'

'I've got something for you,' Amar says. 'Shall we sit inside the car?'

Once inside, he reaches into the glove compartment, pulling out a long box wrapped in silver paper. He hands it to me.

'Oh,' I say a bit doubtfully wondering how to explain a gift from him to my parents. 'You shouldn't have, Amar.'

'It's small. Go on, open it,' Amar urges me since I'm still hesitating.

Under the wrapping paper is a long slim box. Inside is a charm bracelet in silver. The first four links have charms hanging from them. They are the alphabets A and N, then the zodiac symbols for Scorpio and Pisces, our respective Zodiac signs. The fifth charm is a small flower with a blue stone at the centre that sparkles in the light.

'Is it an aquamarine?' I ask Amar.

'Your birthstone,' he grins. 'I did my homework.'

'It's so pretty,' I say trying it on. 'Thanks a ton, Amar.'

'I figured it was time to show you I'm serious,' he says. 'I knew it had to be something small or you wouldn't accept it.'

'Thanks,' I say. 'It's lovely. But please, no more gifts. I don't want you spending your pocket money on me.'

I reach across and kiss him quickly on the cheek. 'Just in case someone I know is passing,' I explain with a grin.

'What time does your dad get home?' he asks. 'I don't want to run into him.'

'Closer to six o'clock. Traffic's not great around this time. Oh, the good news is that Neel has agreed to come to your party. And he'll ask my dad if I can go along with him. All sorted.'

'That's great,' Amar agrees. 'My parents have invited quite a few people. Over fifty at last count.'

'May be best if I'm introduced as a classmate and not as you know, your girlfriend?' I falter at the end of the question. 'It'll be easier for me.'

'You don't want to be introduced as my girlfriend? Why not?'

I pause trying to collect my thoughts around this.

'It's not that I don't want to be known as *your girlfriend*. I'd rather be Naina, your classmate. People get so caught up in the label 'girlfriend', don't you think?'

I glance at him hoping he'll get what I'm trying to say. He looks doubtful.

'Plus, if fifty people are informed we're dating there's more chance someone may tell my parents. And my dad doesn't need to know.'

'Ok,' he says, at last. I realise that *is* the clincher. If my dad hears from someone else his daughter is dating, when he is not aware of it, all hell will break loose.

'But we are, dating?' Amar asks with a frown.

'Absolutely,' I say with a grin. Tapping him on the shoulder, I point a finger at him saying, 'And I hope your ex-girlfriends know that.'

'Ok,' he says looking delighted. 'Jealous?'

'Should I be?' I ask momentarily worried.

'Nope,' he says with finality. 'Not a bit.'

'Where exactly are your exes?' I ask. No harm in knowing if I'm going to run into them or not.

'Mallika moved to the UK with her family two years ago,' he elaborates. 'And Gia moved to Calcutta in March this year. You have nothing to worry about.'

'Ok,' I say cheering up.

'I meant to ask you, what made you decide to start dating me?' Amar asks casually.

I grin, 'If I tell you, you won't believe me,' I say as I tell him what tipped the scales in his favour.

'What? Not my killer smile or my impressive abs?' he jokes. 'Just being decent enough to play the guitar for you?'

'Yep,' I confirm.

Amar shakes his head in wonder. 'And I thought I knew what girls wanted,' he says ruefully.

Vikas comes into view with Twinkle in the lead as usual. My watch tells me it's a quarter to six.

'Time for me to head home,' I say with a sigh. We exit the car reluctantly.

'I'll call you later this week,' I promise just before leaving. 'This Saturday is my friend Mimi's birthday. I'll be at her house in Colaba the whole day. If you're free, perhaps we can meet?'

'Sounds good,' Amar says. 'Any chance of taking you dancing that night?'

'You're kidding,' I say noticing his impish grin. 'I can just see my dad agreeing to that. Like, never. Thanks for the bracelet.'

I watch as Amar starts the car, executes a U-turn and heads back home. I slide the box with the bracelet into my back pocket, pulling my t-shirt over it.

*   *

Mimi's house is one of two in the compound. Her grandfather bought this piece of land years ago and built a house for each of his two sons. The prospect of hosting twenty, fifteen-year-old girls was enough to send her parents over to Mimi's uncles' house for the day.

Happily, we are on our own with huge amounts of food and drink to see us through the day.

After lunch, presents are opened and admired. We linger over dessert exchanging gossip about our classmates. A few girls say goodbye and leave. Those of us that are left, wander over to the small pool outside.

Mimi and I met in kindergarten and continued being friends when we moved over to the main school. When I left to join boarding school, I missed Mimi the most and wondered if I would ever find a bestie again. That was before Neha, and I met.

'I need to know everything about Amar. There weren't many

details in your letter,' Mimi says excitedly as we settle under a tree in the backyard. I give her the details of how we met in school, all the way up to our train journey, finishing with the silver charm bracelet Amar gave me.

'He has good taste,' she declares examining the bracelet. 'Naina, I've got to meet this guy. Got to meet the guy who turned your rules of never dating in school upside down.'

'Well, you're in luck. Amar's coming here to pick me up,' I inform her. 'If my mum calls please tell her I'm around here somewhere. I hope that's alright. We thought of taking a drive around this area.'

'No problem,' Mimi says with a grin. 'After all you've covered for me many times in the past.'

I smile at this remembering the year we turned thirteen. The year Mimi spent being rebellious and giving her parents and me sleepless nights. Thankfully she grew out of that phase and took up tennis instead.

We move over to the swimming pool where a few girls are paddling enthusiastically and perch on the edge, our feet in the water.

'Naina, you have a phone call,' Savita *didi* says coming towards us. Savita joined the household when Mimi was two and never left. Over the years she's gone from being the nanny to the housekeeper.

As I get up to leave, Mimi's friend Sadia, comes over to join us.

'I heard you mention Amar Malhotra,' she tells Mimi as I head inside the house.

Is she talking about the same Amar, I wonder. I'm torn between hearing what she has to say and taking the phone call. I decide to hurry inside. I'm sure Amar is calling to let me know he's on his way.

'Hi, Naina, speaking,' I say into the receiver.

'Hi, Amar, here,' he says. 'I'm on my way to your friend's place. It should take me twenty minutes, max. Will you come outside?'

'Yeah, I can do that,' I say. 'I'll see you soon.'

When I return to my spot by the edge of the pool, Sadia has left.

'What was Sadia saying?' I ask Mimi cautiously.

'Something about Amar's ex, Gia,' she says looking a bit cagey. 'Do you know about her?'

'Amar said they broke up when she and her family left for Calcutta at the start of the year. Why? Did Sadia mention something else?'

'She said Gia took the breakup badly and is still not over it,' Mimi says reluctantly. 'But if Amar said it's over, it must be, right?'

'I guess,' I say trying to sound casual.

As if it's normal to be discussing my boyfriend's ex and their breakup. But I feel a prickle of doubt start somewhere deep down and make its way up.

'Amar should be here soon,' I tell her. 'My mum's sending our car around five-thirty. Can you ask Keshav to wait?'

'Sure, don't worry about that,' Mimi says. 'C'mon I'll wait outside with you.'

I grab my purse and walk outside the gate with Mimi.

Amar is already parked outside the house. As he gets out from the driver's side, the passenger door opens, and a guy gets out from the other side.

As he walks closer, I realise I've seen him before.

'You?' I blurt out.

Recognition dawns on him as well as he looks guilty. It's the guy from the shop who flirted with me before my mom shut him down.

'Naina, this is my cousin, Suhail,' Amar introduces us. Seeing the looks on our faces he asks, 'Wait, have you two met?'

'Yes,' I say.

'No,' Suhail says looking suitably embarrassed.

'Mimi, this is Amar and Suhail,' I make the introductions, so Mimi won't feel left out.

'When Suhail and I met, he was singing *'Does your mother know that you're out*?' I inform Amar and Mimi.

Suhail looks around for a place to crawl into.

'Seriously, dude?' Amar glares at his cousin. 'Is there any female you haven't flirted with?'

'Or tried lines like 'Where have you been all my life?' I add laughing.

'In my defence it was my friend Pavan, who said, not me' Suhail grins. 'Anyway, it's great to meet you, Naina. And Mimi.'

Mimi says a quick Hi and Bye and heads back to her party.

Once we're inside the car, Suhail says, 'Your friend Mimi's cute. Is she single?'

While Amar throws his hands up at this, I grin at Suhail over my shoulder.

'She is at present. But if you guys hook up, it would mean no flirting with anyone else. Can you manage that?'

'For the right girl, I can,' Suhail declares while Amar makes a rude noise. I laugh at their easy relationship.

'How are you guys related?'

'Our mothers are sisters,' Amar says. 'We grew up together. Suhail is three years older than us. He was supposed to be a role model for us. But that didn't work out as planned,' he says smirking at Suhail in the rear-view mirror.

Suhail laughs but doesn't look put out at all.

After dropping Suhail at a friend's place, the two of us carry on. Our first stop is for ice cream at the Parsi Dairy Farm. We wolf down an ice cream sandwich each, at the café. Then clutching a precious kulfi in our sticky hands, we cross the road to catch the sunset at Marine Drive.

Nature doesn't disappoint. Dangling our legs over the concrete wall, we watch the spectacular sunset and lean in for a kiss.

'Happy?' Amar asks leaning back to look at me.

'Very,' I reply. 'It's the small things that make me happy.'

'Me too,' he says taking my hand. 'It's why we're perfect together.'

For some reason that makes me remember what I heard at Mimi's house.

Before I can stop myself, I ask, 'Are you in touch with Gia?'

Amar appears dazed by the sudden change in topic. 'Gia? No. Why did you suddenly think of her?'

'Sorry, for throwing that out there. At lunch today, this girl, Sadia mentioned Gia. Said she took the breakup rather badly.'

Amar looks shocked by what I've just said. Is it because I know so much or because Gia being upset is news to him?

'Sadia is Gia's best friend,' he says slowly. 'Strange of her to say Gia took it badly since we both agreed long-distance dating wouldn't work. It wasn't a spur of the moment decision.'

I shrug, and lean against Amar, feeling silly now for bringing it up. And disappointed because the mood between us has changed. Even though Gia is miles away in Calcutta, her spectre hangs over us now.

'It's almost five-thirty,' I say looking at my watch. 'We'd better get back. But thanks for everything, Amar. I had a great time today.'

'That sounds so formal,' he teases me. 'Am I going to get a thank-you card in the post?'

Laughing, we sprint back to the car.

THIRTEEN

I take another look at the full-length mirror in my room. The cream dress looks good, I decide. The cowl neck is flattering, and the cut of the dress is just right. I throw the sheer wrap that came with it over my shoulders then take it off. I'll add it later if it cools down.

'Hey, sweetie,' my mum says coming into the room. 'You might as well wear these earrings. They match the dress nicely.'

She holds out a pair of simple topaz and diamond drop earrings.

'Mum, these are yours. I can't wear them. What if I lose one?'

'You won't, Naina,' she insists. 'They are the screw on type, so they won't come loose.'

'Perfect,' she says once I put the earrings on. 'You're still a bit skinny but that's alright.'

'Mum,' I say in protest. 'You promised not to call me skinny. If I'm skinny, then it's because of you and dad. It's hereditary, remember?'

She smiles and shakes her head.

Neel and I have this argument with our parents all the time. They fret over both of us being too skinny. When we point out they were skinny too as teenagers (we have photos to prove it!) they say they weren't as skinny as we are now. Really! Next, we'll have to explain how genetics works to them.

We join Neel and my dad in the living room. My dad's having his usual drink of rum over ice and soda while Neel knocks back a Coke. I'm sure it's not Neel's usual drink, but at home, in front of my parents, it is.

'Looking nice, kiddo,' Neel's says with a grin.

'Yes,' agrees my dad, albeit reluctantly. 'Are you sure you want to attend this party, Naina? After all it is Neel's friend's birthday. You can stay at home with us if you want.'

Since that's the story we've told Dad, I need to go along with it.

'I'd like to go, Dad. I've been so busy studying this past week, it'll be good meeting other people tonight.'

'Okay. But remember you need be back by one thirty. That gives you enough time for cutting the cake etc,' my dad reminds us. 'And Neel, I'm counting on you to look after Naina.'

'Dad,' I protest. 'I'm fifteen. I don't need to be looked after. I'm in boarding school, remember? I can look after myself.'

'True, but this is Bombay, not boarding school. If anyone offers you alcohol or cigarettes, you must refuse.'

'Don't worry, Dad. I'll look after her,' Neel says hurriedly before my dad can come up with any more instructions.

'That was close,' I say as Neel drives out of our building. 'Good thing we'd prepared our story in advance.'

'Yeah,' Neel laughs. 'He's stressed out because you never go out at night on your own.'

'Yep, that's true,' I agree. 'But I'm not on my own. You're with me, so I'll be fine. I bet you don't have a curfew when you're out, Neel.'

'In theory my curfew is also one-thirty, but no one is awake when I return so I don't need to worry how late it is,' he shrugs.

I'm pretty sure either mum or dad will be awake when we return tonight. Double standards for sons and daughters! Someday I'll have to address that with my parents.

'Naina, I'll come and wish the twins for their birthday. After that, I'll be at a friend's place nearby,' Neel says. 'That's the phone number I gave you earlier.'

'I've got it in my purse,' I say holding up the small gold clutch I'm carrying. The bag containing gifts for Samir and Amar is at my feet.

'How's your friend, Neha?' Neel enquires.

'She's fine. We talk on the phone every other day,' I say. 'Really helps with revising and staying motivated.'

'Amar's on the phone every day,' Neel says with a grin. 'More motivation?'

I laugh and say, 'You can call it that. But yeah, we discuss what portions we are revising. Helps if the person you date is also into studying.'

Driving down the iconic Marine Drive at night is a sight I never get tired of. Crowds of Saturday night party goers are slowly building up.

'Have you been to their place before?' Neel asks as he turns off Marine Drive, heading towards Cuffe Parade.

'No,' I tell him. 'Been so busy revising, there was no chance. Besides, I knew I'd be here for the party.'

A few minutes later Neel turns into the compound of a tall white building. We park in a spot for visitors and head to the lift. Buildings here are often over ten floors tall and were built more recently while in our area it's common to see older buildings of six floors or less.

We get off at the tenth floor and can tell right away which flat is throwing a party tonight, from the decorations outside and the loud music.

'Here goes,' I say as Neel, and I walk into the flat. I'm suddenly glad I have him with me. Walking alone into a crowd of mostly strangers would have been nerve wracking.

There's a large group of guests near the door as Neel and I enter the flat. I don't recognise anyone, and my spirits flag a little. Walking past them, I'm thrilled when I spot Reena, Arjun, and a couple of seniors from school standing together. I'll have good company tonight.

After exchanging greetings and high fives, I introduce Neel to my schoolmates. Amar comes over just then. Introducing Neel to him, I notice my brother quietly sizing him up. It may not be evident to the others, but I know my brother well enough to read the signs. From the way Neel shakes his hand and greets him, I think Amar has passed inspection.

'Happy birthday,' I wish Amar when I get the chance.

'Thanks,' he says with a warm smile. 'I was expecting something more from you.'

I know what he's hinting at, so I hand the bag containing the gifts to him instead.

'Thanks, Naina, but this wasn't what I meant.'

Grinning at him I say, 'Best to wait when there's less people around.'

Looking at the crowd spread out over the large living and dining area, Amar frowns and says, 'That will be a long while from now. The guest list seems to have gone a bit haywire.'

'It does seem like more than fifty people,' I agree looking around.

'I'd have preferred a quiet dinner with you somewhere. But I had no choice. Come and meet my folks,' offers Amar. 'They'd like to meet you.'

I hang back, shaking my head, 'Not on my own. Maybe later with the whole gang from school.'

Promising to meet up later, Amar heads to the front door to greet more guests. Neel's busy talking to Arjun and two other seniors from school, so I don't have to worry about him for now.

Glancing around the room I'm glad I made the effort to dress up. I spot a few designer bags and dresses, some Gloria Vanderbilt jeans with the iconic swan logo and a lot of sudden sparks of light as gemstones catch the lights overhead.

'Hey,' Reena says joining me on a sofa near the balcony. 'How's the studying going?'

'Good,' I say with a sigh. 'A bit slower than I hoped. How about you?'

'Same here. Slow, but I'm hoping to finish by the end of the holidays. Can't wait for the exams to be over in March,' Reena says. I give a heartfelt nod and raise my glass of orange juice to that.

'Hey, peeps,' Samir yells from across the room when he sees us. Only Samir can get away with that at a formal party. He heads over to us, his signature grin lighting up his face.

After the usual birthday wishes he joins Reena and me on the sofa.

Looking around he beckons someone over. I follow his gaze and realise this must be Dev, his younger brother. His face has the softness of a young boy; only his pallid complexion hints at the ordeal he's been through. He comes closer and I can see his shirt hangs a bit on his frame and his hair is growing back slowly after the operation.

'Dev, come and meet my classmates,' Samir says. 'Reena and Naina, meet the youngest and the nicest of the Malhotra brothers.'

'Hi,' Dev says shyly. 'Nice to meet you both. Naina, I've heard a lot about you.'

'Oh no,' I say in mock horror. 'Hope Samir had a few good things to say about me.'

'Actually, it was Amar,' Dev clarifies as I try hard not to blush.

'Naina, I'm going to head out now,' Neel says.

I look up to see that he has finished his drink and is ready to leave.

'Okay, I'll walk you to the lift,' I say.

'No need,' Neel says.

'It's okay, I can do with a change of scene,' I insist.

Amar joins us at the front door and walks down the corridor talking to Neel.

Waiting for the lift to come up, Neel says, 'Give me a call when you're ready to leave.'

'Sure,' I say. 'It'll be around one o'clock. We'll still be able to reach home before our curfew.'

Once Neel leaves in the elevator, Amar pulls me away from the brightly lit corridor and into a corner near the dark stairwell saying, 'How about that birthday kiss, now?'

'Happy sixteenth birthday, Amar,' I murmur as we break apart from a long, slow kiss that leaves both of us breathless. 'I think we're getting good at this, don't you?'

'Hmm..' Amar says, sliding his hands over my exposed arms. 'You look pretty. I like this dress.'

'Really?' I ask, pleased.

'Really,' he confirms. Starting at my collar bone he follows the drape of the fabric as it dips down saying, 'And I really, really love this part the most.'

'Now, why am I not surprised?' I ask sotto voce.

Amar grins and takes my hand in his, lacing his fingers through mine. 'Listen, I wanted to show you those records we…' he begins, then stops as we hear the elevator reaching the tenth floor.

The lift door opens with a squeak.

Amar frowns. 'Sounds like more guests have arrived. Can we continue this later?'

'I'm holding you to that,' I say.

He gives my hand a squeeze as we head for the lift. Suhail and two other guys are just closing the lift door and greet Amar enthusiastically.

Suhail says 'Hi' and gives me a quick peck on the cheek. He appears preoccupied.

When we reach the front door Suhail says urgently, 'Amar can I have quick word with you?'

I notice he looks worried which is at odds with his usual cheerful demeanour. Sensing he needs to speak to his cousin alone, I carry on into the flat.

'Naina, we've been looking all over for you,' Reena says as soon as she sees me. 'Samir is giving us a tour of the apartment. C'mon.'

I troop up the stairs with Arjun and Reena, as we follow Samir up a graceful staircase that leads to the floor above. I feel the eyes of someone on me and look back at the crowd below. An elegant lady in a pale grey beaded saree is looking up at me. I don't recall meeting her and wonder who she is. Samir turns and waves to her. She smiles and waves back.

'My lovely mum,' he informs us.

Once we reach the top floor Samir shows us around the family area first, and then the bedrooms.

'I used to share a room with Dev but last year he decided he was old enough to have a room of his own. The guest room is now his bedroom,' Samir explains pointing to the first door we pass.

'And this is my room,' he says throwing open the next door with a flourish.

The room starts off a little bare but just past the bed are stacks of canvasses, art paper, and paint supplies in neat organisers. A large corkboard is pinned with various sketches, drawings, and watercolours. An easel stands on either side of large windows that look overlook the sea. The curtains are thrown back and the lights of a few ships pierce the darkness beyond.

'Wow, Samir,' Reena says going over to the windows. 'The view must be great when it's light.'

I tell Samir, 'I'm impressed by how neatly you've organised your art supplies.'

Grinning sheepishly, he says, 'You won't say the same about my wardrobe.'

I laugh. 'You're so much into art, that's understandable.'

'C'mon,' Samir says leading us out of his room. 'Let me show you Amar's room.'

Opening the door next to his he quips, 'Naina you haven't been here, have you?'

Shyly, I say, 'No I haven't.'

The room is the same size as Samir's but here the walls have shelves full of music. Stacks of LP and EP records fill these shelves. More shelves of cassettes end with a small collection of CDs. One wall has an impressive stereo with a pair of matching speakers. In a corner of the room Amar's two guitars lean against the wall.

'This is insane,' Arjun says thumbing through some vinyl records. 'I'd love to hear some of these. They're classics.'

'Guys, guys, I'm starving,' Reena interrupts. 'Someone mentioned dinner is going to be at ten followed by dancing. We'd better head back down.'

I take one last look at Amar's room, before Samir closes the door.

We head down the stairs, as the thump of music erupts from a room. The dancing has begun.

On the way downstairs, Samir stops so suddenly, we all bump into him.

'Oh shoot,' he exclaims. 'Why did she come? She wasn't even invited.'

'Who?' I ask curiously trying to discover who he's looking at.

'Gia,' he says. 'That's her over there.'

Of all the things I expected him to say, that sentence was not one of them.

'Where?' I ask in alarm.

By now we're at the bottom of the staircase, so he doesn't have time to answer. Instead, I get my answer in the form of Gia herself.

'Samir, I was dying to see you. Happy birthday,' a sweet voice says as Samir is enveloped in a perfumed hug.

This is my introduction to Gia, Amar's ex. She is everything I'm not. Small and petite with curves in all the right places set off by a form-fitting silver dress. Light grey eyes, full red mouth on a face framed by sheets of shining hair.

'Gia, meet my classmates. Naina, Reena, and Arjun,' Samir introduces us quickly.

'Hi all,' she says sketching a small wave. 'Where's Amar? I haven't wished him yet.'

'We didn't know you were in town,' Samir says after an awkward pause. 'How did you hear about the party?'

'I met Suhail and his friends at another do. They mentioned it,' Gia says happily. 'I had to come of course. I knew you guys wouldn't mind that I wasn't invited.'

Samir seems at a loss for words.

'I'm still starving,' Reena declares. 'Naina, shall we go and have dinner?'

'Sure,' I say happy to leave this awkward situation behind. 'See you later,' I say in the general direction of Arjun, Samir, and Gia.

'Who's that girl?' asks Reena as we head into the dining room. 'She seems to know her way around here.'

'Amar's ex,' I say shortly since I know Reena will figure it out sooner or later.

'What? You're kidding me,' she says. 'She's come to her ex's birthday do when she wasn't invited. Wow. She has some guts.'

'I guess,' I say unhappily wondering if I should have stayed behind. But I couldn't get over Gia being here in person.

This is what Suhail wanted to warn Amar about. That Gia was coming to the party. Wonder what Amar thought of that.

Ten minutes later Reena and I have filled our plates with food and sink gratefully into chairs. I'm hungrier than I realised and tuck into the food with gusto.

Reena takes a sip of her Coke and calls out. 'Over here, Amar,' as he enters the dining area.

'Hey,' he says coming over to stand by my chair. 'That looks good. I was hoping to have a dance with you if you're done with dinner.'

'I'm done,' I say standing up. Handing my almost empty plate to one of the servers, I follow him into the next room.

I know I should wait till we've had at least one dance together, but I was never good at keeping things inside. As the song winds down I tell him, 'I met Gia tonight.'

From the expression on his face, he knows she's here, but he didn't think we had met. Taking my hand, he leads me out to the balcony. I savour the cool air on my face.

'I'm so sorry she's here, Naina. I had no idea till Suhail told me she was on her way.'

'I know,' I tell him. 'She told us she decided to come here despite not being invited.'

He shakes his head, bewildered. 'Why would she land up here when we ended it back in March? I don't get it.'

'Maybe,' I begin then stop and try again. 'Maybe she still has feelings for you.'

'Not really,' he says. 'It's not like we were serious about each other. Not like you and I.'

I'm thrilled to hear that. But I'm torn between wanting to ask more questions about Gia and not wanting to know any more.

Behind us the lights in the dining area are suddenly switched on. A cake is being wheeled in on a trolley and I can hear guests calling out Amar and Samir's names. It's time for them to cut the cake.

'Go on,' I tell Amar. 'They need you inside. I'll be fine.'

I watch from outside as the brothers and their parents gather around the cake. There's a lot of good-natured teasing as their relations and friends all sing loudly. The cake is cut and one of the servers from the catering crew continues cutting the rest of it.

I spot a small figure in a tight silver dress amongst the crowd closest to the twins. Gia. Of course, she wouldn't dream of hanging back like me to watch things from a distance. She would want to be front and centre.

'Hey,' Reena says coming towards me carrying two plates with a piece of cake on each. 'I didn't see you inside, so I snagged a piece for you.'

'Thanks,' I say taking a plate from her.

'You should be in there, Naina not out here,' Reena says between mouthfuls of black forest cake. 'That girl, Gia is all over the place, hugging and kissing everyone she knows.'

'Yeah, I noticed that' I say trying to eat cake and talk at the same time. 'This cake is yummy.'

Reena nods. 'My parents are coming to pick me up at one o'clock. I'll have to say my goodbyes soon.'

I check the time on my watch. It's close to one already. Time to call Neel. I give Reena a quick hug and say goodbye promising to call her soon.

Inside the apartment a few guests are leaving, as the party starts winding down. Dev sees me and comes over.

'Hi Dev,' I say grateful to find someone who can help me. 'I need to make a call. Where can I find a phone?'

'Come with me,' he says going down the corridor towards an alcove which has a phone. 'Here you go.'

I quickly dial the number Neel gave me and inform him I'm ready to leave, then I hang up. I have to be home by one-thirty, or my dad won't be keen on letting me do this again. He's big on earning trust by following through on a promise. And I did promise to be back on time.

'Samir,' I call out as he passes by. 'Have you seen Amar? I'm leaving in ten minutes; I wanted to say goodbye.'

'Already?' Samir asks checking his watch for the time. 'I saw Amar heading upstairs. I think he went to get some more music. You know where his room is, now,' he smirks at me.

I grin and nod. 'Hey, if I don't see you later, goodbye and all that.'

'Thanks for coming tonight. We'll meet up soon, yeah?'

I give him a thumbs up as I climb the stairs again. At the top of the staircase, I go down the corridor towards Amar's room. The door is open, and light from inside spills onto the landing. Amar's still in there.

'Knock, knock,' I say playfully, matching my words to my actions.

Inside under the muted glow of an overhead light, framed by the huge windows stands a girl and a guy with no breathing space between them. A girl in a silver dress and a boy who looks a lot like my boyfriend. The girl's arms are around his neck.

As I look on, she pulls him closer. Gia and Amar.

FOURTEEN

A part of me is shocked and another part of me thinks, I knew this would happen. As if our entire love story was going to lead to this scene, eventually.

'Amar?' I say his name soundlessly, surprised to find myself inside the room. Somehow, I thought I was still at the door watching all this from a distance.

They turn to look at me. I do what I do best. I flee. Backing away from them, I bump into a chair by the desk. I need to get away from whatever this is, although the sight of Amar and Gia together is burned in my memory.

I catch sight of the bracelet Amar gave me on my wrist. Struggling with the clasp I manage to wrench it off, scratching myself in the process.

I drop it on the desk saying, 'I can't wear this anymore. You can keep it.'

'Naina, wait,' I hear Amar's voice but I don't look back. 'Naina, please.'

Please, please don't come after me. I run down the corridor in my kitten heels. This floor must have a front door too, so I head in the general direction till I find it.

Wrenching it open, I bang it shut behind me and lean against it, weakly. I want to sink on the floor and cry but I can hear Amar calling my name on the other side.

I race down the stairs so I can meet Neel and go home. To the one place where I can put all this behind me. When I reach the landing on the tenth floor, Neel is stepping out of the elevator.

'Neel,' I say, surprised to find it sounds more like a sob. I can't recall when the tears started. I've become *that* girl after all. *I am the girl running down the corridor, sobbing.* How ironic, considering how much I didn't want to be that girl.

Neel turns to look at me and then behind me at Amar who has caught up with me.

'What happened?' my brother asks puzzled. When he left hours ago his sister was happy and in love. And now here I am, miserable and in tears.

'I can explain,' Amar says. 'It's not what it looked like, Naina. Nothing happened.'

'What the hell are we talking about?' Neel asks with an edge to his voice I've never heard before. I've only known him as an even-tempered guy.

'Please,' I interrupt them. 'Can we just go home?'

I press the button on the elevator panel, so it stays on the tenth floor.

'At least listen to what I have to say,' Amar implores. 'She followed me to my room, saying she wanted to wish me. I pushed her away as soon as I realised what she was trying to do.'

'Who is she?' Neel asks. 'Who are we talking about?'

'Gia,' I say shortly. 'Amar's ex.'

Opening the door to the lift, I step inside willing myself to look down at the floor, at my shoes, at anything besides Amar. My face is a mess with tears flowing down my cheeks and onto the front of my dress. Thankfully I didn't attempt wearing any mascara tonight.

'Naina, I think you need to hear what Amar has to say,' Neel says. 'It's only fair.'

'We have to get home before one-thirty,' I say focussing on the one thing that makes sense right now. 'Can we leave, please?'

'Will you call me?' Amar asks.

I nod yes.

Neel says goodbye to Amar and steps into the lift. I exhale slowly as the lift descends smoothly to the ground floor.

On the journey home I tell Neel everything leading up to the moment I saw Amar and Gia together. He hands me a handkerchief. I use it to wipe my tears and blow my nose noisily. It looks familiar. It could be one I've given him for his birthday. I've given Neel and my dad a lot of handkerchiefs as birthday presents over the years.

'Sorry about that,' I tell Neel. 'This is not the way I expected the night to end.'

'Naina, from what you and Amar said, Gia was there to make trouble tonight,' Neel says. 'Perhaps she wanted to get back together with him. I don't think Amar was at fault. And you seeing them together was bad timing.'

'But what if I wasn't there? Would he have kissed her back?' I say as the tears start again.

That is at the heart of my outburst. The reason I ran away. That and the realisation that it hurt so much seeing him with someone else. Even if that someone was his ex. I never thought I was the jealous type. But I couldn't bear seeing Amar getting close to anyone else. And no one is more shocked about it, than me.

'You know what?' my brother asks as we speed past Marine Drive, deserted now but for a few stray dogs and taxis. 'I expected you to stand up to Gia and fight for Amar.'

I look at him and see a grin spreading across his face.

'Neel, do I look like the kind of girl who would fight with anyone?' I chuckle despite the state, I'm in.

'If it's for someone or something you care about, then yeah,' he clarifies. 'Wouldn't you?'

'Oh,' I say turning this over in my head.

If it came down to it, would I fight to keep Amar with me? If I knew he cared as much, then yes, I would. 'I never thought of it that way,' I admit.

Would Amar fight for me if it came to that? I know he would. In fact, that's what he did the first few months after we met; fought to be in my life though I tried keeping him out.

'Neel,' I say to my brother. 'Since when did you get so wise?'

He laughs, 'Since I had to start being a brother to you, for real.'

We both laugh. 'Want to go back and sort it out with Amar?' Neel asks.

'And risk being grounded by Dad? And possibly cry some more? No,' I decide. 'I'll call him tomorrow once I get rid of this awful headache. Comes with all the crying I did.'

Fifteen minutes later we are home. The lights have been left on in the passage and in our rooms, but my parents are asleep. Good to know they trusted us(me) enough not to stay awake.

After a hot shower and a cup of tea, my remedy for all problems, I wrap a quilt around me and sit on the floor of my balcony watching the lights down below. Twinkle who gave us her usual warm greeting when we came in, pushes my room door open and climbs onto my lap.

'Twink,' I say, patting her silky head while taking comfort in her warmth. 'Why does life have to be so full of ups and downs? Is it the same for dogs?'

Her response is to lick my chin enthusiastically before settling down for a nap.

*   *

The next morning, I wake with what feels like a hangover the size of Powai Lake. Given all the orange juice I gulped down the previous night it feels very unfair. But it's probably due to the lack of sleep.

After another hot shower, I stand in front of the mirror and take stock of my reflection. My hair still retains some volume from the blowout I had before the party and my eyes look a bit puffy. Other than that, I look alright.

I wander around our flat looking for signs of life.

'Your parents have gone out for lunch,' Mary informs me. 'And Neel went to meet some friends. Shall I make an omelette and toast for you?'

'Yes, please Mary,' I say, knowing that will make me feel better.

The phone rings and I wander over to pick it up.

'Hello?' I ask cautiously.

'Naina?' A familiar voice asks. I heave a sigh of relief on recognising Neha's voice. I sink into a leather chair nearby.

'Hi Neha,' I say. 'How are you?'

'How are *you*?' she asks, and I know from the emphasis on the last word that she knows what happened last night. 'Are you alright?'

'Yes, I am,' I say. 'You heard what happened at the party?'

'Arjun called and told me. He said you left suddenly; Later Amar told him why. It's awful you had to go through that, Naina. I know you hate making a scene.'

'Yeah. Luckily, I could slip away without meeting anyone, besides Amar, of course.'

'Arjun says he was really upset. That girl, Gia, why was she even there?'

'No idea. But she made more of an impression than I did,' I say with a laugh. 'I think she's used to that though.'

'Listen, Amar called to ask for your number,' Neha says cautiously. 'And I gave it to him. I hope you don't mind.'

'It's okay, Neha, it's time I gave him my number anyway.'

'He's serious about you.'

'And I'm serious about him,' I assure Neha.

'Then you need to tell him that,' she says.

'I'll tell him when we meet next,' I assure her.

'Give him a call and tell him, Naina. He should know you feel the same way.'

'Yeah, I think you're right,' I say. 'I'll do that right away.'

'I'd better run. We're going to see a movie later tonight.'

'Which one?' I ask her.

'*Saagar*,' she laughs. 'You know my dad is a big fan of Dimple.'

'She's my dad's favourite too,' I say. 'Let me know how the movie is. Thanks for calling, Neha. Bye.'

From my perch near the front door, I see Mary go into the dining room with a steaming plate of food. I want to speak to Amar, but I also need to have breakfast or more accurately, brunch since it's well past eleven in the morning.

With food inside me, the day looks much better. Retrieving the handset, I look up Amar's number in my address book and start dialling. The phone rings before I can finish.

'Hi, Naina here,' I say quickly, thinking it must be Amar.

'Hi, it's Gia,' a breathless voice says. 'But please don't hang up.'

I pull the handset away from my ear, wondering if this is another prank on her part. She is the last person I'd want to talk to. She ruined last night for me and made me cry so much my head still hurts.

What cheek of her to call.

I wish I could disconnect the call, but years of being told to be polite to everyone, wins over. Also, I want to know why she's calling. Making a face at the handset, I take a deep breath before answering.

'Hi. How did you get my number?' I ask, knowing I sound peeved.

'I asked Sadia to get it from Mimi, who gave it to her on condition I apologise to you. Which I was going to do anyway.'

'Ok,' I say grinning at that.

I know Mimi would have told Sadia exactly what she thought of Gia, before giving her my number.

'I am so, so sorry for what happened last night, Naina,' Gia sounds contrite.

'So why did you do it?' I ask thinking that is not an unreasonable question.

She lets out a long sigh saying, 'It seemed like a good idea at the time. I knew there'd be a party on the sixteenth for their birthday. I thought it was alright to gate crash it. But not many people were happy to see me there. Not Amar for sure.'

'I was surprised to see you,' I confess to her. 'It takes guts. But you didn't play fair Gia, you know that.'

'I figured there was a chance of us getting back together,' she says. 'I didn't know Amar had a girlfriend. No one mentioned you.'

'My dad doesn't know Amar and I are dating, so I wanted to keep it quiet. Still, it doesn't excuse what you did.'

'No,' she agrees. 'When I saw the look on Amar's face, I knew I'd done the wrong thing. I've never seen him so angry. He was worried about you, Naina.'

'I couldn't stay there after seeing you with Amar. I had to leave.'

'It's why I wanted to call and tell you nothing happened between us. What you saw was me trying to get close to Amar, but he pushed me away,' Gia concludes after a pause.

'I hope you believe me,' she continues. 'Because he's serious about you. I will never live down what I did.'

'At least guests at the party will remember you after last night. No one will recall I was there,' I say with a laugh.

'Which could be a good or a bad thing,' she says with a chuckle. 'Amar's a good guy, Naina. Can't say the same for a lot of other guys. Anyway, I'm sorry for causing so much trouble. Please apologise to Amar as well. Take care. Bye.'

'Thanks. Bye.'

I sit on my bed with a thud. Wow, I was not expecting that. The phone rings again and this time it's Mimi. She's calling from a friend's place, so I quickly update her on Gia's call, and she rings off.

I fall back on my bed, gazing up at the ceiling. So many phone calls and it's not even one o'clock.

The phone rings again and this time it's Amar.

'Hi, Naina, how are you?'

'I'm okay. I've been meaning to call but other calls kept coming in,' I explain.

'I know. Your line's been busy for so long. Are you alright?'

'I'm ok,' I say.

'I hope you believed what I said last night. Gia followed me to my room saying she hadn't wished me and then, well, you saw what happened. I didn't encourage her.'

'I know,' I tell him. 'She told me.'

'She *told* you?' he asks. 'When?'

'She called a few minutes ago.'

'What did she want?' he asks, and I wince at the sharpness in his voice. 'She's caused enough trouble already.'

'She wanted to apologise. I think she meant it.'

'Well,' he says doubtfully. 'I don't know about that. She gate-crashed the party. And then pulled that stunt.'

'True,' I agree. 'I told her it was a cheap trick.'

'I hated seeing you cry. I felt awful, because I had caused it.'

'I know. My head still hurts. The only good thing that came out of last night was realising I don't want to lose you. I'm serious about you, Amar.'

'Do you mean that?' Amar asks sounding surprised, then pleased. 'You've never said that before.'

'I should have. It's true. In fact, Neel says I should have fought for you,' I say.

'Fought for me? How?' Amar asks doubtfully.

'Not sure. Maybe I should have told Gia, 'Take your hands off my boyfriend, you little so-and-so,' I tell him.

'That sounds very um, scary,' he says sounding amused.

'You're laughing at me,' I accuse him.

He chuckles. 'Sorry. I'm trying not to. I can't imagine you fighting with anyone.'

'Who knows. Maybe next time,' I say.

'Nah. There won't be a next time,' he says with conviction. 'Which reminds me, when do I see you again?'

'Yeah, about that,' I say slowly. 'I have a ton of revising left to do and my guess is you do too. I'm way behind the deadline I set myself.'

'I'm behind on my revision too. What do you think we should we do?'

'Instead of meeting, why don't we study the whole day and catch up on the phone at night? It'll save us so much time.'

'Not meet at all?' Amar asks after a lengthy pause. 'For how long?'

'A couple of weeks?' I suggest. 'Till we complete the portions we need to. It'll be hard, but we can catch up at night. After ten o'clock every night, if you're free.'

'That's a good idea,' he concedes reluctantly. 'Should we start from today?'

'Yeah, what do you think?'

'Okay. I wanted to meet you, to make sure you are alright, but you sound better than you did last night.'

'I had a long think about it and realised you were pushing her away when I entered the room.'

'I was, Naina. I wouldn't cheat on you.'

From the passage I hear a key at the front door. Must be my parents, back from lunch.

'My folks are back. I'll call you tonight, after ten?'

'Alright. Back to revising. Talk later, Naina.'

*   *

Over the next two weeks, Amar and I talk every night. In a strange way our phone conversations bring us closer than ever. We don't have to work out where and how to meet or waste time travelling through a crowded city for a rendezvous.

Instead, we use that time to study, then treat ourselves to a phone call after our respective families have gone to bed. The first part of our call is spent going over portions we had trouble with that day. If it's Physics or Chemistry, Amar can help while I help him with Literature and History.

Then it's just Amar's voice on one side and mine on the other with a lot of static between us. To me these calls are more intimate than meeting at a crowded café or stealing ten minutes together at a noisy party.

One night, Samir answers the phone.

'Hi Samir,' I say on hearing his voice. 'How are things with you?'

'Hmm... let's see,' he says slowly. 'Not so good. My best friend Naina has given up on me and doesn't call anymore. She's only interested in talking to Amar. So, I'm all alone.'

'You know that's not true,' I protest. 'I'm busy studying. You must be doing the same. Did Amar tell you we haven't met in a long time?'

'Yep, he did,' Samir says with a long sigh. 'And he put me on the same deadline as the two of you.'

'That's a good thing,' I tell him. 'Isn't it?'

'No,' Samir groans. 'You've got to save me, Naina. He won't let me go out till I finish the days' portion. He's worse than my mother.'

I start laughing. 'You're lucky he's there for you.'

'Maybe,' he says. Then dropping his voice to a dramatic whisper, he adds, 'Ok, to be honest, I'm glad he's making me study, but I complain about it anyway. Just to give him a hard time.'

'Samir, only you would think of doing that,' I say with a giggle.

'I've got to go, now, Amar's here. Chat later, Naina.'

'Okay.'

I smile when Amar comes on the line. Just hearing his voice makes the fact we haven't met for ten days, worthwhile. The last two days we've been revising Biology, a subject both of us love so we don't need to spend too much time on that.

Today, I suggest a game of *This or That*.

'Ok,' he agrees. 'You go first.'

'Tea or coffee?'

'Coffee,' Amar says. 'My turn. City or countryside?'

'Oh, that's hard. City.'

'Cats or dogs?'

'Dogs of course. Last one?' I ask Amar.

'Ok.'

'Five minutes in person or half an hour on the phone?'

He laughs. 'That's a tricky question. Before these calls, I would've chosen five minutes in person but now I'll go with half an hour on the phone.'

'I agree. I love these phone calls. I look forward to them every day.'

'So do I. Oh, before I forget, I have some news for you.'

'Do tell,' I say. 'As long as it's nothing to do with studying.'

'Suhail and I were out today and found ourselves near Mimi's place. He wrote a note with his name and phone number on the back and asked the *chowkidar* to give it to her. Now he's waiting to see if she'll call.'

'I didn't realise he was serious,' I say. 'Mimi and her parents are in Poona for a few days. She'll get the note when they return. Suhail will have to wait till then.'

'Right, I'll let him know not to expect a quick response. Do you think Mimi will call him?'

I consider his question. During her rebellious phase Mimi went through boyfriends at a frightening pace. But since then, she's only dated two guys. Despite his flirtatious nature, Suhail would be a good match for her.

'Yeah,' I say mulling over Amar's query. 'Now that I think about it, they'll be good together. But let's wait till Mimi comes back.'

'Ok, now for the all-important question, Naina,' he says after a pause. 'It's been two weeks since we started revising and we've covered a major portion. When do we meet?'

I laugh,' I was thinking the same thing. But I got side-tracked by your news of Suhail and Mimi. We have earned a chance to meet up, haven't we?'

'I think so.' Amar says quickly. 'I have a great idea of where we can meet.'

FIFTEEN

Meeting Amar after two weeks is like seeing him for the first time. When he arrives at Mimi's place, we are waiting outside. He looks at me and his face lights up with a big smile. He quickly covers the distance between us in a few strides.

'Oh god,' Mimi says just before he reaches us. 'If Suhail looked at me like that, I'd be a puddle of melted nerves by now.'

'I am,' I assure her.

He breaks eye contact long enough to acknowledge Mimi with a smile before looking at me once more.

'It feels like forever since we met,' he says giving me a quick peck on the cheek. In my ear he adds, 'You're looking even prettier if that's possible.'

'I was going to say you look better than ever,' I say with a laugh.

Mimi rolls her eyes at us and shakes her head. 'You guys are forgiven for all the mushiness since you haven't met for over two weeks.'

Amar and I exchange grins.

'Suhail and Samir bought tickets for the matinee show. They're waiting at the theatre,' Amar informs us. 'Are you ready?'

Sitting next to Amar in the car, I try not to keep looking at him. At the first traffic light he puts the car in neutral and takes my hand in his, looking across at me. I look down at our intertwined hands. Why did I ever think falling in love was not worth it? I've known Amar for a few months, yet I can barely recall my life before that.

'Naina, Amar, hello?' I hear Mimi's voice. I realise she's been talking to us, but we hadn't noticed.

'Sorry, Mimi,' I look back at her. 'Could you repeat that?'

'Which part? All I've been saying for the last ten minutes?' she asks me. 'Because I'm pretty sure neither of you heard any of it.'

'The important bits?' I suggest. 'Tell us how you felt when you saw the note from Suhail. Was it a surprise?'

'Total surprise,' she says happily. 'I thought he was cute but didn't think I'd see him again. I called him right away.'

'And how was the first date?' Amar asks.

'Great,' Mimi says excitedly. 'We went for a ride in his open jeep and stopped for lunch at a place off the highway.'

'I'm impressed,' I tell her. 'I feel Amar and I contributed in a small way.'

'In a big way,' she beams.

Amar drops us at the front of Regal Cinema and goes in search of a parking place. Samir is waving to us from the top of the stairs. With him are Suhail and Arjun. Reena and her younger sister, Raima join us a minute later.

When Amar suggested going for a movie, I thought a matinee show would give us a chance to meet and have lunch after that. The choice was between *Roman Holiday* and *Chitty Chitty Bang Bang*. We chose the former as most of us had seen the latter as kids.

'At times like this, I wish Neha could be here,' I remark to Arjun. 'But I'll see her in Delhi in a couple of weeks. Will you be there too?'

'Not this time,' Arjun says regretfully. 'She said both of you have lots of Maths portions to go over.'

'Yes, we do,' I say sadly since all subjects under Maths give me sleepless nights. I hope revising these with Neha will give me a much-needed boost.

After the movie, our little group of eight walks across to the Samovar restaurant for lunch. Located inside the Jehangir Art Gallery it's been a favourite of mine for years. Because it's a weekday and a bit early for the regular lunch crowd we are allowed to pull two tables close together.

Samir and Raima have been discussing the exhibits at the main gallery. They take seats next to each other.

I smile and glance at Samir who smiles back at me. He's smart, funny, and talented. He must have a lot of girls interested in him. How does he deal with that if he's not interested? Watching him chatting with Raima, I know he'll let her down gently if it comes to that.

'Samir wants to visit the main gallery after lunch,' Amar tells me after our orders have been taken by the waiters. 'I'd like to take you back to our place if you are ok with that.'

'And your parents?' I ask taking a sip from a glass of lime juice.

'Mum's is at Suhail's place and dad is at work. I never got to show you around, the night of the party and after that disaster there was no chance.'

'Ok,' I say as our lunch orders arrive. The kebabs, rice and curry are divine. We fall silent as we tuck into the spread. At the back of our minds is the thought that in two weeks' time we'll be back in school, so we had better make the most of a good meal.

Over cups of tea and coffee, the conversation turns to dating and what is expected of a boyfriend or a girlfriend.

'How does a guy prove he's serious about the person he's dating?' Samir asks looking at the four girls in the group. 'Is it flowers, jewellery, a tattoo or a grand gesture?'

Raima giggles and says, 'Jewellery is nice, but a tattoo is a great idea. That shows he's here to stay.'

Reena smiles, 'If he stands up to my dad, I'm sure he's serious.'

Mimi says, 'Just being there for me, is enough.'

I agree with her adding, 'That's what matters.'

'No tattoo, Naina?' queries Samir with a glance in Amar's direction.

'Definitely not,' I say with emphasis. 'That's too final, too intense. People change but the tattoo will remain.'

Amar grins and says, 'I knew that would be your answer, but Samir thought otherwise.'

'Wait, was that up for discussion? Whether Amar should get a tattoo or not?' I ask.

'Yeah, we guys were talking about it, last night,' Samir confirms. 'I suggested your initials or your zodiac sign, but Amar was sure you wouldn't be keen on the idea at all.'

Turning to Amar, I tell him. 'You know me well.'

After lunch, our group splits up. Samir, Reena and Raima want to visit the main art gallery. Mimi and Suhail agree to accompany us to Amar's flat. Saying goodbye to Arjun who is on his way home, we jump into Suhail's jeep.

Large rain clouds are scudding across a sky that has darkened since we went into the restaurant. A few, fat drops of rain fall as we pull into a parking space for visitors.

A young boy opens the door to the apartment asking if we want anything to eat or drink. We decline saying we are too full right now. Suhail and Mimi walk out to the balcony that runs around the family room.

Amar shows me around the room. It's furnished with large comfy sofas in pastel tones and dotted with glass topped tables filled with family memorabilia. I pause in front of a collection of framed photographs. At the centre is a group photo of Amar's family with their grandparents.

It must have been taken before Dev fell sick. Back then he was a smiling boy with wavy hair framing a round face.

'This was before we knew about the tumour,' Amar confirms. 'He was such a happy guy.'

I notice a photo of Samir and Amar, taken a few years ago. They look so young and much more similar than they do now. In the photo, Samir is proudly flexing his unimpressive biceps at the camera, while Amar tries to keep a straight face.

'This photo captures the two of you so well,' I tell Amar.

He grins and laughs.

'Samir. Always the entertainer,' he quips. 'C'mon let's go to my room.'

Amar heads down the passage to his room while I try not to think of the last time I was here. Luckily it looks very different today. The curtains have been pushed back, letting in a strange kind of sunlight that occurs when showers are imminent. It's like a sun shower and looks beautiful from this height.

Closing the door to his room, Amar takes me in his arms saying, 'Alone at last. I've been waiting for this moment.'

I grin since we both feel the same way. Being with friends

was good, but being with Amar is the best. We head for the windows. As we pass a full-length mirror, I pause to glance at our reflection.

'Did you realise we are basically wearing the same thing?' I ask him in surprise.

We're both in white shirts and faded jeans with white sneakers. While his shirt is tucked casually into his jeans, I have knotted the two ends of my shirt at my waist.

'Great minds think alike? Or fools seldom differ?' I murmur to Amar.

He puts his arms around me. Looking at our reflection, he murmurs, 'We look good together, don't you think?'

'You're just biased,' I say to his reflection, but I can't help noticing he's right.

Is it bad luck to admire ourselves in a mirror? Is there a thing like that? I turn away from our reflection hoping we haven't jinxed anything.

'What's up?' Amar asks, noticing the change in my mood.

I shake my head. 'Maybe it's bad luck to admire ourselves in a mirror.'

'I never thought you'd be superstitious, Naina,' he teases. 'Don't worry. Nothing bad will happen to us.'

'I can stay like this forever,' I tell Amar, tightening my arms around him.

'Or, we can go over to the bed,' he says with a grin and a wicked gleam in his eyes.

'Can't. My mother told me to stay away from the bed if I'm in a guy's room,' I counter.

'She did not,' Amar exclaims. 'She probably told you to stay away from *any guy's room.*'

I agree with a laugh.

There's a hesitant knock on the door. Seconds later, the knock is repeated.

'Who is it?' Amar calls out.

'*Bhaiya,* phone call for you,' a boy's voice replies.

Amar groans out loud. 'I just knew my mum would call. I'd better speak to her, Naina.'

He opens the door and takes the cordless phone from the boy.

'Hi mum,' he says running his hands through his hair and walking to the window. 'Yeah, the movie was good. Yeah, I know it's a favourite of yours.'

After a pause he says, 'We had lunch at the Samovar, so we don't need anything right now.'

I watch as he chats with his mum, marvelling at how natural it feels being with him in his room.

Wandering over to the shelves against the wall I start looking through Amar's LPs and EPs. It's an impressive collection of music that includes, jazz, rock, and pop. One shelf labelled 'DAD'S COLLECTION' has LPs of older artists like Jim Reeves, Nat King Cole, and The Beatles, similar to the ones we have at home. Maybe our dads were contemporaries.

At the far end of the room is a window with a ledge below it. It's fitted with wooden drawers along its length. On top of these is a slim mattress with matching cushions. I take a seat in this cosy spot, gazing out to where the rain is falling on the choppy sea below.

On the phone Amar says, 'Don't fuss, mum. If we need anything I'll ask Raju to make it. Suhail, Mimi, and Naina are here. No, it's ok. Fine I'll tell her you said, hi. Bye, mum.'

He disconnects the call, placing the phone on his desk. 'I swear she knows everything that happens here, even when she's not at home.'

'Or one of the maids has standing instructions to call her when guests drop by?' I suggest with a grin. 'Or when you bring a girl home?'

'You may be right,' Amar agrees. 'Whatever it is, she has a good system going.'

I scoot over to make place for him as he joins me at the window. With our shoulders and hips touching, it feels like we are one person. He puts his arm around me, and I settle into the curve of his shoulder. It feels good. *We* feel good.

'Your mum may be worried I'm alone with you,' I tell Amar staring at the endless patterns made by the rain running down the side of the glass.

He doesn't reply. I move back to look at him causing the top two buttons of my shirt to come undone.

Amar looks down at my bare skin, then up at me. He's so close I can feel his warm breath on my skin. He slowly trails a line of kisses from my shoulder all the way to my collarbone. My bones seem to melt away and form a puddle somewhere near my feet.

Suddenly, sunlight streams through the window, shining on us through the rain, our very own spotlight.

'Naina, you don't have to worry. You know you're safe with me, don't you?'

'Yes. I know,' I manage to say. 'It's why I agreed to come here.'

Taking my hand in his, Amar traces the lines on my palm, pretending to decipher them.

'Let's see. I glimpse a tall, handsome guy in your future,' he glances at me.

'Really?' I ask, pretending to think it over. 'Then it can't be you. Must be someone else.'

Throwing back his head he laughs, 'Cheeky. Just when I thought you were all sugar, no spice.'

The rain stops as suddenly as it started and in the silence the clock on the wall catches our attention.

Glancing at it, Amar frowns saying, 'Mum asked our cook to make some snacks for us. He'll up here soon to say it's ready.'

We reluctantly abandon our spot at the window and get ready to go downstairs.

'One day we'll have all the time in the world to be together. No more stolen moments,' Amar promises.

'One day. But not today,' I agree. I suddenly remember a question I meant to ask him. 'Your music collection is amazing. But where are your books?'

'I don't have many, maybe half a dozen,' Amar says looking around his room. 'They must be here somewhere. Why?'

'I thought you read a lot, like me.'

'Umm... no. I don't read much. If I do it's thrillers by Sidney Sheldon or Ken Follett. What made you think I read a lot?' he asks puzzled.

'Let's see,' I say, thinking. 'Because I saw you at the library that day. And because you knew the spelling of *chiaroscuro*.'

Laughing he says, 'That was all it took to convince you I read a lot? I was in the library to borrow Thomas Hardy's book for the book review. And I spotted the word *chiaroscuro* in one of Samir's books on art.'

'Oh,' I say in surprise.

'Disappointed?' Amar asks with a smile. 'Ok, why don't you recommend some books I should read? I'll leave it up to you.'

'Ok,' I say. 'It's a deal. I'd hate to think you're missing out on so much.'

On the way out I scoop up the charm bracelet I had abandoned on Amar's desk. He helps me with the clasp. From his expression I can tell he's happy I remembered the bracelet.

*   *

A week later I'm packing my steel trunk once again, this time with clothes bought over the holidays. My trunk will be dropped off at Reena's place this week and will travel with her back to school.

The balance of my clothes is packed in a small suitcase for my trip to Delhi. Over the years, Neha and I have gotten to know each other's families well so I'm keen to meet them again.

Usually, I'd be counting down the hours till my flight to Delhi, tomorrow. But this year, being away from Amar for a whole week diminishes my excitement a little bit.

Still, I'll get to see him at school in a week's time.

This evening we've arranged to meet again during Twinkle's evening walk.

I reach our meeting point to find he hasn't reached yet. Traffic must be bad, today. Waiting in one place with my dog is not possible since she prefers being on the move when we're outside.

I turn around and head back home at a slow pace, hoping Amar arrives before I reach. However, Twinkle charges ahead as usual and before long, we're only fifty meters from my apartment building.

There's a subdued honk of a car and turning I see Amar parking just behind me.

'Sorry, I couldn't make it on time,' he apologises. 'There was a procession of some sort and traffic was diverted down another road.'

'That's okay,' I say. 'I was hoping I wouldn't miss you. I can't stay out any longer as my dad's taking us to the Golden Dragon for dinner.'

'At the Taj?' Amar smiles.

'Yes, it's a family favourite. Their prawn dishes are to die for,' I say with a grin.

'I agree,' he says. Handing me a paper bag, he adds, 'This is for you. Just some Mars bars and Quality Street chocolates, nothing fancy.'

'Thanks a lot. It's hard to say no to chocolates,' I confess taking the bag from him. I reach out to touch him adding, 'This week is going to be hard being away....'

Just then a white car drives and starts slowing down almost immediately. I freeze mid-sentence. As I watch transfixed, it stops and parks a short distance ahead of us.

It's a white Mercedes with the only number plate I know by heart. It's my dad returning home from work. Sure, enough the car door opens, and he gets out from the passenger seat.

'Amar,' I say urgently. 'That's my dad getting out of the car. Please take the bag of chocolates. Pretend we met by accident.'

There's no time to say any more as my dad joins us on the pavement. Twinkle is ecstatic. She jumps into my dad's arms straight away with short, sharp barks of excitement and settles down happily in the crook of his arm.

'Naina, I thought it was you and Twinkle the moment I passed,' says my dad, tall and distinguished in a suit and tie. Turning to Amar, he introduces himself, 'Hi, I'm Naina's dad. I don't think we've met.'

They shake hands.

'Hello sir, I'm Amar, Naina's classmate,' he says calmly. In contrast, I'm a bundle of nerves, hoping my dad doesn't notice.

'Traffic was being diverted because of the procession. I was passing by and recognised Naina,' Amar continues. 'I stopped to say hello.'

'Traffic was terrible today,' my dad agrees. 'Where do you live, son?'

'Cuffe Parade. But we had some work on this side of town,' Amar explains gesturing to his driver standing beside the car.

'You're a long way from home, then. I think you'd better get going. It will take ages to reach Cuffe Parade,' my dad says leaving no room for argument. 'It was good meeting you, Amar.'

'Good to meet you too, sir. See you Naina,' he says with a brief glance at me.

He walks quickly towards his car. I silently hope he won't get into the driver's seat. My dad will not be happy to see an underage boy, driving. Thankfully he gets into the passenger seat, and they drive away.

'Come along, Naina,' my dad says. 'We need to get ready for dinner. Can't be late.'

I follow him into the car, my mind a whirl of thoughts.

Thank God, we pulled that off.

I'll never get to eat those chocolates after all.

Oh shoot, I never got to say goodbye to Amar properly.

After a long dinner at the Golden Dragon, the four of us whiz down Marine Drive and up Malabar Hill so I can get one last glimpse of the city from the Hanging Gardens.

Neel and I walk ahead of our parents. I tell him of how Dad met Amar that evening.

'Jeez, sis, how did Amar handle it?' Neel asks.

'Quite well,' I tell him. 'Can't say the same for myself. I kept thinking dad would surely guess something's up. But he didn't say anything. Fingers crossed that he believed Amar's story.'

'You know, dad,' Neel says ruefully. 'He didn't get to where he is by believing all the stories he's told.'

'That's true,' I agree slowly.

My dad and his sister, Geeta came to Bombay from Poona. Dad completed his degree in Commerce and started work at an international pharmaceutical company. He worked his way up to the top position through hard work and a strict moral code that he lived by. As his kids, we often found it hard to follow the principles he lives by.

Much later, I'm in my pyjamas, rooting through my closet to see if I've forgotten to pack anything, when my mum comes into my room.

'Did Dad meet Amar today?' she asks me.

'Yes, why?' I look at her, trying to decipher her expression.

'He wants to talk to you. He's in the sitting room,' she says. 'Naina, tell him the truth. No point in lying. If you feel strongly about something, stand up for yourself.'

'Okay,' I say my heart thudding in my chest.

My mum has never, *ever* told me to stand up for myself in relation to my dad. Or looked that serious.

I know now that my dad *knows.*

Making my way to the living room, I enter through the dining room. The two rooms are connected by glass doors that are always open, to create one large area.

'Hi dad,' I greet him in what I hope is a breezy tone. He is at the bar which occupies a corner of the living room.

'Naina, do you want something to drink? Maybe a Coke?' he asks, pouring Baileys Irish cream into two small liqueur glasses. He hands one to my mum who joins us in the living room.

'No thanks,' I tell him.

I take a seat on a sofa facing the balcony. My dad takes his favourite seat facing the TV but with a view of the balcony. We live on the fifth floor, so the view skims the tops of trees to a vacant plot below. At this height the sound of traffic is faint.

'Since you're leaving tomorrow, I wanted to see how your revising is going?' my dad starts the conversation. 'I'm sorry I haven't been able to help you.'

'I've covered most of it,' I tell him. 'I'll revise the rest with Neha in Delhi. So, it's no problem.'

'Ah ok,' he says. After a long pause, he continues, 'Naina, you're a teenager now. I tend to forget that sometimes. Studying in a co-ed school, I know you've some made some good friends.'

'Yes,' I agree, not knowing what else to say.

'This evening, the boy I met, Amar, is he a friend? Do you like him?' my dad asks finally biting the bullet.

I look at my mum who gives me a small nod.

Ok. I guess it's time to confess.

'Yes, I do, dad,' I say. 'And he likes me.'

My dad nods quickly but doesn't say anything. He gazes out of the balcony like he's thinking of something else entirely.

I relax a little. That wasn't so bad.

'You know, your Geeta Aunty and I came to Bombay from Poona,' he says just when I think he's dropped the subject. 'She met a boy in college, and they fell in love. Both were very serious about each other. But the boy's father was not keen on the match, and they were forced to break it off. She was heartbroken for a long time. We were very worried about her.'

Looking at me, he continues, 'That boy's name was Dhruv Malhotra.'

SIXTEEN

I don't say anything. I *can't* say anything. Because I know Amar's dad's name is Dhruv. I heard some guests mention it the night of the party.

'When we were at the station to pick you up, I recognised him,' my dad continues. 'Meeting Amar today, the resemblance was obvious. He's Dhruv's son.'

I don't know what to say. I was expecting all kinds of questions from my dad, but not this. A connection between Amar's dad and mine. Or more correctly between Amar's dad and my aunt.

Life works in mysterious ways.

I take a deep breath, looking down at my hands in my lap. I know what I have to say; still, it's a strange sensation standing up to my dad. Strange, because I've never done it before. In the past, he and Neel have argued over Neel's grades, the amount of time he spends with friends, the amount of money he spends and so on.

I've never had to argue about anything. Being at boarding school, if my grades were good and reports from my teachers were complementary, my parents have been happy.

'Dad, I'm sorry Geeta Aunty had to go through that. But Amar is not responsible for what his dad or granddad did in the past,' I say slowly. 'Any more than I'm responsible for what my granddad has done in the past.'

'That's true,' my dad agrees. 'But I felt you needed to know. Tell me, is Amar serious about doing well in school?'

'Yes,' I confirm. 'He wants to get into engineering college, so he needs good marks in Science, Maths and Chemistry. Like I need good grades in English for a degree in Literature. We help each other while studying.'

My dad nods. 'I've never had to worry about you, Naina so I believe you.'

'Thanks dad,' I say permitting myself a small smile.

'And you're sure your friendship with Amar won't jeopardise your exam results?'

'No,' I assure him. 'It won't.'

'Come here, *beta*,' my dad says getting up from the sofa. He hugs me quickly. 'Whatever you do, remember the two most important things in life.'

'I know,' I tell him getting ready to rattle off the two principles Neel and I have been brought up with. 'You are answerable to yourself first. So don't do anything you will regret later.'

'Exactly,' my dad beams at me. 'Remember these two principles and you will be fine. If you can face the person in the mirror, you can face anyone.'

'Night, dad,' I say giving him a peck on the cheek.

'Night, mum,' I say going over to my mum.

On shaky legs, I make my way to Neel's room and knock on the door.

'Come in,' Neel calls out. He's on the phone, but seeing me he tells the person on the other side, 'Hey, can I call you later? Okay. Bye.'

I collapse on the sofa, face down.

'That bad, huh?' Neel asks laughing. 'You stood up to Dad. You're all grown up now.'

'Aargh, I don't know how I survived that,' I declare into the sofa. Turning over I declare, 'If I'm all grown up, can I have my first beer? After that interrogation, I really need it.'

'Whoa, steady on, champ,' my brother cautions. 'You're nowhere near the legal drinking age, you know that.'

'Didn't stop you, bro,' I smirk at him.

He laughs heartily at that. 'Okay, tell me what happened?'

Pacing up and down the room between his desk and the door, I recount the conversation between dad and me.

'That's not too bad,' Neel comments when I'm done. 'Dad must've been surprised that you didn't back down.'

'As surprised as I was,' I say. 'To be honest, I feel better now he knows about Amar. All that sneaking around gets tiring. However, he can't forbid me from seeing Amar when his only son has been dating for years now.'

Neel rolls his eyes and wiggles his eyebrows at me.

I stop my pacing when I reach Neel's desk, my eyes falling on a letter he's writing. It's addressed to a Rachel and mentions that he'll be in the US next March.

'Who's Rachel? Who are you writing to?' I ask Neel curiously.

'A pen pal,' he explains sheepishly.

'You're dating girls here and you have a pen pal?' I query frowning at him.

'Correction, I'm not dating anyone,' he confirms. 'Doesn't make sense when I leave in three months' time. Hey, are you coming with mum and me in March? To the US?'

'Yeah. By then my exams will be over,' I say. 'It'll give me a chance to visit some colleges and see which one's best for me.'

There's a knock on the door and mum comes in. She frowns at a huge bundle of clothes in a corner of Neel's room.

'Neel, please sort that mess out. If your father comes in, he won't be happy. Naina, remember to take a cardigan and a pair of thick socks. Delhi is quite cold in December.'

Neel grins at my mum.

Adopting a formal tone as if he's interviewing her, he holds out the cordless phone, deepens his voice and asks, 'So Mrs Kumar, what did you think of your daughter today? When she bravely stood up for herself? Were you surprised? Please tell us your thoughts.'

At the end of his speech, he gives my ponytail a hearty tug.

'Ow, stop it Neel. Mum, tell him not to do that.'

Normally she would tell him to stop harassing me.

Tonight, she just smiles and says, 'Goodnight, both of you. Naina don't stay up too late. We must leave early for the airport, tomorrow.'

As she leaves, Neel hands the phone to me saying, 'Please call Amar and put him out of his misery. The guy must have sweated buckets by now.'

Laughing, I start dialling Amar's number as I leave the room.

He answers on the first ring.

'Naina?' he asks.

'Hi, it's me,' I say. 'Sorry I couldn't call earlier.'

'Did your dad believe our story?' he asks at once.

'He did. You looked so calm when talking to him. How did you manage that?'

Amar laughs. 'I thought if I appear calm, he'd believe I was just passing by. But no, I wasn't feeling calm at all.'

I tell him all that's happened tonight. He lets out a low whistle, 'My dad and your aunt? That is so random.'

I laugh. 'I know, right? Turns out the Malhotra boys have been after the Kumar girls for years.'

'There must be something about the Kumar girls, then,' Amar quips laughing.

'Honestly, I'm glad my dad knows,' I continue. 'I don't have to sneak around anymore. Feels so much better.'

'Just a minute, Naina,' he says. Speaking to someone in the room he says, 'I'll be there. Give me a minute.'

Amar comes back on the line saying, 'Listen, we're calling a doctor in America in five minutes. It's about Dev's treatment so I need to be there. But I'll call you at Neha's place tomorrow.'

'Okay, sounds good,' I say. 'Bye.'

'Have a safe flight. Missing you already. Bye,' Amar says as he hangs up.

SEVENTEEN

Our bus slows down to turn left into the school campus, and we all let out a cheer. Back to school! Two days of travel has left us exhausted; all we want is a hot bath and a change of clothes. Neha and I exchange a glance, this is the last time we'll return to school as students.

When the bus stops in front of our hostel, we alight from it, cautiously. The last fifty miles of road were in a bad condition, but at least we're in one piece.

While we were away, our hostel got a fresh coat of paint. A faint smell of paint and distemper greets us inside. Our rooms, beds and cupboards have also been painted.

Jo and Priya join us in the corridor to help get our luggage into the room. They reached before lunch and are in the middle of arranging their cupboards. We all start talking at the same time; we have so much to catch up on.

Neha pushes her trunk closer to her cupboard saying, 'This is the last time we'll be arranging our cupboards.'

'Not us. Jo and I will be back next term,' Priya informs us. 'I've decided to return for the eleventh and twelfth standard.'

Jo smiles at Priya. She was worried she'd have to find a new roommate. Now she and Priya can share a room as seniors, on the second floor of the hostel.

Neha and I have chosen not to return for the next two years. Our parents are keen to have us back home since we've been away since the age of ten. This school has been our safety net, an idyllic haven for so long. From boarders, we'll become day students. Feels strange just thinking about it.

Just two months long, this term will be the shortest one ever. From now till the end of February we'll be revising like our lives depend on it. Which in a sense it does. The board exams start in the last week of February and end at the start of March. The day after our last exam, we'll leave school for the last time.

'You and I are going to have a lot of 'lasts' this term,' I remark to Neha from my bed.

'It's so short, it'll be over before we realise,' Neha observes, sounding subdued.

'We must keep in touch,' Priya says. 'Otherwise, we'll grow apart quickly.'

We nod in agreement, promising to stay in touch. However deep down we know making a promise is easy, keeping it will be harder. Each of us has chosen a different path to get to the career of our choice.

Neha wants to be a doctor; the next few years will be stressful for her. She'll be studying long after we finish. Jo wants to become a teacher, a great choice given how caring and patient she is. Priya's dream of becoming a stewardess means she'll have to do a course in travel and tourism. I've always wanted to write, so a degree in English is my first goal after which I'll see what else I need to do.

Reena pokes her head in. 'Hi girls. Welcome back. Naina, you have a visitor.'

'Who is it?' I ask her. 'Amar?'

'Yes,' she confirms with a grin.

Picking up a roll-on lip gloss, I glance in the mirror so I can apply a fresh coat. Behind me I see Priya and Neha look at each other, and giggle.

'What's up?' I ask returning the gloss to the glass bowl I keep it in.

'No use applying gloss when you're meeting Amar,' Neha smirks.

Blushing, I leave. 'See you at dinner.'

Going down the hostel steps, I pick out Amar's silhouette against the light of the streetlamp.

'Hey, you,' he says in that familiar voice.

As we move away from the light; Amar throws his arms around me in a tight hug.

'Did you get prettier in just one week?' he teases me.

'I tried,' I joke. 'It's good to see you too.'

We take the long route towards the dining hall. Most of the lane is in darkness so it's not used by many students.

'I got you this,' I say, handing Amar a book wrapped in brown paper.

'Wait,' he says handing me a package wrapped in paper. 'I got you a book too.'

We exchange a chuckle. 'C'mon,' I urge. 'Let's open them together.'

Amar's gift to me is a special edition of *Little Women* and mine to him is *The Little Prince.*

'I love it,' I tell him turning the book over. The beautiful dark green cover is adorned with illustrations of the four March girls and has quotes from the book on the inside covers.

Amar unwraps my gift to him and says, 'Cool. I've heard of this book. But I thought it was meant for young kids.'

'I think you'll like it,' I say, then I amend it to, 'I hope you'll like it.'

Because I was with Neha in Delhi, we couldn't spend New Year's together, so meeting Amar tonight means a lot to us.

We look at each other in the semi-darkness, neither of us wanting to drag our eyes away. When we lean in for a kiss, I realise how much I've missed him. It's like an ache somewhere deep inside of me. In a few short months I've gone from being reluctant to date to not wanting to stay away from him. My rules were abandoned sometime before our first kiss.

'Mm…peppermint,' Amar says licking his lips. 'Is that your lipstick?'

'Lip gloss,' I clarify, smiling.

'I missed you so much, it hurt,' Amar says as we break apart and continue walking.

'Same here,' I agree.

'Naina, I'm going to say something, but I don't want to scare you. And you don't have to say anything in return,' Amar says a little breathlessly. 'I'm in love with you.'

'I feel the same way,' I say, much to his surprise.

My words appear to set something free in him. He reaches for me, pulling me tightly against him. When we kiss I'm surprised to feel him tremble, his shoulders shaking from some emotion he's keeping in check as he buries his face in my neck. Amar doesn't get emotional often; seeing this side of him is a surprise. Is it because we were apart for a week or something else? As we pull apart, his next words clarify what it is.

'You know,' he stops walking, searching for the right words. 'I've realized I need to tell you how I feel. What we have, helps me deal with things. I get so caught up in trying to be the responsible son, grandson and older brother, that I forget to tell you the important stuff.'

'Amar, I understand,' I take his face in my hands. 'You have so much happening in your life right now. Helping your parents with Dev's treatment, being there for your brothers. All this, on top of the coming exams. I'd like to help if I can.'

'Thank you,' he whispers. 'You are helping. I didn't want to burden you with my stuff.'

'Your stuff is my stuff too. All of it,' I say lightly. 'It's what makes you who you are and it's why I love you.'

We continue walking, lacing our arms behind our backs. I just saw Amar for who he is, a scared, insecure teenager trying to juggle way too much for his age. That shakes me to my core, wishing I could help him somehow.

I created a virtual prison for myself with my no-dating rules, so I'd never fall in love and experience the inevitable heartbreak. Amar has done the same by always being in control, in charge and on top of any situation. I couldn't sustain my world and Amar is finding he can't either.

'We're just teenagers, Amar,' I remind him. 'We can't be expected to deal with adult issues too.'

'Let's always tell each other what we're going through' he declares. 'Then nothing can come between us.'

I shiver suddenly and Amar looks at me in surprise. 'Are you feeling cold?'

'No,' I say. 'I just had a funny feeling. Look, I even got goosebumps on my arms.'

He takes his jacket off and drapes it around me. 'Must have been a cold breeze.'

I agree with him, but I can't shake off the strange, heavy feeling that came out of nowhere.

EIGHTEEN

After the middle of January, the days seem to speed by like a cassette tape on fast forward.

Our teachers have completed the entire syllabus and are now revising portions we've found difficult. Or areas that a lot of us answered incorrectly in the tests. And yet, the feeling of not knowing enough, never leaves us.

Most of us are in a state of mild stress with board exams a few weeks away. Last week we started solving old exam papers to get an idea of what questions to expect.

Today, we are in the middle of another session. We choose some benches in the shade of a tamarind tree and spread out schoolbooks and papers on the cool cement surface.

'Alright,' Neha says rifling through a sheaf of old exam papers. 'Naina, you get English and History, Reena you get the Hindi paper, Amar you get Physics and Chemistry and I'll keep the Maths papers.'

'I'll take Biology,' Samir offers. 'I like the subject.'

'That's because you're a favourite of Shilpa Ma'am's,' Priya adds with a laugh. 'Jo and I will work on the Geography paper.'

'I'll help you with the Maths paper, Neha,' Rahul says joining our group.

'Sure, here you go,' Neha says giving him two sheets.

We get busy, although at the back of our minds is just one

thought: get through the next few weeks and life will be so much better.

We'll be free. But for now, this is our reality.

Half an hour later Reena puts her pen down saying, 'I don't want to cause more stress, but these papers are tough.'

'Reena, if you find the Hindi paper tough, imagine how bad it'll be for me,' I say glumly looking up from my answer sheet. Hindi has never been my strong point.

'How's the English paper?' Amar asks me.

'Not too bad,' I say. 'Some questions are confusing, though.'

'Same with the Maths paper,' Neha says. Pulling packets of biscuits from her bag she passes them around.

'These are the toughest ones from previous years,' Rahul reasons with us. 'Meaning, they aren't all from the same year. One tough paper should be balanced out by a couple of moderately tough ones.'

'Fingers crossed,' Priya echoes the faint hope in our minds.

We end the session, sitting on tables, going over each paper methodically. Then all the answer sheets are circulated amongst us, so everyone has access to the correct answers.

Eventually, the faint peal of a bell signals it's time for lunch. We walk in silence, clutching our papers and books, feeling dispirited, like the stuffing has been knocked out of us.

When we pass a group of guys studying in the shade of another tree, we offer a feeble wave.

'Hey guys,' Rahul says. 'How's the studying going?'

'Not too bad,' Praful, our classmate answers.

Another classmate, Jai, waves at us from his perch on the branch of a tree.

'What are you studying, Jai?' Reena asks noticing a colourful book in his hands. It doesn't look like any of our drab schoolbooks.

'Oh, it's the latest James Hadley Chase,' Jai holds the book up so we can see the cover.

'You're reading that, with the exam only weeks away?' Reena voices the obvious question.

He shrugs and laughs. 'Look it doesn't matter how much I study; I'm going to fail anyway.'

His statement would be shocking if it wasn't also true.

Although our test marks are never made public, over the years, we've learnt who scores the highest marks and who scores the lowest. Jai isn't good at academics or sports, nor does he have any other talent. But he's never worried about any of that.

I've secretly wondered how he and his friends get promoted to the next class, year after year.

Seeing how surprised we are by Jai's answer, Praful says, 'It doesn't matter. Jai is the only son, so he doesn't have to worry. His future is secure.'

Jai's dad reportedly owns three garment factories based near Madras. And by all accounts the family is very wealthy. That's what Praful's referring to.

'Don't your parents expect you to study?' I ask hoping I don't sound judgemental, just curious.

'Nah,' Jai says placing a finger on the page he's reading so he won't lose his place. 'They know I'm not good at academics.

Besides, how will these exams help in running my dad's factories? Practical knowledge is best. In fact, I won't bother getting a certificate for these exams.'

'What if you need a certificate later for some reason?' Amar asks Jai. 'Maybe for a loan or something?'

'I can always buy one,' Jai laughs, 'In fact, I can buy one with First Class marks on it. For the right price, you can buy anything.'

We nod and walk on. We've all heard of forged certificates but never considered getting one.

I mull over Jai's logic; if he's going to inherit everything from his wealthy dad, why bother with exams?

'Do you think what he said makes sense?' Jo wonders climbing the steps slowly.

'For him it does. We don't have rich fathers who are okay with us failing at exams,' Neha says.

'What if we all had rich fathers who didn't care about exams?' Samir asks with a grin.

'We'd all be reading the latest James Hadley Chase,' quips Rahul.

'Or PG Wodehouse,' I add thinking of the Jeeves omnibus lying unread in my cupboard.

'Or Asimov,' says Priya, who's big on sci-fi books.

Cheered by the thought of living in that fantasy world, we join the trickle of students on their way to lunch.

*   *

At ten o'clock Anita Ma'am comes around to wish us goodnight.

'Can we have the lights on for one more hour, please?' Priya sounds worried.

Our hostel warden shakes her head saying, 'The reason we insist on lights out at ten is, so you get eight hours of sleep. You need to rest after studying all day.'

As soon as our warden leaves, Priya pulls the bedcover over herself and continues studying with the help of a torch. I'm quite glad to have the lights off, I could do with some sleep.

'Goodnight, all,' I say stifling a massive yawn.

Much later, I feel someone shaking me awake. I groan hoping they'll go away, so I can carry on sleeping.

'Naina, wake up,' Neha says, her voice sounding loud in the dark. 'Naina, c'mon wake up.'

'What's the matter?' I ask struggling to sit up.

Neha and Jo are sitting at the foot of my bed, torches in hand.

'It's Priya,' says Jo. 'We think she's sleepwalking.'

'What? How do you know?' I ask in surprise.

'For the last two nights, I've seen her wake up, go to the door and out into the corridor,' Jo explains. 'I followed her tonight. She's in the garden, sitting on the stone bench.'

Pushing my feet into my flip flops I follow them out into the corridor. The wide passage is bathed in moonlight. In the centre of the quadrangle is a lawn with stone benches on one side. A motionless figure sits on one of these benches.

'Are you sure she's asleep?' I whisper to Neha.

'I walked past her, and she didn't say anything,' Neha whispers back.

'We shouldn't wake people up when they're sleepwalking,' I remind them.

'Can we guide her slowly back to bed?' Jo suggests.

Neha and I look at each other, unsure of what to do.

'Look, she's getting up,' Neha says.

We move aside, so we aren't in Priya's way. She passes right by us and returns to our room. Once inside, she lies down on her bed and continues sleeping. Jo covers her with a sheet.

'I think that's it for tonight,' Jo says. 'Do you think she's sleepwalking because of the exams?'

I shrug. 'It seems likely. We need to tell Anita Ma'am tomorrow.'

Next morning Priya seems tired and testy.

'Did you sleep well, last night?' Jo asks her.

'I'm not sure,' Priya sounds worried. 'I haven't been sleeping well. I feel tired every morning.'

When she hears of her sleepwalking episodes, Priya is not surprised, just relieved. At least she knows why she's been tired and run down lately. When we inform our warden about Priya's sleepwalking incidents, she suggests asking the school doctor for advice.

After class, Jo and Priya schedule a visit to see the doctor.

'How did it go?' I ask Priya on their return.

'He says I need to reduce my stress by thinking of something other than the exams just before I go to sleep,' Priya says shaking her head in disbelief. 'How do I do that, this close to the exams?'

Over the next few nights, we revise together just before bedtime to boost Priya's confidence in herself. And before we fall asleep, we remind ourselves of the trip we're going on, right after the exams.

We've been planning this trip for a year. The day after our last paper, we'll pack up for the last time, send our luggage to our respective homes and stay in Bangalore for a week.

My dad's company has a guesthouse that comes with a cook, a car, and a driver. We plan to relax and recover for two days. After that, we'll hit the city. Watch out Bangalore!

Finally, the exams are only two days away. Just when our stress levels couldn't get any worse and our brains feel close to bursting with months, years, of accumulated knowledge. We're all so *over* revising at this point; we just want to get the exams done and behind us.

'How many of you are going on this trip?' Amar queries as we us exit the senior school one evening.

'Jo, Priya, Neha and me,' I tell him. 'We planned this long before you and I met. As a farewell gift to ourselves. We don't know when we'll all meet again.'

'No boyfriends allowed?' he asks with a smile.

'No,' I confirm. 'But I'll see you in Bombay.'

'Yeah,' he nods. 'Only for two weeks though. Aren't you going to the US with Neel and your mother?'

'Yep. My dad can't join us as he needs to be in the UK, on work.'

'How long will you be away?' Amar asks.

'A month,' I confirm. 'I want to check out colleges that offer Creative Writing degrees or post-grad diplomas.'

Seeing the look on his face, I take his hand saying,' It'll go by quickly. You'll be busy partying with Samir and Suhail.'

'Still, it won't be the same without you,' he says.

'Have you thought any more about studying abroad?' I ask him.

'I put those plans on hold when Dev fell sick. But my parents are keen I do my degree in Architecture.'

'Maybe we'll get into colleges that are close by?' I suggest. 'That won't be so bad.'

A black Ambassador car slows down and stops near us. From the back of the vehicle, a window is rolled down. A man leans out. 'Does this road lead to the school guesthouse?'

'Yes,' I say. 'Follow this road to the end and it will lead you there.'

'Thank you,' the guy says giving the driver directions. As he rolls the window back up again, a second Ambassador slows down then follows the first one down the metalled road.

Both cars have an official logo on the back that I recognise at once.

'Naina, we've seen those people before, haven't we?' Neha joins us.

'Yes,' I say. 'It's the examiners from the CISE board. They're here to conduct the ICSE and ISC exams.'

'How do you know?' Amar asks puzzled.

'We see them every year around this time. And both those cars had the official logo at the back.'

'Which means it's time,' Amar concludes.

'Yes,' Neha and I say together.

―――――――――――――――――――――――――

NINETEEN

Half-way through the week, I decide the exams are not so tough after all.

I mean sure, I had a couple of fails; in History, a major question was on a subject I failed to study. I answered it anyway hoping I'll get some marks for attempting it. I feel sorry for whoever gets to mark my Hindi paper; I'm not proud of my answers.

However, in Geometry, the theorem Neha had explained the morning of the exam was in the paper. I was able to work it out perfectly. QED. Score!

And I'm hoping my English and Economics marks will balance everything out.

Each paper that we finish, means one less subject to worry about and one more area of my brain that's now free to think of other things. No more calculus and algebra for me. Ever.

If I never have to puzzle over *'Two trains that leave a station travelling in different directions'* again, I'll be happy.

With just one exam left on Friday, the mood is cheerful on Thursday evening. The thought of being done with exams tomorrow, is enough to make us relax. Our last exam is Geography which a lot of us like. It's not a tough subject so we have a chance to score well.

A few suitcases are already out in readiness for tomorrow. Our classmates are smiling and laughing for the first time in a long while. Tonight, there'll be only a few of us pacing the corridors and fewer still studying by torchlight after ten o'clock.

'Naina, here's your autograph book,' Jo says handing it to me. 'Mandy from upstairs gave it to me.'

'Thanks, Jo,' I say opening the book to look at the entries. There are a lot of 'Hope to hear you singing on the radio soon' and 'Looking forward to seeing you on stage someday'.

I smile at these comments. I consider my voice average; certainly not good enough to take up singing professionally. But I do hope to be a writer someday.

Some pages are stiff with photos that have been stuck inside. These range from childhood snaps to ones taken on holiday. A couple of pages have dry flowers pasted on them; a faint fragrance still clings to them.

'Lovely, isn't it?' asks Neha. 'My book is full as well. Oh, before I forget, Samir gave me this envelope. It's the snaps he took last week.'

Sliding the photos out of the envelope, I lay them out on my bed. The group snaps the Samir got us to pose for are so good. Compared to the official photos of the entire batch, in these we look relaxed and casual. The ones he took of Neha, Arjun, Amar, and me are perfect, certainly worth framing.

After lights out, we continue chatting for a while in the dark.

'Only two sleeps left till we leave school,' Neha points out as we drift off to sleep.

* *

The minute the buzzer goes off at the end of the last exam, we erupt from the classroom, ignoring the disapproving looks of the board examiners.

Freedom! From school, timetables, and exams.

We did it! We survived the tenth standard exams.

Standing in the school courtyard, we cheer and yell, throwing our books and papers up in the air. They fall in heaps all us. They're no use to us anymore.

Eventually, noticing the frowns of a few teachers and ultimately the principal, we leave the school building for the last time.

Amar joins me outside. 'Naina, we did it!' he exclaims as we exchange high fives.

Moving over to a bench on the side of the path, we grin as the rest of our batch streams past us, tired but excited. Samir, Reena, and Rahul join us, the latter two still discussing the paper we just answered.

'Guys and girls,' Samir says holding up his hand. 'That's it. We are done with school. No more discussions of test papers, please. Our real life starts now.'

Laughing I say, 'Ok, let's do that last tour of school like we planned. Where's Neha?' I ask, looking around for her.

She joins us saying, 'Sorry, I'm late. I was going round the classrooms thanking our teachers.'

'Oh. I never thought of that,' I say in dismay. 'I'll do it at dinner tonight.' I love that about Neha. She always knows the right thing to do at the right time.

'C'mon, let's get started on that tour,' Samir says.

We start our last trip around school at the entrance sitting on the stone slab one last time; then cross a bridge over a stream we have paddled in many times, till we are under the stone arch almost obscured by a canopy of a pink bougainvillea flowers.

Onto the main auditorium building, the scene of hundreds of

practice sessions, dozens of play rehearsals, and hours of leading the school in song during morning assembly. Hard to total the number of hours I've spent under its roof, over the last five and a half years.

'Hey, how come the swimming pool is covered in plastic?' Rahul asks, when we reach the building which houses the open-air pool. 'I've been so busy studying; I haven't been here this term.'

'It's being renovated,' Reena says. 'That's why it's covered in tarpaulins. Shall we take a last look?'

'Count me out,' Samir says firmly. 'Swimming pools and I don't go together. You guys carry on.'

Leaning against a tree, he gestures to us to carry on. I remember how much he hates swimming pools.

The rest of us climb the few steps to peer over the metal fence, but the thick plastic prevents us from seeing much.

'Well, so much for a last look,' I say with regret. 'This is where I learned how to swim. Not very well, but enough to get by.'

'Me too,' Neha says. 'I remember being terrified. Not so much of the pool but having to walk around in my swimsuit.'

Reena and I laughingly agree.

From the pool we walk past the junior and senior school, past the squat arts department building, the tennis court, and the basketball courts till the road ends in front of a line of junior hostels.

'This is where it all started,' Reena points to a building. 'Do you recall us all being in the same dormitory when we joined? We were only ten years old, so it was alright.'

'Wait, boys and girls together in one building?' Amar asks incredulously. 'No way.'

'Oh yes,' Rahul clarifies with a laugh. 'All together and all homesick at the same time.'

Amar and Samir shake their heads in disbelief.

'They couldn't do that anymore,' Neha remarks. 'Girls and boys are in totally different hostels, now.'

'So, this is it,' Samir says throwing his hands out. 'Our last day here. Tomorrow, it's back to Bombay.'

'Not all of us,' I remind him. 'Neha and I will be in Bangalore for a week. Along with Jo and Priya.'

'See you at dinner,' Amar calls out as the guys carry on down the road to their hostel.

Reena climbs the stairs to our hostel; we tell her we'll join her in ten minutes.

Neha and I continue walking slowly, making for the hill, our go-to place on countless Sundays.

'It really *is* time to leave, Naina,' Neha muses. 'I'm going to miss this place so much. We did all our growing up here. There's a part of me that will always be here. Do you think we'll find it difficult outside?'

'To be honest, I have wondered about that,' I confess. 'But we have to leave someday, either now or after the twelfth standard.'

'True. But here we are big fish in a small pond and out there...' her voice trails off.

'Out there we won't be able to see the edge of the pond or count the number of fish in it,' I say with a laugh. 'And that's scary and exciting.'

'Thank God we have supportive parents. And great boyfriends,' Neha jokes poking my arm. 'Even you Naina, the original I'm-never-going-to-date girl. Where is she now?'

Giggling, we turn back once we reach the foot of the hill and start walking towards our hostel.

Our mini-bus leaves at ten tomorrow morning and there's a lot to do before that.

Our luggage needs to be packed and ready and our room needs to be cleaned for the next occupants; four ninth standard girls waiting to move from the main dormitory to our room.

*　　　*

With the exams behind us, our last night feels like an anti-climax. We've dreamed, planned and waited for this day for so long. Now that it's here we have no idea what to do with ourselves. After dinner we stand around in groups chatting, too excited to return to our hostel.

We have no homework, tests, or classes, nothing to prepare for, the next day. And that's precisely why the school wants us to leave so soon after the exams. Students with nothing to do are dangerous to have around.

'How about one last midnight walk?' Neha suggests when Arjun and Amar join us.

'I'd like that,' Arjun says taking Neha's hand. 'I'm not going to see you till the holidays. It's going to be strange without you.'

'I know,' Neha agrees. 'Anyone else wants to join us for a midnight walk?' she asks Samir and Rahul who have joined us.

'I'm up for it,' Samir remarks. Looking up, he continues, 'It will have to be a short walk. Looks like it's going to rain tonight.'

'Yep,' Rahul agrees. 'The forecast mentioned a possible thunderstorm.'

'Alright,' I say. 'A quick walk to wrap things up. See you later.'

We spend the next hour saying goodbye to the seniors on the second floor. From there we move to the main dormitory on our floor and continue our goodbyes. Soon we are reminiscing about events we shared together and get all teary-eyed. Lots more addresses and phone numbers are exchanged. This is starting to feel very real and very final.

By the time we do a last clean-up of our cupboards, close our suitcases, and have a shower, we are very sleepy and tired.

'Maybe we shouldn't have planned a midnight walk, tonight,' I venture to Neha collapsing on my bed. 'All I want to do is sleep.'

'Me too,' Neha agrees. 'But how do we let the guys know?'

'We can't,' I remind her. 'The hostel doors are closed. They'll wait for us at the crossroads at midnight. If we don't get there, they'll think something's wrong.'

'Let's set the alarm on our clock to wake us at eleven-thirty in case we fall asleep,' Neha suggests.

Jo and Priya decide not to join us as they still have a lot to finish.

Not surprisingly Neha and I fall fast asleep. Jo wakes us just before the alarm goes off.

'Thanks Jo,' I whisper sitting up in bed and peering out of the window. From the way the branches of the trees are moving outside, the wind appears to be quite strong now. 'It looks like a 'dark and stormy night' tonight.'

'Put your waterproof jacket over your t-shirt,' Neha tells me tying the laces on her sneakers. 'In case it rains, we'll still be warm and dry.'

'All done,' I shrug my jacket on and follow her to the door of our room. Turning to our roommates I say, 'We won't be out late.'

'Be careful, you two,' Priya cautions us. 'If it's wet and windy, tell the guys it's not worth walking tonight and come back.'

'We will, don't worry,' Neha says.

Just as we reach the crossroads, four guys emerge from the shadow of the arts building. All of them have waterproof jackets on. Out here the wind sounds louder, but it hasn't started raining yet. The sky is full of stars and the moon is a big, bright circle of light.

'Hi,' Arjun greets us softly. 'We thought you may have changed your minds, given the weather.'

'We almost did,' Neha tells him. 'But we decided to take a chance.'

By common consent we decide to go to the formal garden, the one with a pond at the centre.

'No sign of any of the guards,' Rahul remarks taking the stairs two at a time. 'They must be expecting rain.'

The five of us perch on the edge of the pond while Samir sits on the grass. The ornamental fish are nowhere to be seen.

'The fish must be resting,' I say peering into the water to locate them. But the reflection of the moon on the water is unbroken by anything.

'I'm going to be the only one here tomorrow night,' Arjun sounds dismal. 'All of you will be at home or in Bangalore.'

'I'll be in Delhi with my family,' Rahul says. 'I'm taking a flight from Madras. It'll be the first time I'm flying by myself.'

'Oh, I'll be doing the same after our week in Bangalore,' Neha says. 'And so will you, Naina, right?' she says turning to me.

'Yes,' I confirm.

'What about you, Amar, Samir?' Neha asks them.

'We're flying from Bangalore to Bombay tomorrow afternoon,' Samir says. 'We'll have to think about college admissions soon.'

'Oh no,' Neha groans. 'I don't want to think about college just yet. It reminds me I'll be studying for many, many more years.'

'How many more?' Amar asks her.

'At least another ten years, depending on what subject I want to specialise in,' Neha says. 'I'll be studying long after all of you have stopped.'

'Wow,' Samir says. 'That's tough to think about. Arjun, what do you plan to do?'

'Engineering,' Arjun answers with a smile. 'I'll be studying for a few more years, but not for as long as Neha.'

'Hey guys,' Samir says stifling a yawn. He gets up and stretches, 'I'm heading back to the hostel. I'm very sleepy. See you on the bus tomorrow.'

'It's a minivan,' Neha corrects him. 'Since there's only a few of us travelling.'

'Oh good,' Samir says grinning. 'We can choose a good restaurant to have lunch at.'

'I'll go along with you,' Rahul gets up and joins Samir. 'See you all tomorrow.'

The wind has died down a bit, however it's still cool for the beginning of March.

'Naina, it's your birthday in three days,' Neha says suddenly. 'Sweet sixteen! We'll be in Bangalore on the fourth.'

Next to me I hear Amar sigh; it's a sore point between us. He wanted to join us to celebrate my sixteenth birthday together. But I reminded him, we had planned this much, much before the two of us met.

I slip my hand in his. 'I'll make it up to you when I return to Bombay, I promise.'

'You know the best way to end our last night here?' Neha asks us. 'By going to the prettiest place in the campus.'

I look at her and I suddenly know what she's going to say.

'The fireflies,' we say together and start laughing.

'Are you sure? It's getting late and it's going to rain soon,' Amar points out.

'Pretty please, Amar?' I say sliding my arm around his waist. 'It's the last time we'll ever see the fireflies. I really want to see them one last time. Please?'

Seeing how intent I am, he relents saying, 'OK let's do it. But only for five minutes. We shouldn't get caught in the rain or thunderstorm.'

The four of us hurry down the path leading to the stream. It must have rained somewhere upstream going by the increased level of water. However, the flat steppingstones are still visible for us to cross over to the other side.

The fireflies appear a lot less than before, but we're thrilled to see them one last time.

'I'll always remember this place,' Amar says wrapping his arms around me. 'The place where we first kissed.'

This time our kisses are different from the last time we were here. Now we're sure of our feelings for each other. There's no hesitation from either of us.

'Listen,' Arjun says, the urgency in his tone getting our attention at once. 'Can you hear that? It's the sound of rain coming this way.'

We fall silent, listening to the sounds around us. In the last five minutes, the weather has changed dramatically. The wind is now rushing through the field we are in, with alarming speed.

A sharp, earthy smell of rain hitting dry earth permeates the air.

Petrichor. A word as evocative as the smell.

The stars are no longer visible. Instead, above us the sky splits apart as the first flash of lightning strikes. We wait for the sound of thunder but there's an eerie silence instead.

'C'mon,' Amar says as we head towards the stream. 'We still have time to make it back.'

For the first time that night I feel a prickle of worry. Will we make it back before it starts raining? Getting caught in a thunderstorm is not the way we wanted this night to end.

We don't say much as the four of us hurry silently through a night that's suddenly gone from exciting to dangerous.

We slow down only when we spot the dim glow of the streetlight at the crossroads. We've managed to stay ahead of the rain. Now we're a short sprint away from our hostels.

'Neha, Naina, you'd better hurry,' Arjun says. 'You have a few minutes before the rain arrives.'

'See you guys tomorrow,' I say hurriedly as Amar hugs me quickly. Our lips meet hurriedly before I turn away. 'Take care, you two.'

We don't say much as we charge up the road, fearful of getting caught in a storm we can hear all around us now.

The first, fat drops of rain hit us as we scale the wall, dropping noiselessly into the garden. Another lightning strike is followed by a sharp burst of thunder chased by a long, ominous rumble.

Jo and Priya are waiting on the staircase outside our room. The look of relief on their faces says it all.

'Thank God, you made it back safely,' Jo says as she hugs us. 'We were so scared when we saw the lightning.'

Neha and I grin at each other.

'Wow, look at that,' Priya points to the courtyard.

We watch as the sky dissolves into chaos caused by vertical sheets of rain falling on the ground. Tree branches shudder and sway with the force of the wind hitting them. The entire courtyard is lit by a flash of light followed by a crash of thunder.

Summer's first thunderstorm has begun.

TWENTY

I wake up to an ominous silence.

The calm after the storm.

Is anyone else awake? Rolling over, I realise I'm all alone in the room. Did all my roomies wake up early on our last day at school? Very strange.

Getting up, I pad across to the window, pushing back the curtains. The storm has left a trail of destruction everywhere. Leaves and branches lie in haphazard piles on the ground. Mounds of debris are scattered across the usually bare cricket field.

The rain has created rivulets in crazy patterns in the mud outside our window. A small tree has been uprooted and lies on its side.

It's surreal seeing so much destruction when everything is so still and quiet.

Yawning, I head to the loo. Surely, at least one of my roommates must be around somewhere. I splash some water on my face so I can feel more awake and less drowsy.

Crossing the corridor, I notice a group of girls in front of Anita Ma'am's room. They look like they're in shock. I wave to Reena as she exits the warden's room, but she gives me a strange look that's almost embarrassed or...sad?

What on earth is going on? Pulling my hair up into a top knot, I walk down the corridor to clear up the mystery.

The girls see me coming and scatter into smaller groups. Is it my imagination or are they avoiding making eye contact with me?

When I see Neha coming towards me, I smile at her saying, 'Good morning, I was looking for you.'

She doesn't answer. Her face is blurry, like she's been crying. I'm about to question her, but she guides me wordlessly into Anita Ma'am's room.

Inside, it's awfully quiet. Jo and Priya are seated on chairs. They too look like they've been crying.

So, it's bad news of some kind, that's why everyone's miserable. I try and prepare myself.

'Naina, we've been waiting for you. Come, sit,' the warden says guiding me to the sofa.

'What is it?' I ask, fearing the worst. 'Is it bad news about my parents? Or my brother? Please tell me.'

'Your family is fine, don't worry,' Anita Ma'am says. I heave a sigh of relief. 'But we do have some bad news.'

'Who is it? What happened?' I ask once more.

Our warden looks at Neha and then says, 'There was an accident last night. Well, this morning, really. One of the boys fell into the swimming pool. He is in a serious condition. We don't have any more information.'

'Which boy?' I ask, a heavy feeling gripping me. 'Is it someone I know?'

'It was Samir,' the warden says slowly. 'Your classmate, Samir Malhotra.'

'In the pool? No, no that's not possible,' I say shaking my head.

I lean against the sofa in relief. 'Samir hates pools, hates getting into water. It must be someone else.'

I know Samir would never go *anywhere* near that pool, ever. I'm so relieved it's not Samir, but I'm also scared it might be someone else I know.

Neha gets up from her chair and comes towards me saying, 'Naina, it is Samir. They pulled him out of the pool. He's very serious. He is in a coma.'

I get up shakily from the sofa saying, 'Neha, they must be mistaken. He hates pools, hates water. He didn't even come to have a look at the pool, yesterday. Remember? Why would he go there?'

Her face crumples up and tears stream down her face.

'It can't be Samir. Tell them it's not him,' I implore her.

She doesn't say anything. Her face tells me the truth. It is Samir who fell into the pool and is in a coma.

I walk towards her, putting my hand out to comfort and, reassure her. But I never make it. My legs give way beneath me.

I feel hands reaching out to catch me, as the world goes black.

TWENTY-ONE

My head feels like it's been split into two, as I open my eyes slowly and stare up at the ceiling. Moving carefully, I turn over.

Neha is already sitting up in bed, a pillow behind her head.

'Happy birthday, Naina,' she says in a bleak voice.

Her tone brings everything back with a rush.

I struggle to sit up, hoping my headache doesn't get any worse. Propping my pillow behind me, I glance across at her.

'Thanks,' I say in a dull tone. 'I was hoping it was all a bad dream, but I guess it's not.'

'No,' Neha agrees. 'I wish we were celebrating your birthday under better conditions.'

'I know. Poor Samir.'

Both of us hardly slept much last night or the night before that. In fact, ever since we heard of Samir's accident sleep has evaded us. Crying repeatedly has not helped either. The first two days after the terrible news, that's all we did.

Mum knocks and pushes the door open. 'Good morning both of you. Happy birthday, honey,' she wishes me but not as cheerfully as she would normally have done. She hugs and kisses me. 'It's going to be okay, Naina. I'm sure your friend will get better.'

Shaking my head, I say, 'Mum, Samir's in a coma. No one knows when he'll come out of it.'

'What time are you going to the hospital?' my mum asks. 'Do you want me to go with you?'

Neha shakes her head saying, 'It's okay Aunty, we'll go by ourselves. They don't want too many people visiting.'

'Alright. Have a shower and some breakfast. You'll feel a little better.'

As the door swings shut behind my mum, Neha and I sigh and sink deeper into the bed.

Nothing can make us feel better unless we can undo what happened that night. And that's not possible.

What we know about the events leading up to the accident, was narrated to us by Rahul. We've gone over it all so many times and it still doesn't make sense. How could everything go so wrong in the space of a few minutes? Why did three bullies change our last night at school from exciting to dangerous, to almost fatal. How did one wrong turn end with Samir lying in a coma in hospital?

*   *

After leaving us that night, Samir, and Rahul headed back, keen to finish packing and get to bed quickly. It had been a long day for everyone.

At the door of the hostel, they ran into the A2Z bullies. The three seniors had been waiting for an opportunity to rag Samir, but never got the chance.

For their luck, he was there that night, with only Rahul for company. No Amar or Arjun to look out for him. No teachers to watch out for. Not even Neha and I, to tell them off.

'Hey Samir, Rahul, where have you guys been?' Aadesh hailed them like long lost friends accompanied by his usual scowl.

'Lucky guys, it's your last night here.'

'Yeah, from tomorrow you'll be back home enjoying good food and drink,' Zoravar said with a gummy grin that revealed all his teeth. 'You'll forget about us.'

As they talked, the three bullies slowly closed the front door of the hostel and spread out in a line, preventing Samir and Rahul from entering the building.

'Look, guys.' Rahul said. 'We've had a long day, and we still have packing to do. We need to get into the hostel.'

'Well,' Appu said looking at his two cohorts for support. 'You guys shouldn't be out so late. It's against the rules, you know. Why don't you come for a walk with us? Hmm? Keep us company.'

'C'mon guys,' Samir said. 'We don't have to do anything you say. We aren't freshies anymore.'

'I don't see anyone else around, so maybe you *have* to do what we say,' Zoravar said flexing his arms, cracking his fingers, and walking menacingly towards them. 'Know what I mean? There's no one to fight for you or to protect you.'

'Let's go for a walk,' Appu said again. 'Let's see how you can entertain us. Show us what you can do. Sing, dance, recite poetry. We're not picky.'

This time there was no mistaking their intent. Get the two boys away from the hostel, so they could 'entertain' them, whatever that meant.

Samir and Rahul tried to get past the bullies once more, but they were no match against the three of them.

Deciding to change tactics; they ran round the side of the hostel. The plan was to throw pebbles at a window till someone woke up and let them into the hostel.

That's when things started going wrong.

Without the help of any lights and with the weather getting worse, Samir got separated from Rahul. Sensing their chance, the bullies ran after him. To avoid them, Samir ran down a long dirt road thinking it would lead back to the hostel at some point.

It didn't.

Meanwhile, Rahul succeeded in waking up Satish who opened the front door for him. The two guys roused Prem, a senior and they started looking for Samir.

This was roughly around the time we were on our way back to the crossroads trying to stay ahead of the thunderstorm.

By now Rahul and the boys were getting anxious. There was no sign of Samir and the first few drops of rain had turned into a drizzle.

A quick search of the area around the hostel told them Samir wasn't there. They widened the search to the arts building thinking he might be inside.

'Samir's not in this building,' Prem confirmed after checking both the doors and the windows. 'Do you think he would have gone further than this?'

'He's not at the hostel and not here, he must be out there somewhere,' Rahul said worriedly. 'Look, there's Amar and Arjun. They'll be able to help us find him.'

After telling Amar and Arjun what had happened, the five boys started searching again in earnest. They were hampered by the rain, lightning, and the wind.

By now the streetlights had either gone out or were obscured by the rain. They had one torch between the five of them.

At some point they decided to go down the dirt road from the hostel. That's when they stumbled upon Samir's shoes in the mud. Nearby, a wooden ladder was propped against a building that didn't look familiar to anyone.

Thinking he might have climbed up seeking refuge from the bullies, they clambered up the ladder.

Once they were inside, they realised what it was. The building that housed the swimming pool.

The ladder had been placed there by workmen while they renovated the pool.

They found an unconscious Samir in the pool. In the dark he had stumbled and fallen in. Luckily for him, the water level was low because of the renovation.

They pulled him out and started CPR immediately.

While the rest of us slept, the boys alerted the hostel warden and the headmaster. The school van took Samir, Amar, and a few boys to a hospital in the nearest town.

The doctors there decided he needed to be moved to Madras or Bombay right away.

Our classmate Jai had insisted on going in the van. From the hospital he called his dad and through his connections, Samir and Amar were air-lifted to Bombay the same morning.

I learned all this after I came to. The only thing anyone could speak of that morning was Samir's accident and his chances of coming out of the coma.

The excitement of leaving school was replaced by a gloomy, despondent feeling and tears. Lots of tears. We packed, said goodbye, and left quickly. The teachers were glad to see us go. The school could now get back to its usual schedule.

Our week-long trip to Bangalore was cancelled. No one felt like celebrating or going anywhere. Jo and Priya left for Madras. Neha and I went to Bangalore hoping to get a flight to Bombay, so we could visit Samir at the hospital as soon as possible.

Most flights out of Bangalore had been cancelled or postponed because of the storm. With the help of Neha's dad, a Brigadier General in the army, we got a flight to Bombay on Monday. At the airport they told us we were lucky to get tickets.

But this morning, we don't feel lucky. We feel terrible. We're alive and well while our best friend lies hooked up to machines in a hospital. Machines that help him breathe, feed him intravenously and monitor all his vital signs.

'I'll be at the hospital this morning,' Reena informs me when she calls to wish me. 'I'll meet you there. They aren't allowing anyone but family to see Samir. He's in the ICU since his condition is still critical. But we can meet Amar and the family.'

'Reena, have you spoken to Amar after the accident?'

'No,' she says. 'I saw him yesterday, but he was so busy I didn't get a chance. Maybe you'll get to speak to him today.'

*   *

At ten in the morning, we join Reena in the foyer of the hospital and take the lift to the third floor.

'Do you know if the Malhotra family are here?' Reena asks the lady behind the desk.

She checks a large register. 'They were here the whole night. They waited till a specialist examined the patient and left. They'll be back later, maybe after lunch.'

We wander over to the large plate glass windows at the end of the floor.

'What do we do Naina?' Neha asks me. 'Do you want to wait for Amar to return?'

I shrug and say, 'We don't know how long they'll be away. I'll call him at home.'

'Not much we can do here,' Reena agrees.

'It's odd to hear Samir being called 'the patient', I shudder. 'He's our friend, a living, breathing person.'

'True, but to them he is a patient in the ICU,' Neha explains.

'Can you see yourself working in a hospital like this?' I ask Neha curiously. To be honest, I don't care much for hospitals.

'Yes, I do,' she muses slowly. 'Think of all the lives saved here every day. The hard work and care that goes into making each patient better.'

She sounds so passionate; I know she'll make a great doctor. Her ultimate dream is to become a heart surgeon.

'There's Suhail, Amar's cousin,' I'm relieved to see someone I know. 'He'll know when Amar plans to return to the hospital.'

Suhail looks surprised to see us there. 'Hi Naina. Didn't think I'd see you here. Weren't you going on a trip somewhere?'

'The trip was cancelled,' I tell him. 'We were too worried about Samir. No one felt like going.'

Suhail nods.

'We were hoping to see Amar and his parents here,' I explain. 'Is Samir better? What do the doctors say?'

His expression becomes serious while he struggles to overcome his emotions. 'The doctors don't say much, you know what they're like. His condition is stable, so they are optimistic, but they won't give us any other details.'

'Does Samir respond to anything? You know like sound or light?' Neha asks.

'Nothing yet. But the specialist who saw him this morning says there's a good chance he'll do that soon. We're waiting for that to happen.'

'Amar will be back in the evening,' Suhail continues. 'They're all exhausted. The doctor advised them to get some rest at home. I offered to be here, just in case.'

Reena glances at her watch saying, 'It's eleven o'clock now. The office at St Xaviers opens at noon. I need to collect the syllabus and admission forms today.'

We urge Reena to go ahead with her plans. Admission into schools and colleges in Bombay is a long process. Not only because the number of applicants is huge but also because we've studied in another state for the past five years. That adds another complication to the whole process.

'Have you spoken to Amar?' Suhail asks me.

'No, not after the accident,' I tell him. 'How is he?'

'He's okay,' Suhail says cautiously. 'He's had to become the responsible older brother overnight. And that's not an easy thing.'

'I can imagine,' I murmur, my heart going out to him. Having successfully seen his youngest brother recover from cancer, he has to negotiate a new crisis now.

'What I don't get is why they were out that night,' Suhail says shaking his head. 'They knew a storm was approaching yet they were out so late.'

'It was meant to be a short walk, a farewell to our school,' Neha tells Suhail. 'Nothing like this was meant to happen.'

'You were there too?' Suhail asks doubtfully.

'We both were,' I confirm. 'We took a short walk around campus and returned to the hostel. That's all. After that it all went wrong….' I say trailing off. Looking back now, the walk seems trivial given what happened at the end.

'Amar never mentioned the two of you were there. He said they went for a walk, and Samir got separated from the rest of them. And then, well you know the rest,' Suhail says bitterly.

When a nurse approaches Suhail, he excuses himself. 'They need me at the reception desk. It's best if you return in the evening or tomorrow, Naina.'

'Can I try calling Amar at home?' I ask.

Suhail shakes his head. 'No one answers calls any more. There are just too many people calling. You can leave a message.'

Going down in the lift, I remark, 'I'm surprised Amar never told him we were there.'

'Probably to protect us from getting into trouble,' Neha says. 'In case there's an enquiry or something.'

'That sounds like something Amar would do. How did a silly walk in the dark become such a disaster?' I say regretfully. 'I wish we'd never gone out that night.'

The minute we get home from visiting the hospital, I dial Amar's home number.

The phone rings repeatedly. After a few minutes, a guy answers in Hindi. He says the family is at home but are not taking calls. I give him my name and number and ask him to tell Amar I called. He agrees, but from the tiredness in his voice I know mine is just one more message that will join the dozens of others recorded today.

We celebrate my birthday with dinner at the Shamiana at the Taj Hotel. The plan was to celebrate my birthday with a party thrown by my parents. But I insisted on cancelling it.

'How is your classmate?' my dad asks once our order is placed. 'Did you get to see him?'

'No,' I say. 'Only family members are allowed because he's in the ICU.'

'I was thinking of not going ahead with the US trip,' I inform my family when the food arrives.

My comment is greeted with shocked silence.

'I don't understand,' my dad remarks. 'Why would you want to cancel your trip? You insisted on joining your mum and brother.'

'That was before Samir's accident,' I say. 'Now it doesn't seem fair to be going, when his condition is so serious.'

'Naina, your being here will not help in any way. You just said only family members are allowed to see him,' my mum points out. 'They and the doctors will do what's best for him.'

'A change of scene will do you good,' dad insists. 'Besides, you need to check out colleges for your degree. It makes sense for you to go.'

Neha gives me a small smile and squeezes my hand. I sit back defeated.

*   *

'Your parents are right, you know,' Neha says on our way to the hospital the next day. 'Samir's family will do all they can for him.'

'I know but I wish I could help in some way,' I say gloomily. 'I wish you could stay here for a few more days, Neha. I could use the company.'

'I want to. But I need to start applying to colleges. And so do you,' she points out. 'You need to collect the forms before you leave next week. Promise?'

'I'll start first thing tomorrow,' I assure her.

At the hospital, we manage to squeeze into a lift after a twenty-minute wait. On the third floor, we skirt past a large crowd gathered in the waiting area and look around for Amar and his family. Reena and Mimi join us. Four months after they first met, Mimi and Suhail are still together.

'Amar and his parents are with the doctor,' Mimi tells me after we exchange a hug. 'I told him you and Neha would be in today.'

'How is he coping?' I ask her.

'As well as possible,' she says after a pause. 'There he is, coming down the corridor with his mum.'

It's five days since we met but it feels like a lifetime. So much has happened that I feel I hardly know the boy talking to his mum.

The last time we met our concern was returning to the hostel without getting wet or catching a cold. Trivial things compared to what he has to worry about now.

There's a strange lump in my throat. I want to go over and talk to Amar, console, and support him. Instead, I stay where I am. There are so many family members around that I can't face meeting them under these circumstances.

When Amar looks my way, I raise my hand attempting to catch his attention. His expression doesn't change so I'm unsure if I was successful or not.

'Amar,' Reena calls out. He turns, raises his hand, and walks towards us.

I wait while Neha and Reena ask him about Samir. He's lost some weight and looks like he hasn't been sleeping well.

'Hi Amar,' I say quietly when the others fall silent. 'How are you?'

'Not too bad,' he answers distractedly. 'I got the message you left for me but didn't have the time to call you.'

'That's okay. Is there any update on Samir?' I ask him.

'Not much. The doctors are still optimistic, but we can't see any change.'

'Can we see him?' Reena asks. 'Or is that not allowed?'

Amar shakes his head. 'Sorry, they are very strict about that. They won't even allow our relatives to see him.'

'That's understandable,' Neha says. 'I'm flying to Delhi today, but I wanted to see you before that.'

'Thanks Neha,' Amar replies. He looks back to where his parents are. 'I've got to go back. The doctors are changing his medication and we're having another meeting in five minutes. Thanks for coming to the hospital.'

He turns and leaves. I could be any girl in that waiting room. Not *the* girl he professed to love, less than a week ago. But then these aren't normal circumstances.

After ten minutes Neha and I say goodbye to Mimi and Reena and walk down the stairs. We've timed our visit well but it's a long way to the airport and we can't afford to take chances with Bombay's traffic.

'Neha, are we terrible people?' I ask her.

'What? No. Why would you say that?' she says looking puzzled.

'Was it a mistake to have suggested a midnight walk on our last night at school? If we hadn't, Samir would be fine instead of being in the ICU.'

'Naina, it's true we suggested a midnight walk. But we didn't force anyone to come. And it's the bullies who are responsible for this, not us,' Neha sounds adamant.

'I noticed Amar and you didn't say much to each other,' she adds after a pause.

'It felt trivial wanting to talk to him alone. He has so much to deal with right now. With his parents and relatives there, it didn't feel right.'

'Whatever happened doesn't change your feelings for each other,' she points out.

The lump in my throat feels even bigger. I turn and gaze at the traffic outside.

TWENTY-TWO

The next few days are a blur of collecting forms from colleges and obtaining a tourist visa to America. Forms, original certificates, and endless copies of everything litter my desk and cover the dining table.

In between, Twinkle decides to take a nap on some papers, which requires a fresh round of copies.

But finally, it's all done. An American visa proudly adorns each of our passports. Neel and I gaze at the innocuous page in wonder. He's got admission to a college in Massachusetts. My mum and I have been sponsored by my mum's younger sister who lives there. We'll be away for a whole month, and we leave in two days' time.

With my days spent filling out forms, I have had no time to visit the hospital and I've been relying on Mimi to provide updates on Samir.

'Any news of Samir?' I ask Mimi over the phone one night.

'I was going to call you,' she says sounding excited. 'Amar said Samir's finger moved for the first time today. It's what they've been waiting for, Naina.'

'Really?' I say shocked and happy. 'I'm so glad to hear that. Mimi, this means he's going to get better. I just know he will.'

'They've been reading and playing his favourite songs lately,' Mimi says. 'I'm sure that helped a lot. Will you be there tomorrow?'

'Yes. I've seen Amar just once since I got back.'

'Are you going ahead with your US trip?' Mimi asks.

'I wanted to cancel it, but mum and dad wouldn't let me,' I tell her. 'Anyway, I'll see you at the hospital tomorrow.'

I call Neha immediately to share the news with her.

'That's the best news we've had so far,' she says happily. 'I wish I could be with you at the hospital tomorrow.'

'Me too.'

Going up in the lift the next day, I feel better than I have on previous visits. I scan the waiting room for Amar. His mum and dad are sitting with some relatives. The mood feels cautiously upbeat.

I join Suhail and Amar who are near the window, chatting.

'Hi Suhail, Amar,' I greet them.

'Hi Naina,' Suhail says with the ghost of a smile. 'Did you hear about Samir? This morning, he moved two fingers on his right hand.'

'That's the best news yet,' I tell him glancing at Amar. He's looking out of the window and doesn't say anything.

Suhail says, 'I'm going to get something to drink. Do you want anything, Naina?'

'Sure,' I say. 'I wouldn't mind a Coke or a Fanta.'

As Suhail leaves, I glance again at Amar. He barely acknowledges me standing next to him. This is an Amar I've never seen before.

'Amar,' I tell him with a smile. 'This means Samir will come out of the coma soon, doesn't it?'

He doesn't respond.

'Amar?'

He looks away from the window, then at the floor, finally at me, almost reluctantly.

'Naina, I don't think you should be here,' he says, no emotion in his voice.

I look at him in confusion. 'Sorry?'

He looks away again and exhales slowly. 'I didn't want to do this, but it's the right time. I don't think you should visit Samir anymore.'

'I don't understand,' I tell him still confused. 'What are you saying? You want me to stay away from the hospital?'

'Yes. Because if it wasn't for you, we wouldn't be here.'

I freeze on hearing these words.

'What? That doesn't make sense. I didn't cause Samir's accident.' My words spill out in confusion. Does he know what he's saying?

Still looking at some point outside the window, his voice hardens as he says, 'If you hadn't insisted on going to see the fireflies that night I would have been with Samir. And this.... this accident would never have happened.'

My breath comes out in a rush like I've just been punched in the stomach.

Amar thinks I'm to blame for Samir's accident, because I suggested going to see the fireflies.

I shake my head in disbelief.

'I can't believe you said that' I tell him.

'You know it's true,' he says in the same dull voice. 'The ten minutes we wasted there could have saved his life. Those guys never bullied him when I was around. If I'd been with Samir, I'd have protected him like I always did. He wouldn't be in the ICU right now, fighting for his life. My family wouldn't be suffering like they are now.'

I feel a bit lightheaded listening to his accusations. That I indirectly caused Samir to fall into the pool and into a coma seems astounding to me. Samir, who I love as much as I do my own brother.

Now I understand why Amar has been so cool and distant with me. Why he never returned my calls. Why he can't even bear to look at me right now.

Trying to make sense of why it happened, he's traced it back to the ten minutes we spent watching the fireflies that night. And blames me for wanting to go there.

I look back at the people in the waiting room. At Amar's parents, relatives, and friends. Then I look at Amar and me standing by the window, our reflections indistinct and blurred in the glass, like we are already breaking apart.

'You really believe this?' I ask taking a step towards him.

He moves away saying, 'Yes, I do. Sometimes you can be quite selfish, even childish. And it can cause accidents like this.'

'I blame myself for not protecting Samir,' he continues. 'I've always looked out for him. So, I can't do this with you anymore. It doesn't feel right.'

I'm amazed at how calm I am. It's surprising I haven't dissolved into tears yet. Perhaps subconsciously I knew this was going to happen. God knows there have been enough clues for me over the last two weeks.

If anyone else had blamed me, I'd have objected but hearing Amar accuse me, knocks all the fight out of me. On some level, I know we are teenagers trying to deal with a terrible situation and failing badly. But I can't see a way out of this, from where I am. Sometimes love just isn't enough.

I try one last time to appeal to Amar.

'Do you really think I should go? You really want me to leave?' I ask him in a low voice.

'Yes. I think you should go. Please leave,' he confirms still focused on some distant point outside the window.

I turn and leave. I don't look back.

TWENTY-THREE

Eight years later

'Mitch, wake up,' I say knocking on the door. 'Wake up or you'll be late for class.

After a pause I call again, 'Mitch?'

On the other side of the door, an alarm clock goes off. There's a clatter as it falls to the floor, hitting the mosaic tiles. It's a miracle it still works. Or it could be a new clock. Hard to tell.

A voice mumbles something.

'Mitch?' I call out again.

'Yep, I'm awake. Thanks, Naina,' Mitch yells.

Satisfied, I carry on down the corridor to the kitchen. As the youngest in the family, I was usually the one being dragged out of bed reluctantly. Now in a reversal of roles, I'm the oldest one around and by default the 'responsible' one. The irony is not lost on me.

Filling the electric kettle with water from the water purifier, I place two large mugs and a tea pot with tea leaves on the counter. I cover the leaves with boiling water and put the lid on leaving the infusion for the required five minutes.

Carrying my steaming cup of tea, I rescue my copy of *The Times of India* from the front door and head to the balcony.

Five floors below me, our neighbourhood is starting to wake up.

Sounds of cars, dogs and people float up to the flat. The cries of vegetable sellers and guys selling fresh eggs are faint but discernible from the main road.

Six months ago, I moved back to Bombay, (soon to be Mumbai) from the US. Neel's fiancée, Rachel (yes, they started off as pen pals) asked if her friend Mitch could stay with me while she did her degree in classical Indian dance. Michelle Marie Roy or Mitch is half Bengali and half American and so good at classical Indian dance, that I refuse to show her what little I recall from my years at school.

A young girl with long, brown hair, clad in a long t-shirt with *'You've got this!'* printed on the front, wanders out and drops into a chair opposite me.

'Morning,' I grin at Mitch, my tenant for the last four months. Well, in truth we are both tenants of my parents to whom we pay rent for this flat.

Mitch rubs her face sleepily and says,' Remind me why I opted to take an extra class that starts at nine in the morning?'

'Because you love Indian culture so much, you wanted to cover as much as possible in the year you're here,' I remind her.

'True. I just wish it started a bit later,' she grumbles.

'There's a pot of fresh tea in the kitchen,' I say helpfully. 'A mug of tea may help.'

'I need something stronger than a cup of tea, but it'll have to do,' Mitch remarks heading for the kitchen.

I linger over my tea thinking back to when my family lived in this flat. Mornings were a mad rush with everyone up at seven-thirty or earlier. My mum's main goal was to have us at the table for breakfast but that didn't always work.

Two years ago, my dad retired, and my parents moved to Poona, now Pune. This flat lay vacant except for the times my dad stayed here to attend business meetings in the city.

My mum keeps urging me to hire a full-time maid but the thought of having someone around all the time doesn't appeal to me. I work long hours and Mitch is away at class or out late with friends. A part-time maid cleans the flat every other day while another maid comes in to cook three times a week. I know my mum thinks this arrangement is inadequate, but it works for us.

'See you later, Naina,' Mitch yells as she heads for the front door. 'Don't wait up for me tonight.'

The front door shuts with a thud and I'm alone again. Time for a shower, change of clothes and a slice of toast if I'm lucky.

An hour later, I close the door, balancing a slice of toast spread with marmalade in one hand and my bag and a folder full of loose papers in the other.

'Good morning, Pinky Aunty,' I greet our next-door neighbour. She's buying fresh eggs from a vendor. I watch as she dunks each egg into cold water, waiting for it to sink to the bottom. Eggs that fail this test are rejected as not being fresh enough. I recall my mum doing the same thing years ago.

'Hi Naina,' she eyes the slice of toast in my hand. 'Is that all you're having for breakfast?'

'Yes, Aunty,' I say. Seeing her frown, I quickly add, 'I'll have something at the office later. See you.'

I hurry into the lift before she says anything else. I know she'll be shaking her head over how our generation doesn't eat right or look after ourselves enough. But honestly who has the time to have a full breakfast of scrambled eggs, toast, sausages and fried tomatoes like we used to? Work takes up most of our day and socialising takes care of the hours after work.

However, the thought of that breakfast makes my stomach give a ruminative rumble.

Manoeuvring my Maruti Zen past dozens of other cars in the building, I turn onto the main road. Lately, cars on the road seem to get larger and more in number while the roads stay the same size.

My office is in Tardeo; close enough to drive to, but not so close that I can walk there. I park and walk up the two floors to my office. I work as a book reviewer at a women's magazine. I love the buzz of being part of a magazine, of having a page and a by-line with my name on it. Having been away from the city for so long, I now have my finger on the pulse of Bombay, soon to be Mumbai.

After work, I often go to a book launch or a reading by an author. Or if I'm lucky I get to attend a new play or visit the latest art exhibit at one of the galleries.

'But that counts as work,' Neha remarks on one of our Sunday evening calls. 'When do you go out with friends? And what about boyfriends, Naina?'

'These are my friends too,' I point out to her. 'Well, almost. They're colleagues who are friends, too.'

'And guys? Are you dating anyone?' Neha persists. 'The last guy you dated was months ago. He was the weird one, right?'

'Hmm... a little. When he heard I worked at a women's mag, he went to great lengths to show me what a feminist he was,' I grin. 'When he was anything, but a feminist.'

'Who was the one who called you fragile?' Neha asks.

I groan and say, 'Now he was weird. He turned out to be a control freak so I stopped seeing him immediately.'

On the way to my department, I say 'hi' to a few colleagues. Monday mornings can be a shock to the system for some people. Not everyone is in a good mood. A lot of us work a half day on Saturday so Sunday is our one full day away from work.

Grabbing a pen and notebook I take a seat in the meeting room. Every week starts with a meeting by our editor, Saira, a dynamic thirty-something, who runs the magazine with a combination of intelligence, charisma, and energy.

Beena, the magazine's art critic stops by my desk after the meeting.

'I'm going to the opening of a new art gallery tonight. Interested?' she asks me.

Recalling that Mitch may not be home tonight, I agree.

*   *

Holding back a yawn, I unlock the door to the flat later that night. My watch informs me it's just after ten o'clock. Dinner was half a chicken roll and a couple of kebabs; part of the finger food they served at the gallery opening. The floor lamp in the sitting room is on, so Mitch came in at some point to shower and change, before heading out again.

There's a flashing red light on the phone; someone has left a message. I'm about to press play when the phone rings.

Lifting the receiver I say, 'Hi Naina, speaking.'

'Hi Naina, this is Samir. How are you?'

'Hey gorgeous,' I say with a smile. 'How's life?'

Samir's laugh cuts through the crackle of the transatlantic line. 'That's supposed to be my line, Naina.'

'Well, going by the photos you sent me, it describes you

perfectly. The long hair, laidback attitude, colourful clothes. You look like a true artist.'

'Like a struggling artist,' Samir corrects me. 'I'm still at the start of my career, you know. Breaking into the art scene in America is tough.'

'I've no doubt you'll make it big someday, Samir,' I assure him. 'What's up? Did you call earlier? I was about to play the message on my machine.'

'Yep, that was me. I figured you would be back after ten o'clock, Indian time.'

'I just got back from a work thing,' I inform him. 'How's Paul?'

'He's fine. We're having brunch right now,' Samir says. 'Paul says a big 'hi' to you.'

'Thanks. I'm glad you both are happy,' I tell him wandering out to the balcony. It's such a clear night, I can see the lights on some ships out at sea.

'Naina, the reason I called was to give you some news,' says Samir slowly.

'Oh, ok,' I say wondering what it could be.

'Amar is in Bombay.'

Before I can stop myself, I ask, 'Who?'

'Amar, my twin brother and your...'

'Oh, I remember Amar,' I interrupt Samir before he can complete the sentence. 'Sorry, I had a brain freeze right then.'

He was going to say your ex-boyfriend and I'd rather not hear those words.

'He's been in the city for the past two weeks,' Samir explains. 'He returned to Bombay, just like you did.'

I swallow and exhale. Clutching the phone to my ear, I sit down carefully not wanting to say anything. In the years since Amar and I broke up, I've avoided meeting him, successfully. And I don't plan to change that any time soon.

'Naina?' Samir enquires cautiously.

I think of something to say and come up with nothing. Making a big effort, I inject some feeling into my voice and say, 'Your parents must be happy, Samir.'

'They're thrilled,' he agrees. 'And he's happy too. In fact, that's why I called. Amar wants to get in touch with you and asked for your number.'

'Oh,' I say stunned by his words. In a shaky voice I add, 'I don't see why. We haven't been in touch.'

'Exactly. He wants to meet you and apologise,' Samir says. 'Apologise for what happened the last time you met.'

Sighing I say, 'There's no need for an apology. I've moved on from that, years ago.'

'Naina, he feels awful about the way things ended between the two of you and wants to make amends. He feels you both need closure,' Samir says.

I close my eyes and take in gulps of air. Closure, the word that says it all yet does so little.

'Samir, we were teenagers, kids really. And those were not normal circumstances. Everyone was so worried about you. I don't hold it against him. And I don't need an apology. Please tell him that.'

'Are you sure?' Samir persists. 'Amar said he left messages for you, but you never called back. And there was no reply to the letters he sent years ago.'

'You know, I was away in the US for two months and when I got back, my focus was on securing admission to a college. I never got round to replying. Honestly, it's not a big deal.'

After a pause Samir says guardedly, 'You don't want to meet him, do you?'

'It's not that. I'm just so busy,' I say frantically. 'Work takes up a lot of my time. Then there's friends, my parents, my brother, the list goes on and on.'

'And boyfriends?'

'Yeah, boyfriends too,' I agree. 'You know how busy life can get.'

'Ok I'll let him know,' Samir says. 'He'll be disappointed.'

'Samir, please tell him it's all good from my side. And who knows, we may meet somewhere. This city can feel like a small place sometimes,' I say, hoping we can drop the subject now. 'By the way, when will you be here next?'

'Sometime this year,' he says slowly.

'Oh good,' I say happily. 'I'd love to see you and Paul again.'

'Ok, Naina it was great catching up with you.'

'You too, Samir. Take care and keep in touch. Bye.' I say glad to have heard the last on that subject.

'Sure, will do. Bye.'

I throw the phone on the sofa and slump into the chair I'm sitting on.

Amar's back, in Bombay. He's in the same city I'm in.

I try to wrap my head around that. This city of millions that always feels so large and unwieldy, feels very small tonight. Why did he have to return to Bombay? I've avoided meeting him or talking to him for eight years.

I close and lock the balcony doors, turn off the lamp, and head down the passage to my room.

Once inside, I stand in front of a full-length mirror, looking curiously at my reflection. What do people see when they look at me? I never grew past five feet eight inches, but I'm not as skinny as I used to be. This is relative; however, my parents still consider me to be underweight.

My hair's shorter; it now ends a few inches past my shoulders. I usually wear it loose, allowing it to wave naturally.

My wardrobe is a mix of Indian and Western clothes like a lot of my friends. The rest of me is the same, a little older and hopefully a lot wiser. Too wise to fall madly in love, the way I did at fifteen.

But if I close my eyes, I can still glimpse the sixteen-year-old girl, that I was eight years ago. The girl who returned from the hospital that day, heartbroken and bewildered. Puzzled and haunted by doubts that maybe, just maybe she was guilty after all. Else why would her boyfriend of six months accuse her of causing a terrible accident to his twin brother and break up with her, all in five minutes?

I open my eyes and walk away from my reflection.

It doesn't take much college level psychology to realise I never really dealt with the fallout of my breakup with Amar. When the first guy I ever dated, didn't want me around anymore, my world crumbled. Samir was still in the ICU, his recovery, uncertain at best. It couldn't get much worse than that. I knew Amar had lashed out at me in grief. He blamed himself for not protecting his twin and by association he blamed me too.

Leaving for a month-long trip with my mum and brother,

allowed me to delay dealing with any of it.

'Why don't you stay for another month?' my aunt suggested as our departure date drew near. 'We haven't spent much time with you.'

'Can I stay?' I pleaded with my mom, hoping she'd say yes.

'Are you sure it won't be too much for you?' my mum asked her younger sister. 'You'll be busy with Sunil starting high school this year.'

'Don't worry. His school starts much later. We'd love to have Naina for another month if she wants to stay,' my aunt said hugging me tightly.

'Alright,' my mother agreed.

Dad agreed to the extended holiday after my aunt convinced him I would be no trouble at all.

'Naina, a friend of yours called today,' my dad said towards the end of the call. 'It was Amar. I told him you were away for a month.'

'Thanks Dad,' I said turning away so the others couldn't see my face.

'He's sent a letter,' my dad added. 'And put his name and address on the back. Oh, wait, another letter came in this morning. That's from him too. Should I forward them to your aunt's place?'

'There's no need,' I informed him. 'I'll read them when I get back to India.'

The letters. Samir mentioned them during our phone call, tonight.

After a quick shower, I slip into a strappy, cotton nightie and pad across the corridor to the study. This used to be Neel's room but since he is unlikely to return, my parents converted it into a study-cum-guest room.

Kneeling in front of a bookcase I reach behind a stack of dusty encyclopaedias. My fingers search for and close around a long box. I draw it out, placing it on the floor.

Grabbing a duster from the kitchen I give the bookcase and its contents a good clean. I spend a minute looking through our collection of atlases and encyclopaedias. They were such a vital part of growing up in the eighties; used so often that dust never had a chance to settle.

Carrying the box to the desk, I place it under the light. Do I really want to open it? Will it prove to be my Pandora's Box?

I pry the lid off. Inside is a collection of items I haven't looked at for years. Right on top is a cloth pouch containing dried flowers, that Amar and I collected on our last day of school. Under this is a box with the silver bracelet he gave me. Years of tarnish cover the links and the delicate charms. The oblong box sits on a limited edition of *Little Women*, his last gift before we left school.

Putting all of this to one side I continue my search. Next is a bunch of cards from Amar. Cards to mark Christmas, New Year and Valentine's Day when we were together. His last card was to wish me all the best for the exams.

What's missing is a card for my sixteenth birthday.

At the very bottom of the box is a pile of letters, held together by a white ribbon. With difficulty, I undo the knots, setting off a small cloud of dust.

Using the date on the front of each, I arrange the letters in order on the desk. Amar sent one letter every month for five months after we broke up.

I don't know what's in them because I never opened and read them.

TWENTY-FOUR

When I walk in to work on Friday morning, there's a note from my editor asking me to see her.

'Hi Saira, can I come in?' I ask, pausing at the door to her office.

'Naina, come on in,' Saira says when she sees me. Closing a mock-up of the next issue of the magazine, she pulls a paper from a folder. 'I looked at your suggestions for future articles, and I like the one about Indian female authors living abroad. Can you do a first draft by Monday? I want to see what angle we can take on it.'

'I'm on leave, Monday and Tuesday,' I remind her. 'Can I hand in a first draft by Wednesday?'

'Wednesday, let's see,' she says consulting her calendar. 'Yes, that should be okay. We can still make the next issue. Are you going anywhere special?'

'I'm going to Pune for the weekend,' I tell her. 'I haven't been to see my parents for a while.'

'Ah, I remember now,' Saira says with a smile. 'You haven't taken leave since you joined us, have you?'

'No,' I agree. 'But I enjoy working here so I don't mind that.'

'Good, I'm glad to hear that,' Saira says. 'Anything planned for your stay in Pune?'

I shake my head, saying, 'Just chilling out with my folks. Oh, and I'm attending a wedding while I'm there.'

Saira raises her eyebrows at that. 'You're single, right?'

Seeing my nod, she adds, 'Watch out for matchmakers at the wedding. You know, the aunties. They'll be looking out for someone to set you up with.'

I laugh and say, 'I've told my mum to give me time, so I'm good for a while. I'll have the draft on your desk first thing on Wednesday.'

'Alright,' Saira says. 'Have a good break.'

I return to my desk thrilled at the thought of writing an article in addition to my usual book reviews.

Sitting in my chair is Kishore, a marketing manager for the magazine. Ever since I joined, he's been asking me to go on a date with him. I'm firmly against dating people at work. It's a rule I've stuck to since I started working. My rule hasn't deterred him from trying, though.

'Hey lovely,' he says. 'Have you made up your mind?'

'Kishore, I've told you before, I'm not interested,' I say trying to retrieve my chair.

'All I'm asking for is one date,' Kishore says giving me what I assume is a smile that has worked wonderfully on other girls. 'You don't know what you're missing.'

'I'll pass,' I say firmly. 'Now if you don't mind, I have to get back to work.'

'Ok, but think about it,' he urges as he leaves with another winning smile.

'You know he's been going steady with a girl for years, don't you?' Anita, my colleague asks me. 'They're practically engaged.'

'I'm not surprised to hear that. He probably tries his luck with every new girl at the magazine.'

'Yeah, he does,' Anita agrees with a laugh. 'I saw him chatting to the new girl in HR yesterday.'

I work steadily for the next few hours and manage to jot down some points for the article Saira has assigned to me. Having gone out every night this week, I'm rather tired.

Before leaving, I tidy my desk as much as possible. Not surprisingly piles and piles of books are stacked around my desk and chair. A bookshelf behind me is full of even more books. They are arranged by type, but as soon as I've got them in order, a fresh lot arrives, and the system is thrown out of whack again.

At the gate of the building, I notice all the cars ahead of me are turning left. When it's my turn, I'm forced to do the same since a long procession of people and cars is blocking my usual route home.

I haven't been down this road for years, so I mentally try and figure out a way back home. At the traffic light, I look around for a road that I can turn into once the lights change. This area has been developed a lot recently going by the new buildings and shops.

Suddenly my eyes fall on a large sign, and I freeze. Above a brand-new office space, the sign reads '*Malhotra and Sons, Interior Designers and Architects*'.

I quickly look away. Samir had mentioned his family was opening another office on this side of town; I never realised it was this close to my office. Rooting around in my dashboard, I grab a pair of sunglasses and put them on, then casually sneak another look.

The Malhotra family has been in interior design all these years, Amar must have added the architecture division since he's a qualified architect now. Is he at this office today? Or is he at the old office near Cuffe Parade?

I nervously look away reminding myself I'm no longer the shy girl I used to be. This is the grown up, professional me, who doesn't fall apart so easily.

The light turns green, and I join the dozens of cars and taxis that surge forward and drive away, my heart beating a little faster.

I make it back home after just one wrong turn. Kicking off my sandals in relief, I open the balcony doors to let the evening air in. A gust of wind washes over me. Summer is a month away, but the days feel warm already. Standing outside, I savour the coolness of the tiles under my feet.

I haven't had a chance to read Amar's letters since I retrieved them from the study. Or more accurately, I've avoided thinking about them. They'll take me back to a time I'd rather forget. When I left India, I thought I'd left that chapter of my life behind not realising I took it with me wherever I went. The past has a way of never leaving you, till you turn around and face it squarely.

The phone rings, pulling me back to the present.

'Hi, Naina here,' I say cautiously.

'Hi bestie,' Neha as usual sounds upbeat. 'How are you? You sound a bit off. What's up?'

'Oh Neha, hi,' I say in relief. 'I'm fine. Just a bit tired, that's all. How come you're calling for the second time this week? All good at your end?'

'Oh yeah, no problem,' she replies. 'I know we spoke on Sunday, but I thought I'd give you a quick call today. Do you have a minute?'

'For you, of course,' I say. 'What's this about?'

'Well,' she says and then stops. In the pause that follows I know what she's going to say. Sure, enough she continues with, 'I had a call from Amar last night. I think you know what it was about.'

This time I'm prepared. Choosing a chair near the balcony I say, 'I think I do. He asked Samir to call me too.'

'He really wants to meet you, Naina. Don't you think it's time the two of you met?' she asks me.

'Not really,' I tell her.

'That means you aren't over him,' Neha declares.

'Or I am *so* over him, there's no need to meet him,' I say.

She sighs, then I sigh.

'Why are you sighing?' Neha asks indignantly. 'I'm the one doing the hard work. By the way he sounds good.'

'Who? Amar?'

'Yep. He already had a nice, deep voice. Now he's got a bit of an American accent, so he sounds even better,' Neha says.

'I didn't know you liked Amar's voice,' I laugh. 'How come you never mentioned it before?'

'He was your boyfriend so obviously I couldn't,' she says reasonably. 'Look why don't you meet him this weekend? Get it over with. Then no one will bug you anymore.'

'I'm away in Pune this weekend. I'm going for the Sharma wedding, remember?'

'The one that's meant to be the wedding of the year?' Neha asks. 'I forgot about that. When are you back?'

'Tuesday. I'm leaving on the early train tomorrow.'

'Say hi to your mum and dad for me. Its's been ages since I met them.'

'Sure, I will,' I assure her.

'Will you at least think about meeting Amar?' she pleads. 'I think he deserves that much.'

'I will,' I promise her. 'This is the only topic we don't agree on, isn't it?'

'It is. But we've agreed to disagree, so it's ok,' she says. 'I just want to help.'

'You are helping,' I tell her. 'And thanks for taking the time to call me. I know your free time is precious to you.'

'Speaking of that, I'd better hang up. I've got to be at the hospital. Take care, love you.'

'Love you too, bye.'

I exhale slowly and put the phone down. First Samir and now Neha. Seems like Amar is working his way through my friends, till I agree to meet him. Now that both of us are in Bombay, it's inevitable we'll meet somewhere. Maybe closure is what we need.

I step out of a cool shower and into an old t-shirt and long cotton skirt. Mitch and I are having dinner at home tonight, a rare occurrence.

But first it's time for a glass of wine. From the fridge I take a bottle of white wine, chilled just enough, then two wine glasses and the house keys. I leave a note on the kitchen counter for Mitch telling her where I'll be.

Pulling the front door shut, I climb the stairs to the sixth floor and carry on till I reach the terrace above it.

A few residents have created a homely place to sit and enjoy the breeze up here. A couple of rattan chairs with comfy cushions and a rickety side table sit by the side of the water tank. I walk to the end of the terrace and peer over the ledge at the road below.

'Hi Naina,' Mitch greets me from the door to the terrace. 'Oh, it's so cool up here. Is it wine o'clock yet?'

'It definitely is,' I say grinning at her. She opens the bottle deftly and pours a glass for each of us. 'How has your week been?'

'Thank God it's Friday,' she quips taking a generous sip of wine. Licking her lips she adds, 'This is a very good wine. Where is it from?'

'New Zealand. On my way back to India, I visited my aunt in Auckland. She recommended some wines to bring back with me,' I tell her.

'Oh, I forgot to tell you, Neha called yesterday. She didn't want to leave a message,' Mitch says. 'It sounded important.'

'She called again today, don't worry,' I say.

'All good?' Mitch asks.

'Yeah, kind of,' I say, not knowing where to start. 'It's a long story.'

'We have a great bottle of wine and all the time you need,' Mitch points out lowering herself into one of the armchairs.

Looking at her I decide it may be worthwhile to tell her what's on my mind. She's a good listener and has given me good advice before.

'Ok, but if you want me to stop just let me know,' I say. 'Like I said, it's a long story.'

Settling into the curve of the wicker chair, I look up at the stars and start talking. Once I begin, the years roll away and it feels like I'm sixteen again. I tell her how Amar and I met, my initial reluctance due to my dating rules, our first kiss and the dates we had in Bombay.

It's only when I get to Samir's accident that I falter and almost stop. My voice shakes while I relive the abrupt ending to my relationship with Amar.

When I finish, I relax. It feels good telling Mitch all of it because she is an impartial listener, not having lived through any of it. And retelling the events gives me a better perspective.

'Wow,' Mitch says slowly. 'That must've hurt a lot. Was Amar your first boyfriend?'

'Yep,' I say carefully.

'He sounds like a nice guy except for that last bit,' Mitch remarks. 'More a doer than a talker, I gather.'

I nod. 'He was, maybe still is. After that, I decided I was done with nice guys. Look where that got me. After Amar, the guys I dated were anything but nice.'

'Did that work out?' she grins.

I smile. 'No, but dating bad guys is very entertaining. If you remember to only date, but not fall in love with them.'

Mitch laughs. 'Very true. Don't fall in love and don't try to change them. Been there, done that.'

'It's like a rite of passage, isn't it?' I muse. 'Dating different types of guys just so you know which sort you *shouldn't* end up with. Also, I never date anyone for longer than three, max, four months now.'

'After that, what do you do?'

'I take a break and move on to the next. Works beautifully each time.'

'Let me guess, your dating rules are back in place too,' Mitch observes.

'I've tweaked them, but the essence is the same. Don't give your heart to anyone and you won't have it handed back to you in pieces.'

Mitch pours the last of the wine into our glasses. 'What was in those letters that Amar sent?'

I pause. 'I don't know, I've never read them.'

'What? How come?' she asks in surprise. 'Aren't you curious to see what's in them?'

'At first, I was too heartbroken to read them and later, too angry. I wasn't around when he sent the last few letters. I had already left India.'

Exhaling, I add, 'There's something else. My brother once remarked that if you feel something is worth fighting for then you should fight for it. I never fought for my relationship with Amar. The chance of being rejected again was too much. I still feel guilty about that.'

'You've got to read the letters, Naina,' Mitch urges me. 'See what he has to say.'

'I'll read them after dinner,' I inform her knowing it's time I did.

I'm finally ready to see what the letters contain. I need to see things from Amar's perspective.

TWENTY-FIVE

12TH March 1986

Dearest Naina,

I never thought the first time I wrote a letter to you; it would be to apologise for being such a jerk. I'm not good at writing letters but I figured I'd get better by writing a lot of them if we were studying in different cities or countries like we talked about.

Instead, here I am asking you to forgive me for the terrible things I said the last time we met. I have no excuse except to say I haven't been myself lately. I think you'll agree with me on that.

Seeing Samir lying on a cold bed hooked up to a machine in the ICU for the last week has changed me and not in a good way. Still, none of that justifies what I said to you. I was hurting and I ended up hurting the one person who could help me get through this.

Soon after you left, Suhail came back with a bottle of Coke for you. I had to tell him what happened between us and now he thinks I'm a jerk too. So does your friend, Mimi. Not to forget my parents who heard all about it from Suhail. Let's just say I'm no one's favourite person right now.

The best news I wanted to share is the doctors are very optimistic about Samir coming out of the coma. They have allowed us to move him to a private room. We spend a lot of time reading, talking, and singing to him. I wish you and Neha were around to talk to him too. Suhail cracks a lot of rude jokes; in the hopes he can hear them as well. To balance everything out, he says.

Naina, this letter is also to wish you a belated sixteenth birthday. If things had gone to plan, your parents and a few of us were going to throw you the best party ever! Sadly, that never happened. I didn't even remember to wish you that day.

Yesterday, I called to speak to you, but the maid said everyone had left to go abroad. When you return to India after a month, this letter will be waiting for you. I hope it helps convince you that I care for you. A lot. As much as I did before and then some. Because now I know what it's like not having you around. And I hope you feel the same way about me.

I'm looking forward to picking up where we left off in a month's time.

Lots of love, always.

Amar

While reading the first letter from Amar, I stop a couple of times to blow my nose before I'm able to finish. Tears are running down my cheeks. A few have landed on Amar's letter, soaking the fine paper, and blurring the words.

The rest of the letters are strewn on my bed. Four letters to go. This is not going to be easy.

Mitch pops her head round the door to check on me. Seeing my face in a mess of tears she says, 'Do you want me to hang around?'

I sniff back more tears, saying, 'No, thanks. I need to do this on my own.'

'Alright, but I'll be in my room if you need me,' she says closing the door behind her.

The second letter has *Hand delivered - April 1986* written on it in Amar's handwriting. The envelope feels heavier than the others and appears to have something besides a letter inside it. Two small, silver charms fall out when I slit the envelope open. One is an exquisite heart decorated with filigree work; the other is a firefly with an opal gemstone on the body of the insect. The charms are not as tarnished as the bracelet, but they have left marks on the letter paper.

14th April 1986

Dearest Naina,

I spoke to your mum last night. She said you plan to spend another month in America. I'll have to wait a while longer to deliver my apology to you in person. I didn't get a reply to my first letter; I don't know how you felt about it.

I bought two more charms for the bracelet I gave you. I hope you'll add these to the bracelet. I decided to get a firefly because I realise now fireflies were an important part of our time together in school.

You may have heard Samir is out of the hospital and recovering at home. It will be a while till he is a hundred percent alright but being home has made a big difference to his condition. He too had a lot to say about the last time you and I met. I'm sure he's never, ever going to forgive me.

I keep thinking about you and wondering what you're doing in the US. Whenever I read a good book or a see a movie I like, I want to call you and tell you about it. Then I remember you are no longer just a phone call away. At times like these I'm glad I have the photos Samir took of us so I can look at them and recall the great times we had together.

I'm keeping this letter short because I'm waiting to tell you everything else when we meet at the end of the month.

Love always.

Amar

The next two letters are just a single sheet each containing an update on Samir. The address on the back of each is a house in New Jersey. The twins and their mother stayed there for two months as part of Samir's recovery. By then I had returned to Bombay and started my first year of junior college.

Leaving my bed, I pad to my bathroom where I splash cold water on my face. It feels swollen and hot from all the tears I've cried. In the kitchen, I make myself a mug of hot chocolate and return to my room.

The last letter is going to be the hardest to read, I'm sure. Setting my hot chocolate down, I make myself comfortable, then slit open the envelope.

15th July 1986

Hi Naina,

This is my last letter to you. I haven't received a reply to any of my previous letters, so I've got to face the fact that you have chosen to move on.

If I could go back in time and take back what I said to you that day in the hospital, I would. But life doesn't work that way. I'm sorry we never even dated for a year. I'll live with the knowledge that I caused the end of our relationship.

I know this was your first relationship, the first time you dated anyone, and I regret it ended so abruptly. I hope this doesn't make you doubt yourself or your ability to love someone else in the future. The fault was not yours but mine. Maybe it was naïve of me to think you'd want to continue being a part of my life.

I'll remember the good times we had and hope someday we'll meet again.

Have a great life.

Au revoir as the French say or till, we meet again.

Take care,

Amar

I can't hold back my sobs, so I don't even try to do that. When Mitch comes in to check on me again, I hold the letter out to her. She reads it and her eyes get watery too.

'Oh Naina,' she says hugging me tightly. 'He really cared for you. What harm is there in meeting him since he wants to?'

Drying my eyes on a tissue, I nod, 'I think I need to meet him and put an end to this. Maybe we do need closure.'

'Do you think he's with someone now?' Mitch asks.

'I'm sure he is. Perhaps that's the reason he wants closure. I'll contact him when I return from Pune. I'm ready to close this chapter so we both can move on.'

TWENTY-SIX

Taking another look at my reflection I decide it's too much. I'm standing in front of a mirror at my parent's house in Pune in a heavily embroidered lehenga and blouse in the palest pink shade I could find. My hair is freshly washed and pinned back to show the curls created at the salon earlier that day. Around my neck is a simple choker and from my ears hang matching earrings. Gold bangles clang every time I move my arms and rings on my fingers make any movement difficult. It's too much, way too much.

'Mum,' I call out. 'Can you come here for a minute?'

'What's wrong?' my mum asks hurrying into the room. She stops when she glimpses my reflection in the mirror. 'What's the matter? You look lovely, Naina.'

'Isn't it too much? Do I look like a Christmas tree? The long skirt, the blouse, the long scarf, and the jewellery. I need to take something off,' I declare.

'No sweetie, it looks perfect. You look so pretty,' she says with a catch in her voice.

I glance at her noting the soft, misty look in her eyes, the slight tremble in her voice.

'You're going to be a gorgeous bride someday,' she says adjusting the scarf while checking my reflection in the mirror.

And there it is. The reason I don't attend weddings often. When I do, my mum gets all teary-eyed and sappy thinking of my wedding.

'Mum,' I tell her with a stern look. 'You promised you wouldn't bring up my wedding. And you've already broken your promise. I'm not getting married for years and years.'

'Oh Naina,' she says with an audible sniff. 'Not years and years. Maybe a few years?'

'Only when I'm really ready to get married,' I remind her.

I pull the long scarf over my exposed midriff in a bid to cover that area, but my mum admonishes me saying, 'Don't fuss Naina. You're supposed to show a few inches of midriff.'

'Oh, ok,' I give in with a sigh. 'Will I know anyone at the wedding?'

'Savitha Aunty and her daughter Pallavi will be there. And our neighbours, the Singhs will be there with their son Mohit.'

On our way out I wave to my dad, happily settled in his favourite armchair with a whiskey and soda by his side.

'Are you sure you don't want to join us, Dad?' I ask him, though I know what his answer will be.

'No thanks,' my dad replies in evident relief. 'They are showing '*Sholay*' again tonight and I don't want to miss the fight sequences.'

According to my dad, the best part of any Bollywood movie are the fight sequences. He loves watching the same movie repeatedly to figure out how the fight sequences were shot.

The wedding is being held at a five-star hotel which glows in the distance like a beacon guiding us towards it. Traffic starts slowing down as we near the hotel. Normally I'd be happy to drive on Pune's roads but the ensemble I'm wearing makes it hard to negotiate these roads. When my mum suggested getting a driver, I happily agreed.

Our car turns into the huge compound of the five-star hotel. The wedding hall has its own entrance on the side, so we join a large crowd in the reception area. Mum is immediately recognised by a group of ladies.

They make straight for the two of us, smiles in place while they take in every detail of my outfit. Suddenly the jewellery I'm wearing doesn't seem excessive.

'Sonia, so nice to see you,' a lady in a chiffon saree says, embracing my mother. She quickly turns to me. 'And this must be Naina.'

'Hi Savitha,' mum greets her. 'Yes, this is Naina. Is Pallavi here?'

The rest of the aunties crowd around us and are about to start a conversation with me when a girl dressed in an inky black embroidered long skirt, and blouse grabs my hand.

'Hi aunties, bye aunties,' Pallavi says cheekily sketching a wave as she pulls me away from them. 'Aren't you glad I rescued you in time? They were about to start the twenty-question drill. You can thank me later.'

'Thanks,' I tell Pallavi as we join a group of twenty-somethings on the other side of the room.

To match her black outfit, Pallavi has done up her eyes with smoky black and grey eyeshadow and finished the look with dark burgundy lipstick. The goth makeup works well with her black ensemble.

Our group drifts into the reception area which is really two large rooms opened to accommodate the huge crowd. The group I'm with is a mix of guys and girls from Pune and Mumbai. Those of us living in Mumbai sigh over how nice it is driving in Pune's traffic while the Punekars envy the shopping and discos we have in Mumbai. A case of the grass being greener...!

After dinner and dessert, we sit around chatting lazily. Mohit and I have been flirting for a while, but I don't want to take it to the next level. His parents live next door to mine so that puts a damper on things.

'Next stop for the night is the disco,' declares Pallavi. 'Naina, did you bring an outfit to change into, like I told you?'

'Oh no,' I tell her. 'I totally forgot about that. Holding back a yawn, I add, 'Truthfully though, I won't last a trip to the disco. That last tequila shot was a bit much for me.'

'No problem,' Mohit says. 'If you need to go home and change, I can pick you up later.'

'Honestly, I'm done for tonight,' I tell him. 'I took the early train in, so I'm quite tired.'

'Are you sure?' Mohit asks looking disappointed. 'It's too early to end a Saturday night. I thought Mumbaikars were real party animals.'

'Maybe tomorrow?' I suggest to him.

'Ok,' he says seeing me stifling another yawn.

I say a quick goodbye to the group and head towards where my mum and her friends are sitting.

'Mum, are you ready to leave?' I ask her.

'Let's stay for a little longer,' my mum says. 'There's a few people I still need to meet.'

'Ok,' I agree reluctantly. 'I need to find a loo. I'll be back in ten minutes.'

My mum waves absentmindedly at me as she turns back to her friends. I head towards the doors of the main hall and continue down the broad corridor. It looks promising and must lead to the restrooms.

But halfway down the passage, after passing lots of doors leading into empty halls, I'm no closer to finding a loo.

Seriously, this is a five-star hotel so it must have dozens of loos, right?

I come upon another corridor that intersects the one I'm walking on. Glancing at it I decide it's worth a try and start walking. However, the rest of it is so dark and badly lit, it seems unlikely there'll be a loo there.

Turning back to the main corridor in despair, I run headlong into someone.

'Watch where you're going,' I say, annoyed that I've got to deal with this on top of everything else.

'You too,' a voice from my past replies. 'Naina?'

'Amar!'

I'm taken aback. Where did he spring from? Did I manifest him into existence? Because I'm positive the corridor was empty a few seconds ago.

I planned to contact him later but seeing him in front of me is unsettling. There's a tight sensation in my chest and my feet feel unsteady. Amar puts out a hand to help as I take a step back. My scarf chooses this moment to leave my shoulder and fall silently to the carpeted floor. Amar retrieves it, handing it to me.

In all the scenarios I played and replayed in my head of what I'd say when I finally met Amar again, this was not one I'd thought of. In my versions, I was always cool, calm, and collected while I appraised Amar from a distance and delivered some witty one-liner about meeting again after so long.

Yet here I am, sans any one-liner, witty or otherwise.

'Hi Naina. This is a surprise,' Amar says recovering before I do.

'Hi, what are you doing here?' I ask, voicing the first thing that pops into my head. Not up there with the most intelligent thing I could say but it's the best I can come up with.

'Attending the Sharma wedding. Are you here for the same reason?'

'Yes,' I reply. 'I'm here with my mother.'

I fiddle with my bag, place the scarf back on my shoulder and wiggle my toes in the two-inch heels I am wearing. But I can't think of a single thing to say.

'You look fab,' Amar says. 'This outfit suits you.'

'Thanks,' I say. Since I'm still bereft of words I fall back on the fool proof question nicely brought-up girls use when in doubt. 'How are your parents?'

'They are fine, thanks,' Amar replies.

That is my cue to segue into, 'That's good. My mother's waiting for me, so I have to leave. It was nice meeting you, Amar. Take care,' I turn away and start walking back the way I came.

'Naina, wait,' Amar says. 'If you have a few minutes, can we talk?'

The corridor, which was deserted till now, is suddenly busy with guests. Most are heading for a pair of doors ten meters ahead of us. Those doors lead to the elusive loos I was searching for.

'Here?' I sound reluctant. 'It's rather crowded.'

'We could try those doors,' Amar suggests pointing to a pair of glass doors at the end of the corridor. 'They might lead to a balcony.'

Walking to the end of the passage with Amar I try to keep my emotions in check, my expression neutral. He is wearing a long cream-coloured tunic with matching trousers, formal Indian dress reserved for weddings. His hair is much shorter than before and he's sporting a two-day stubble.

He must have caught the eyes of a few girls tonight. How come I never saw him at the reception?

We pass through the doors and onto a large balcony. Amar closes the doors behind us. It's cool outside and surprisingly well-lit. Above us a luminous sign spells out the name of the hotel in ten-foot-high letters.

'It's quite cool here. Is that alright?' Amar asks me.

'It's alright,' I answer, wrapping my scarf around my shoulders.

A round table with four chairs has been placed in the middle of the balcony but neither of us chooses to sit down. We lean against the parapet wall, instead. I'm not yet ready to have a long conversation with Amar. I need a bit more time.

'How long since you've been back in India?' Amar asks.

'About six months,' I say. 'What about you?'

'A few weeks. I wanted to get in touch ever since I returned,' Amar tells me. 'I asked Samir and Neha to call you.'

'They both did,' I inform him. 'I meant to contact you, but I've been so busy with everything. You know how it is.'

'I know,' he nods. 'Work, family and friends.'

'Yep,' I agree, then without thinking I add, 'And boyfriends.'

'Are you dating someone?' he asks immediately.

Berating myself for having started this topic, I follow through with the lie.

'Yes, I am,' I confirm.

'Would I know him? What's his name?'

'I doubt you'd know him. His name is….' I cast around for a name and come up with, 'Ashwin. His name's Ashwin.' It's the name of a restaurant we passed on our way to the hotel.

'I'm happy for you,' Amar says seriously. 'Look, I know you must be busy this weekend, but can we meet sometime, since we're both in town?'

I shake my head, 'We're really busy this weekend. It's going to be difficult. Why don't we schedule something for when we're back in Bombay?'

'Ok,' he replies but I can tell he isn't happy. 'In case you're free, give me a call. Just a minute, I'll be back.'

Going through the glass doors he flags down a waiter. A few minutes later he's back with a piece of paper.

'I'm staying at my aunt's place. This is her number. It's just me staying there. If you have the time, give me a call so we can meet,' he urges.

'Ok, thanks,' I'm careful not to promise anything definite. 'It was good seeing you. Bye.'

Stepping back into the corridor, I finally enter the restrooms. Closing the door of the last cubicle, I put the lid down and sit on it.

Leaning back, I go over my meeting with Amar. Did that just happen? How is he at the same wedding in Pune as me? Is it a coincidence? Or is the universe giving me a sign we really need to talk and get past our past.

I'm miffed at myself for not handling the situation better. Where is the girl who swore she'd be rude and distant the next time they met? The girl who would give Amar a taste of what it felt like to be dumped so suddenly, is nowhere in sight. When it came down to it, I couldn't do it. At the core of Amar's outburst that day was his concern and love for Samir and that I can understand only too well.

On the way back home, my mum asks if I enjoyed the wedding.

'It was alright,' I tell her, mulling over the coincidence of Amar and I attending the same wedding.

'You seem a bit preoccupied,' mum remarks looking at me. 'Did something happen tonight?'

'Yes,' I say reluctantly. 'I bumped into Amar. You know the guy from school.'

'The guy you dated. Your first boyfriend?'

I nod to her. 'I'm glad you had a chance to catch up,' says my mum.

'We didn't talk much. Amar wants to meet again this weekend.'

'And you agreed?' my mum persists.

'I didn't say yes. I need to think it over.'

'Haven't you thought it over for long enough? It's been what, eight years?'

'Yes, but it still hurts, mum.' I tell her.

'What if you had been in his shoes? And you were crazy with grief over Neel? Think about that,' my mum says as we pull into our driveway.

On her way upstairs she pauses. 'You may be punishing yourself more than Amar.'

Changing into a t-shirt and a pair of shorts I wander into the living room. I dial Neha's number hoping she'll be home by some miracle.

'Hello, this is Neha,' she says when the call goes through.

'Hi, it's me,' I tell her. 'I need some advice from you. How come you're home tonight?'

'Every few months Arjun puts his foot down and insists we have some 'together' time. Tonight, is one of those nights. What's up?'

'I met Amar tonight. At the wedding. He was attending the same wedding that I went to.'

'What? Wow, that is some coincidence. How did it go? I hope you two had a chance to talk,' Neha says.

'Not for long,' I inform her. 'I was still in shock over meeting him, so I bailed out early. But he wants to catch up again this weekend. Should I agree?'

'You know what my answer is going to be Naina,' she says softly. 'Don't you?'

'Yeah,' I agree. 'You want us to meet, I know you do. I asked my mum, and she said the same thing. She even played the Neel-card. You know- what if I was in Amar's shoes, how would I have reacted?'

'Ooh, that's a hard one,' Neha declares. 'Let me know how it goes, ok?' she says before ringing off.

One last phone call and then it's decision time.

When Neel, my brother answers the phone, he sounds happy that I'm calling him. With both our schedules and the time difference we don't get to talk as much as we'd like to.

'Hey, it's my favourite sister,' he says enthusiastically. 'How are things with you Naina?'

'Neel, I'm your only sister,' I retort.

'Same thing,' he says, not in the least put out by my reply. 'What's happening there? How are mum and dad?'

'Everyone's fine here. I need your help Neel,' I tell him. I tell him about the decision I need help with.

'Happy to help,' he says promptly. 'Let's see now, which one was Amar? Wait, I remember him. Shortish guy, not very bright and not much to look at either.'

'Not at all,' I reply indignantly. 'Amar's six feet, smart and certainly not bad looking.'

My brother's laugh echoes down the line. 'I think you have your answer, sis.'

'What do you mean?'

'You defended Amar with such passion, I think you still have feelings for him. There's your decision.'

'Neel, it's a good thing you are such a long distance away from me right now,' I say vexed and thankful at the same time.

After ringing off, I retrieve the piece of paper that Amar gave me from my bag. On the way back to the living room, I go through the bottles in my dad's bar till I find a bottle of red wine.

Pouring myself a glass, I glance at the clock. It's a quarter to twelve so I consider my options. Should I call Amar now or tomorrow morning? On a Saturday, this close to midnight, I'd expect him to be at a party or asleep. If I call now, I can leave a message letting him know we can meet at a park, nearby.

Punching in the numbers, I go over the message I'm about to

leave. I listen to the ringing, hoping the answering machine will pick up the call.

'Hi, Amar speaking.'

'Oh,' I'm surprised to hear his voice. 'I thought you'd be out. I planned to leave a message for you.'

'Naina?'

'Yeah, hi, it's me,' I say quickly.

'You wanted to leave a message for me?'

'Yes, but now that you've answered, it's ok,' I tell him.

'Just, ok?' he asks. I can hear the amusement in his voice.

'It's fine. You know what I mean, Amar.'

'Yeah, I do,' he concedes. 'What message were you planning to leave?'

'Can we meet tomorrow after breakfast? There's a park about a hundred meters from my parents' place.'

'I can meet you there,' Amar sounds relieved as he notes down the name of the park.

Taking another sip of the wine I continue, 'You know, I asked three people tonight what I should do and all three advised me to meet you. Three out of three is a great score.'

'Who did you ask?'

'My mum, Neha and my brother.'

He's quiet for a moment, 'Somehow, I feel you made the decision on your own before that. What tipped it in my favour?'

I hesitate, 'It was the letters.'

'My letters? But I sent those years ago.'

'I know, but I read them only last week.'

Amar is so quiet that I wonder if he has put the phone down and left.

'Amar?'

'I'm still here. I was thinking of what would've happened if you had read them earlier,' he confesses. 'Would we have gotten back together?'

I pause. 'For years I wasn't in the right mindset to even think about them, let alone read them.'

'I understand, Naina and I'm truly sorry,' he says. 'If I could take back what I said that day, I would.'

'I know, but at the time it hurt. To be honest it still hurts a bit, but then I think of how Samir came through and it's all worthwhile.'

I never hear Amar's reply because all at once I hear a scream from upstairs, followed by the sound of footsteps running down the corridor.

TWENTY-SEVEN

'Naina, Naina,' my mother calls out. The panic in her voice is unmistakeable. 'Naina, come quickly.'

'Naina, where are you?'

'Amar, can you hold on? My mum's calling me.'

I don' t wait for his answer as I climb the stairs hurriedly, the phone still in my hand. The door to my parent's bedroom is wide open. From inside I can hear mum talking to dad.

'Mum, what's the matter?' Fearing the worst, I rush into the room.

'It's his heart,' my mother's voice falters when I reach my dad who's sitting up in bed. 'I think he's having a heart attack. Call the hospital, please.'

My father looks pale and tired. His breath comes in short, sharp gasps while his hand clutches his heart.

'Don't panic,' he tells me in a faint whisper when I lean closer. He points to a notepad on his bedside table so I grab it quickly. In my father's clear handwriting is the name and number of a hospital nearby.

I dial the number on the notepad while mum places another pillow behind my dad and rubs his arms and chest. Belatedly I realize I forgot to tell Amar what the emergency was before I ended the call.

'Dad, please, please don't say anything more. Just relax. Let's get you to the hospital first,' I implore. He gives me a weak smile. We continue talking to him while making sure he's as comfortable as possible.

The next fifteen minutes appear to crawl by while waiting for the ambulance to arrive. I've never been happier that my parents opted to retire to Pune because the city is small enough for the ambulance to reach promptly.

It takes all my self-control not to break down when I see my dad being carried downstairs on a stretcher. Only one family member is allowed inside the ambulance so mum climbs in and sits next to dad. An oxygen mask covers most of dad's face but he already looks much better.

'I'll follow the ambulance and meet you at the hospital,' I assure my mother as the vehicle prepares to leave.

The ambulance doors close with a dull thud and the driver gently eases away from the kerb.

I'm about to get into my parent's car and follow, when I notice a car approaching our gate. It slows down, stops and a guy gets out. I look up curiously, wondering who's visiting at this late hour.

'Amar,' I say surprise. 'What are you doing here? How did you find our house?'

'From what I heard on the phone, I thought you might need help,' he explains. 'You said the park is close to the house, so I drove here looking for an ambulance.'

I quickly tell him about my dad's condition and that I'm on our way to the hospital.

'If you like, I can drive you to the hospital,' he offers.

'Amar, you don't need to do this,' I point out. 'I can handle it.'

He's quiet for a moment, then says, 'Naina, I want to help. Don't make the same mistake I did all those years ago. Let me drive you to the hospital'

My chest feels tight suddenly when he mentions the past, but I agree. 'Okay.'

Amar opens the passenger door for me while I climb in.

'I didn't expect to see you here,' I remark as Amar drives quickly, the sparse traffic making it easier for us.

'When I heard you mention heart trouble on the phone, I assumed it was your dad and took a chance.'

'I'm glad you did. Thanks,' I tell him gratefully, shivering in my thin t-shirt and jeans.

'There's a jacket in the back,' Amar offers turning the air-conditioning down. 'This may be a delayed reaction to the shock of tonight.'

I push my arms through the sleeveless jacket and turn the collar up. A faint citrus fragrance clings to the garment. Some things don't change. Memories that I locked away for so long threaten to surface again. Surprisingly I still like woody, citrus fragrances on guys.

'Is that better?' Amar asks as we turn into the hospital. I manage a nod.

At the entrance, I get out quickly while Amar parks the car. The reception is almost empty but the lady behind the desk waves me through after I sign in and give her my dad's name. The familiar smells of a hospital hit me. It's been so long since I've been in one. The last time may have been when Samir was in hospital.

Amar and I hesitate before walking into the room, anxious about my father's condition. Inside, we're surprised to see my dad sitting up in bed, propped up by pillows behind him, an oxygen mask hanging loosely around his neck. A young guy in a white coat is checking his blood pressure.

'Dad,' I exclaim, hurrying to the bed. 'What happened? Are you feeling better?'

My father gives me a weak smile. 'It was a mild heart attack, nothing to worry about.'

'He's not out of danger, yet,' mum clarifies, joining me. 'But it's not as bad as we feared. We'll have to make major changes to our lifestyle.'

My dad grimaces on hearing that. He is a big foodie and loves a good single malt whisky or a well-aged rum. Any mention of change to his lifestyle is bad news to him.

'You'll have to be here for two to three days, Mr Kumar,' the doctor remarks, as he writes on the clipboard. 'You're lucky this was a mild attack, a warning sign for you to start taking care of yourself.'

'Will I have to eat only bland food and give up whisky?' Dad asks tentatively.

The doctor smiles. 'Why don't we review this after two days and then decide? I'll see you again tomorrow.'

I introduce Amar to my parents although both of them remember him. After all he was my first boyfriend so they know a lot about him.

While mum fusses over dad, I tell Amar, 'I'll be here for a while. You can carry on if you need to.'

'You'll need to get things from home if your parents are staying here,' Amar suggests. 'Let's consult your mum and start making a list.'

I'm surprised that he knows exactly what to do till he reminds me, 'I've done this before, remember?'

*   *

Amar holds his hand out to help me up when we get to the summit of the hill. Seated on a stone bench, we take in the view of the city below us.

This last week has been tough on my family. I stayed back to help mum and dad through it. Though my dad is back home, we are still worried. A steady stream of visitors keeps us busy during the day. My father brushes off questions by saying it was 'just a mild attack' but mum and I have quietly worked out a new regimen for him.

Thinking back to when Amar dealt with something similar as a teenager makes me sorry I didn't try and reach out to him after our breakup.

Amar left on Monday and drove back to Pune this weekend. He's been really helpful to me and great company for my dad. Who would have thought!

Today we've been walking and chatting for a while, catching up on eight years of events. It feels good talking to him. It feels like going home, easy and familiar. I've missed the friendship and camaraderie we had and though I try and ignore it, I know I'm still attracted to him.

'Earth to Naina,' Amar smiles at me. 'I lost you for a minute, didn't I?'

I smile too. 'I've missed this, missed talking to you.'

'So, have I. Maybe we can spend time together in Mumbai.'

'I'd like that. But I don't really date.'

He grins. 'What a coincidence. I don't date either.'

I laugh out loud. 'Look at us, using every defence mechanism we can, to avoid getting hurt again. We're pathetic.'

'I have something to confess,' Amar says. 'Me attending the Sharma wedding last week, wasn't a coincidence. I knew you'd be there.'

'How?' I ask incredulously. 'The only person I told was...'

'.... Neha.

'And she told me,' Amar confirms.

I'm dumbstruck. For Neha to do something like that would mean she really, really thought we needed to meet.

'She said it's the only time she's ever done it,' Amar says. 'And she'll never do it again.'

'I'm still shocked. You drove all the way to meet me?' I ask incredulously.

'Yes. Because of Neha, I knew exactly where you 'd be that night. It was worth the drive.'

We take a minute to look at one another. However, my reluctance must be evident because Amar continues, 'There are no guarantees in life or love, Naina.'

'I know that' I admit to him. 'But we found our way back to each other....'

'....and that must mean something,' Amar concludes.

'Where do we go from here, Amar?' I wonder out loud.

'What if, we drive back to Bombay together?' Amar suggests slowly. 'Instead of you taking the train?'

'I'd like that,' I admit. 'What if… we stop somewhere for the night instead of driving straight back?'

The look on his face changes from pensive to puzzled to ecstatic as he works out what I'm trying to say.

Laughing he says, 'That can be arranged.'

'After all what could *possibly* happen between two people who are not dating?' I ask rhetorically.

'My thoughts exactly,' Amar smiles as we lean closer, our lips meeting again after years apart.

*   *

ACKNOWLEDGEMENTS

Thank you to the editors, beta readers and proofreaders of this book. They were the first people who read my manuscript and helped make it better.

Thanks are also due to the many teachers who inspired my love of the English language and literature through school and college.

Finally, the biggest thanks go to my parents, who encouraged my writing endeavours from an early age. Dad, Mum, I wish you were around for this.

ABOUT THE AUTHOR

Kavery Madapa

The author grew up in Mumbai (then Bombay) and completed her degree in Literature and a diploma in Communications.

Printed in Great Britain
by Amazon